**The breath caught in Kate's throat. She knew who he was. She should have known the minute she set eyes on him.**

Kit took the pistol from its holster, turning it in his hand so that he was holding the barrel as he offered her the handle. She inhaled a deep steadying breath, staring at it for a moment before she accepted it from him.

He opened his coat, exposing his chest.

'Close your eyes if it makes it easier.' He guided the muzzle to press it against his heart. 'One squeeze of the trigger and it is done.'

She stared at his heart with determination in her eyes but he could feel how much the pistol's muzzle trembled against his chest.

The moment stretched between them.

'Do it, Kate,' he urged.

# AUTHOR NOTE

Kit Northcote (Captain North) and his fate have been present in the background throughout the *Gentlemen of Disrepute* mini-series. If you are wondering what has happened to this particular disreputable gentleman in the years he has been missing, THE LOST GENTLEMAN will give you the answer.

Kit is undoubtedly flawed, but I hope you will agree that he is a worthy hero, nonetheless, and that he deserves Kate Medhurst as his heroine.

Kate is not your average Regency woman! In writing a romance about pirates set in an era when women were seen as the weaker sex I had a lot of fun turning certain preconceptions on their head.

I sincerely hope you enjoy reading Kate and Kit's story as much as I enjoyed writing it!

# THE LOST GENTLEMAN

## Margaret McPhee

® and TM are trademarks owned and used by the trademark owner and/or its licensee. Trademarks marked with ® are registered with the United Kingdom Patent Office and/or the Office for Harmonisation in the Internal Market and in other countries.

First published in Great Britain 2015
by Mills & Boon, an imprint of Harlequin (UK) Limited,
Large Print edition 2015
Harlequin (UK) Limited, Eton House, 18-24 Paradise Road,
Richmond, Surrey TW9 1SR

ISBN: 978-0-263-25547-8

Harlequin (UK) Limited's policy is to use papers that are natural, renewable and recyclable products and made from wood grown in sustainable forests. The logging and manufacturing processes conform to the legal environmental regulations of the country of origin.

Printed and bound in Great Britain
by CPI Antony Rowe, Chippenham, Wiltshire

**Margaret McPhee** loves to use her imagination—an essential requirement for a scientist. However, when she realised that her imagination was inspired more by the historical romances she loves to read rather than by her experiments, she decided to put the stories down on paper. She has since left her scientific life behind and enjoys cycling in the Scottish countryside, tea and cakes.

**Previous novels by the same author:**

THE CAPTAIN'S LADY
MISTAKEN MISTRESS
THE WICKED EARL
UNTOUCHED MISTRESS
A SMUGGLER'S TALE
   (part of *Regency Christmas Weddings*)
THE CAPTAIN'S FORBIDDEN MISS
UNLACING THE INNOCENT MISS
   (part of *Regency Silk & Scandal* mini-series)
UNMASKING THE DUKE'S MISTRESS*
A DARK AND BROODING GENTLEMAN*
HIS MASK OF RETRIBUTION*
DICING WITH THE DANGEROUS LORD*
MISTRESS TO THE MARQUIS*
THE GENTLEMAN ROGUE*

**And in Mills & Boon® Historical *Undone!*:**

HOW TO TEMPT A VISCOUNT*

*\*Gentlemen of Disrepute*

For Nicola Cornick,
whose wonderful Regency romances
inspired me to write, and whose company
is as wonderful as her books.

With grateful thanks.

# Chapter One

*May 1812—Caribbean Sea*

The sea was a clear green-turquoise silk, rippling and sparkling with crystal-flecked waves. The sky overhead was vast and expansive; the type of sky that only this part of the world held, a vivid never-ending blue, cloudless. It was only ten in the morning, but the sun had already unfurled its bright strength, bleaching the oak of the small American pirate schooner *Coyote's* wooden deck pale and baking it.

Kate Medhurst could feel its warmth beneath the bare soles of her feet and was grateful for the shade of the dark awning that stretched over this section of the quarterdeck—that and the cooling sea breeze. It sent the dark silk ribbons of her straw bonnet flicking and dancing against her neck and the muslin of her black skirts hugging her legs, but Kate noticed neither. Her attention was fixed solely on one thing—the ship coming into view in the distance.

There was the sound of a raven's caw, a slightly sinister call, out of place here in the middle of the ocean.

'A raven on the mizzen mast. A portent that our luck is about to change,' one of the men murmured from the deck before her. Kate knew the superstitions the same as every man on the ship. But unlike them she did not touch her forehead, making the sign to ward off evil. She did not believe in such omens, but superstition was a very real thing to most of those who spent their lives on the waves, so she did not mock them.

'For the better,' she said, 'if what is coming our way is anything to go by.' Through the spyglass she held to her eye she followed the course of the large black-hulled merchant schooner, struggling against the wind.

She snapped the spyglass shut and turned to Tobias, standing by her side. He was a tall man, over six foot in height, with a skin lined and weathered to a nut brown and hair that hung, from beneath his tricorne, in long matted braids interwoven with beads and feathers. His nose was flat from it having been broken in too many drunken fights in the past. With his looks and his faded, frogged frock-coat, Tobias was the very image of what one expected a pirate captain to be, with a temperament to match. He was still staring up at the raven with a vicious look in his eye.

'She's flying the Union Jack, but I cannot see her name.' Kate spoke not to Tobias, but the small, sturdy older man standing on her left-hand side— Sunny Jim. The bandanna wrapped around Sunny Jim's bald head had once been red, now it was a grubby faded pink, pale in comparison to the mahogany-darkened leather of the skin of his face and neck. She passed him the spyglass. 'Can you?' She frowned, knowing the name of every British ship she had ever attacked.

Sunny Jim frowned even more than usual, shaking his head as he passed the spyglass to Tobias for appearances' sake. 'Not yet, ma'am.'

'What does a name matter?' Tobias asked as he peered through the glass.

'Probably nothing.' But it bothered her more than the large black bird that still sat on the mast top watching them.

At the sight of the ship, Tobias grinned, revealing his missing front teeth. His gold-hoop earring glinted in the sunlight and reflected golden dots of light to dance upon the tattoo inked upon his neck. 'Nice,' he hissed.

'A straggler from the merchant convoy that passed at dawn, no doubt,' she said.

'Fallen behind, all alone, without the protection of those mean, son of a gun, Royal Navy frigates.' Sunny Jim almost managed a smile. 'Oh, dear, oh, dear, oh, dear. We can't leave her out there all on her own now, can we?'

'We certainly cannot,' Tobias agreed. 'We should slit their English throats.'

'There will be no slitting of throats.' Kate exchanged a glance with Sunny Jim, then shot Tobias a fierce curbing look.

Tobias's upper lip curled. 'You are too soft on them.'

'Not soft at all,' she countered. 'Hit them in their pockets and leave them alive to bear the pain and witness to the fact that America's seas are just that. America's. It is enough.'

'And supposing I disagree?' He looked at her with angry challenge in his eyes.

'Again? You seem to be disagreeing with me over much these days. This is not the time to be having this discussion. We will deal with it when we get back to Tallaholm. For now, you are on my ship, under my command and you do as I say.'

'Do I? When so many think *I* am *Coyote's* captain?' He stepped closer, trying to intimidate her.

'You do, you young cur,' Sunny Jim said with soft deadly menace and pulled his cutlass free from its scabbard. 'You would do well, Tobias Malhone, to remember that you're a nobody playing a part. There's only one true captain of this ship and, for all your fancy coat, it ain't you. So if the Captain says it's enough then it's enough. *Comprendez?*'

Tobias gave a sullen nod and backed off from his challenge, for now. 'If you say so, *Captain.*' He placed just a slight sneering emphasis on her title.

'I do.' She met his gaze unflinching. 'Are you going to be a problem for me today, Tobias?'

He looked at her for a long second before answering. 'No.' He sneered at her. 'Not today.'

She understood well the implication. Not today, but another. But unbeknown to Tobias, the problem would be gone by then. 'Then we can get on with the job at hand. They are low in the water line.'

'Heavily laden with cargo,' said Sunny Jim.

'Our favourite kind of merchantman.' She turned her gaze from the prize to Tobias. 'Make ready. Let us see if we cannot lighten the merchantman's load a little to speed her on her way.'

'Aye-aye, Captain,' Tobias said softly and without the cynicism this time. He grinned almost to himself, then spoke more loudly to the men who stood poised and waiting, 'Take her about, boys, we've got a date with an English merchant schooner.'

There was a raucous cheer of approval, before the small loyal crew raced to action. Kate pushed her worries over Tobias to the back of her mind for now and watched from her place beneath the awning, with Tobias standing ahead, giving the small orders. The black canvas sails unfurled to catch the wind and the ship began to move.

'Hoist the flag,' she commanded.

A smile curved her lips as *Coyote* sped towards her prey.

Kit Northcote, or Captain North as he now went by, snapped his spyglass shut and slipped it into the pocket of his faded leather coat. The coat had once belonged to a pirate, now it was worn by someone markedly different—someone leaner, harder, honed; although he still wore the black shirt beneath, the shabby buckskin breeches and his tall boots.

'They are coming.' His gaze was fixed on the distant ship.

'Is it La Voile?' Reverend Dr Gabriel Gunner, his friend, asked.

'The hull is a single black-striped sienna brown, the sail is black, and she is flying the Stars and Stripes as well as La Voile's own flag.'

'A skull with a mouth that is the smiling curve of a cutlass painted red with dripping blood. He is artistic. You have got to give him that.'

'I will give him more than that when he arrives.'

Gunner laughed. 'The captain is going to get the

nice little surprise that he deserves. Does he think he can just keep attacking British merchantmen and get away with it?'

'I expect that is exactly what he thinks.'

'Do you know that La Voile is thought to be single-handedly responsible for reducing British transatlantic trade by almost twenty per cent? How can that be? How is it even possible?' Gunner asked. He was tall and surprisingly slender for a man who had spent many years at sea. Freckle-faced and with hair that in colder climes was red, but now in the bright sun of the waters off the Gulf of Mexico was golden beneath the straw hat he always favoured. He had clear, honest blue eyes and long bony fingers that could wield a prayer book, scalpel and cutlass with equal precision.

'La Voile operates under the protection of both a pirate overlord and authorities who turn a blind eye to his illicit actions. He has one vessel and a small loyal crew—low costs, tight control. He hits fast and hard. Takes what cargo he wants and leaves the merchantman and crew intact and *in situ*— a novel concept in the pirate world. He's clever. Clever enough to hit only easy targets and leave the big well-defended jobs to others. Clever enough to find the inevitable stragglers every convoy leaves behind. And clever enough to avoid being caught despite the best efforts of His Majesty's navy.'

'Lucky for us,' said Gunner.

'Very lucky,' agreed Kit and thought of the astronomically large sum they were being paid to do this job.

La Voile's ship, *Coyote*, was no longer a speck on the horizon. 'My, but he *is* fast.' Gunner spoke aloud what Kit was thinking.

'Almost as fast as us,' said Kit.

Gunner smiled. 'Do we take him dead or alive?'

'Alive,' said Kit. 'The bounty is higher. They want to make an example of him and hang him in irons themselves. Be gentle with this particular American pirate, Reverend Dr Gunner.'

'If you insist, Captain North.'

The two men exchanged a wry smile of understanding.

The crew on the deck hurried about as if in panic, feigning a ship that was trying to escape the jaws of a predator. The Union flag fluttered from the jack, its red, white and blue crosses and diagonals clear in the Caribbean sunlight. Men appeared as if they were trying to adjust sails.

'Is everything ready?' Kit asked.

'Exactly as you specified.'

Kit gave a nod and, slipping the spyglass from his pocket once more, studied the black-sailed *Coyote* as she closed the distance.

'Interesting,' he murmured and focused on the

three figures standing at the ship's helm beneath the black awning. 'They appear to be arguing over a woman.'

'A woman?' Gunner screwed his face in disbelief.

'And a respectable looking one at that.'

'A hostage?'

'She is neither bound nor gagged.'

'Abducted,' pronounced Gunner.

'More likely.' Kit could see the distinct threat in the body language of the taller pirate towards the woman. The sunlight glinted on the steel of both men's half-drawn cutlass blades.

'Is La Voile one of them?'

'I believe so. Look for yourself.' He passed the spyglass to Gunner that he might study the three figures.

'How big a fall in the bounty if we deliver him dead?'

'Enough.'

'You convince me, but I cannot deny that I would prefer a more personal approach to the spilling of his blood.'

The two men stood together on the deck of *Raven* and waited for La Voile to step into their trap.

It was the sight of the captain of the merchant schooner that sent the first shiver of apprehension rippling down Kate's spine. There was something about the dark steady focus of his eyes that reminded her of the unnerving stare of the raven that had sat overhead on the mizzen mast not so long since. She pushed the absurd thought from her head and tried to ignore the unease that hung about her like a miasma in the air. This was a hit, just like any other, she told herself, but her eyes checked again for long guns, despite the spyglass having already told her they were absent.

'Not a gun in sight,' said Tobias as if echoing her thought. 'Not a hint of resistance. They are yielding just like all the rest of the British yellow bellies. Cowards! For once I wish they would give us a real fight!' He spat his disgust on to the deck.

'Unarmed and faced with our long guns pointing straight at them? Don't be a fool, Tobias. We should be thankful that their common sense makes things easier for us,' she said.

*Coyote's* long guns had that effect on the British merchant ships Kate selected, allowing an easy progression to locking the two ships together by means of grappling hooks before throwing down the boarding planks. The nameless ship was no exception.

Kate's crew followed the same procedure, the same routine they were so practised at they could have undertaken it with their eyes shut. She watched the Tallaholm men disappear down the merchantman's ladders to her cargo deck. All they had to do was take their choice pick of the goods being carried and *Coyote* could sail away. Same as ever she did. Easy as taking candy from a baby. Yet that same unfamiliar apprehension and anxiety pulled again at Kate, stronger this time.

Her gaze scanned over the merchantman's deck, finding nothing out of the ordinary, before returning to the ship's captain once more. There was something about him, something she could not quite figure out. She examined him more closely. He was lean of build with that stripped, strong look that came from years of hard manual work. She could tell by the way his shabby faded coat sat on his broad square shoulders, from his stance, and the way the shadows cast from his battered old tricorne hat revealed sharp cheekbones and a chiselled jaw.

Under his hat his hair was dark, and his skin had the golden tanned colouration of a man who had spent time at sea. Beneath his coat she could see a shirt and neckcloth, both black as any pirate's. Buff breeches were tight on muscular legs. On his feet he wore leather boots that had once been brown, but were now salt- and sun-faded to a noncolour that defied description. The long scabbard on his left hip was empty. Its sword lay with the other weapons her men had taken from him and his crew, thrown in a paltry pile on the deck before them.

The tip of young John Rishley's sword hovered close to the captain's chest, should any of his crew decide to defy their captors. John had proven himself a valuable member of *Coyote's* crew, but Kate still wished Tobias had sent an older, more experienced member of her crew to hold the merchantman's captain.

All of these thoughts and observations took place in seconds, her gaze absorbing it in one swift movement before returning to his eyes. Dark eyes beneath the brim of that hat. Eyes that were looking right back at her. The shiver ran over her skin again. Someone walking over her grave, her grandmother would have said. She did not break the gaze, because it was his eyes that were ringing every warning bell in her body. There was something about those eyes of his. What was it…? As she stared into them, she realised.

The captain did not look like a man who was nervous for his life or his livelihood. There was nothing of fear in him, not one tiny bit. His stance was relaxed and easy, too easy. There was an air of quiet, almost unnatural calm that she could sense even across the distance that separated them—him on the deck of the merchantman, her watching from beneath the awning on *Coyote*. What she saw in that resolute, unflinching dark gaze of his was cold, hard, very real danger. She glanced at Tobias.

'Something is wrong. Get the men out of there.'

'What…? Hell, woman, nothing's wrong.' Tobias was looking at her in disbelief, as if she had run mad.

'Do it,' she insisted.

He glared at her but, at last, grudgingly gave the command.

But it was too late. In that tiny second everything changed. It happened so fast that there was nothing she could do. One minute the situation aboard the merchantman was quiet, controlled, run of the mill, the next, all hell had broken loose. The British produced weapons, and such a host of weapons that she had not seen aboard any mere merchant schooner before. They fought, hard and fast and with an expertise that surpassed *Coyote's* crew. It was over almost as soon as it had begun. Easily handled, so that within a minute her crew on the deck of the merchantman were lying face down on its deck; all save young John Rishley, who was being held like a shield before the dark-eyed captain, the boy's head pulled back to expose his pale vulnerability. A cutlass now glinted in the captain's hand, as the wicked curve of its blade pressed against the youngster's throat.

'Sweet heaven!' Kate whispered beneath her breath as her blood ran cold at the sight.

At that moment the rest of the British emerged

from the schooner's lower deck and cargo hold. Her men, who had ventured down there for the prize, were being led, bound and gagged.

It was not a situation in which Kate had ever found herself before. Her mind was whirring, her eyes flicking this way and that, seeking a means of escape for them all, but there was nothing. No way out—not with the merchant captain's blade hard against John Rishley's throat, if the man really was just a merchant captain, because Kate had seen a lot of British merchant captains, but never one like him. The boy was nineteen years old. Kate knew his mother and his sisters, too. His Aunt Rita taught Sunday School back home in Tallaholm. And Kate had sworn to them that she would do all she could to keep the boy safe. Now a British blade was pressed to his throat and the sight of it stirred such dark terrible memories that almost paralysed her with fear.

He frogmarched John Rishley before him, crossing the boarding plank over which *Coyote's* crew had walked without the slightest suspicion of what was awaiting them on the other side. A lanky fair-haired fellow, who wore the robe and collar of a priest, followed in his wake.

'When did you add abducting women to piracy, La Voile?' The merchant captain's gaze was fixed on Tobias. His English accent sounded foreign to her ear, but even so she could hear there was something educated about it. His voice was low-toned, serious, unemotional.

*They thought her abducted?* She opened her mouth to tell him the truth, to step up to the mark and own responsibility, for everything about him told her he was not just going to let *Coyote* and her crew go. There was a blade at a boy's throat. This was serious. The masquerade was over.

But Tobias stepped forward first. 'Who the hell are you to question me?' he growled, donning the role of the captain he was coming to believe he really was.

As she and Tobias and Sunny Jim watched, the raven flew down from its perch high on the top of the mast, to land gently upon the merchant captain's shoulder. He did not bat an eyelid at the raven's presence. The bird sat there quite happily, preening its black feathers that shone blue in the sunlight, as if it were his usual perch.

The breath caught in Kate's throat. She felt her heart kick, then gallop fast. Her stomach dropped right down to the deck beneath her feet. *Not a merchant captain, after all.* She knew who he was. She should have known the minute she set eyes on him.

'He is the one they call North.' Her throat was so dry that her voice sounded husky. Because she knew in full the implication of the man standing before them with his sword ready to slit John Rishley's throat—for her crew, and for herself.

'Lord help us!' Sunny Jim whispered on her left-hand side.

She could hear the murmur that spread through her crew, could see the widening of their eyes, could hear someone beginning to pray.

Lord help them indeed.

Those dark eyes turned their attention to Kate. Now that she knew who he was she could have retreated from that gaze, but her pride would not let her.

'At your service, madam,' he said, and gave her a tiny bow of his head before returning his gaze to Tobias. 'Let the woman go.'

Tobias laughed. 'You can have her…if you leave my ship.'

'I will leave your ship.' North smiled and it was a smile that was colder and more cutting than other men's glares. 'You *are* the pirate La Voile?'

'I'm La Voile, all right.'

'Good,' said North. 'I would not want to take the wrong man.'

'Like hell am I coming with you!'

North pressed the blade harder against John Rishley's neck. 'You want me to slit his throat while you watch? Or will you yield to spare him?'

Kate had to press a hand over her mouth to stop

herself from crying out. Her heart was racing. She felt sick with fear and horror and rage. As her hand tightened against the handle of the long knife hidden beneath her skirts, she felt Sunny Jim's grip around her wrist.

'Don't!' he whispered fiercely. 'Let him think you abducted. There's too much at stake, Katie.' The old man's slip of the tongue, to use her girlhood name, showed just how serious the situation was. His crinkled pale blue eyes stared meaningfully into hers, reminding her of exactly how much was at stake both here and back at home in Tallaholm.

'Go ahead. Slit it.' Tobias grinned and shook his head, an excited expression on his face. He glanced down at the long blade of his cutlass, as if watching the way the sun glinted on the sharpness of the steel. Then suddenly with a great swing of his cutlass he ran at North, yelling, 'But I'll never yield to you, you English dog!'

'No!' Kate screamed, knowing Tobias's foolhardy action would cost John Rishley his life.

It happened so fast that she could not have told how. One minute John Rishley was North's shield, the next he had been thrown, alive and well, into another British grasp and a single slash of North's blade had felled Tobias. She could see the dark stain spreading rapidly across Tobias's chest, see the blood growing in a glistening pool on the scrubbed wooden deck beneath him.

Shock stole her breath.

The silence that followed was deafening. The seconds seemed to stretch.

Nobody moved.

Nobody spoke.

Kate stared. Tobias's eyes were still wide open, dead and unseeing, staring with the same shock that she felt freezing like ice through her blood.

The priest, who seemed to be North's second-in-command, walked over to where the body lay. Crouching down, he touched his fingers against Tobias's neck.

'Dead as a doorpost, I'm afraid,' he pronounced softly, and gently swept the man's eyes shut before murmuring the words of a final prayer and getting to his feet.

'More is the pity. But we'll take him dead just the same.' North gave a nod.

With incredulous horror Kate watched as four of the British crew lifted Tobias's body between them and carried it across the boarding plank to the bigger schooner.

North's eyes shifted to where Sunny Jim's hand still held Kate's wrist. 'Release her to us.'

'And if we don't?' Sunny Jim demanded. His grip

was gentle for all the ferocity of the part he was playing before North.

North's gaze flicked coldly to Tobias's lifeless form before returning to Jim's. 'We'll kill every last man amongst you.'

She did not doubt North's assertion, neither did anyone else. Every pirate and privateer who sailed these oceans had heard the stories of North the Pirate Hunter.

Sunny Jim's eyes slid momentarily to Kate's in veiled question. He would fight for her to the death, they all would, but she could not allow that, not all these men who had served her so loyally.

'I am not worth one man's life, let alone thirty,' she answered. 'Surely you see that?' Words that could be those of a prisoner held against her will.

But Sunny Jim's expression was stubborn. He had known both her grandfather and father and he was not a man to cut and run.

'Give us the woman and the rest of you may go free,' said North.

'You think we would believe a story like that?' Sunny Jim sneered at North.

'You should—it is the truth. I have no interest in bringing in *Coyote* and her crew as a prize. My commission is purely for La Voile.'

She felt the hope that North's words sent rippling through her crew. They did not fully believe him, but they wanted to. She knew it with a certainty, because she felt the same way, too. North could not be trusted, but, if he wanted, he could kill them all anyway and take her just the same.

Sunny Jim knew it, too. But still he wavered.

'You must yield me to them,' she said, as if pleading with her captor, when in truth it was the command he needed to hear.

He gave a nod, his gentle old eyes meeting hers in understanding and salutation. 'If you want her so much, take her. And let us pray you do not lie, Captain North.' In the role he was playing Sunny Jim threw her hard towards North.

The force of it made her stumble and almost fall, but North caught her and in one movement swept her behind him.

'Oh, I do not lie, Mr Pirate. You need have no fear of that.' She could hear the ironic curve on his mouth as he uttered the cool words.

But he was not smiling when he glanced at the priest. 'Escort the lady to safety, Reverend Dr Gunner.'

The priest gave a nod and when he gestured ahead, she had no choice but to follow him, leaving behind *Coyote* and safety, and step with feigned willingness across the breach that divided her world from his.

* * *

On the British ship Kate stood by the bulwark, her grip so tight upon the rail that her fingers ached, watching them, watching North, watching what would come next.

Those crew who had been captured upon North's ship were returned across the plank to *Coyote*. All of her men were lined up there, on their knees, most still bound and gagged. There was nausea in her stomach, an icy dread in her blood.

'Will he kill them?' she asked the priest, her eyes lingering on the scene on *Coyote's* deck.

'North does not lie. He will not take their lives, ma'am.'

But priest or not, Kate could not trust the words.

North moved.

Her heart missed a beat.

But he did not spray the deck red with blood as she feared. Instead, true to his words, he sheathed his cutlass and walked away, leaving them there as he returned to his own ship. In less than a minute all physical connections between the two ships had been severed, the boarding plank and pricey grappling hooks sent plummeting into the waves without a second glance.

As North's ship manoeuvred carefully away from *Coyote*, Kate's gaze held to Sunny Jim's, but neither of them dared show one single sign. Behind her she could hear the creaking of the rigging and the crack of unfurling canvas and the movement of men busy at work. And before her, the distance of the ocean expanding between them as North took sail.

She was aware that North and the priest were somewhere behind her, but Kate did not look round. She just stood there and watched while the wind seemed to speed beneath North's sails to leave *Coyote* further and further behind.

Until, at last, the dark shadow fell across her and she knew that North had come to stand at the rail by her side.

One second. A deep breath.

Two seconds. She swallowed and hid all that she felt.

And only then did she turn to face the man who was the infamous pirate hunter North.

Those dark eyes were looking directly into hers with a calm scrutiny that made her nervous.

'North, Captain Kit North,' he offered the unnecessary introduction. 'Under commission from the British Admiralty to bring in the pirate La Voile.'

The hesitation before she spoke was small enough not to be noticed. 'Mrs Kate Medhurst,' she said, using her real name because it would mean nothing to him and because successful deception was best attained by sticking close to the truth.

He took her hand and just the feel of his fingers against hers made her shiver.

'You are cold, Mrs Medhurst, now that our speed increases.'

She hated that he had seen it, that tiny sign of weakness, of fear. 'A little,' she agreed by way of excuse.

Before she could stop him he slipped off his coat and wrapped it around her shoulders.

She could feel the warmth of him still upon it, smell the scent of him too much in her nose— leather and soap, sunshine and masculinity. It surrounded her. It enveloped her. Bringing him close to her, making it feel like a gesture of intimacy that she did not want to share with any man, least of all him. She itched to tear his coat from her, to dash it at his feet, this hard-eyed handsome Englishman who was her enemy in more ways than he could imagine. But Kate knew she could not afford to yield to such impulses of emotion and controlled herself as carefully as ever she did.

'Thank you,' she said, but she did not smile.

'You are safe with us.'

*Safe?* The irony of the word would have made her laugh had the situation not been so dire. 'Even if I am an American? And there is—' she hesitated in order to choose the word carefully '—disharmony between our two countries?'

'Even if you are an American and there is disharmony between our two countries.' There was the smallest hint of a smile around that hard mouth. 'You are welcome aboard *Raven*, Mrs Kate Medhurst.'

'*Raven,*' she said softly. *Of course.*

'The name of the ship.'

The name that, had she seen it, would have made all the difference in the world.

'They said there was no name upon your ship,' she said.

'La Voile was not meant to see it.'

'It was a trap,' she said slowly, her blood chilling at the extent of his cold calculation.

North smiled. 'The name would have tipped him off.'

'Yes,' she agreed. 'I am sure it would have.' And knew it for the certainty it was. 'Why take just La Voile and not *Coyote* and the rest of her crew? Why leave behind the greater part of the prize?'

'I am not interested in prizes. My commission is for La Voile and only La Voile.'

'I did not realise he was so important to the British. Surely compared to Jean Lafitte, he is just small fry?'

'He is a big enough burr and one with the potential of becoming a rallying anti-British figurehead, much more so than Lafitte. Admiralty wish to cut off the head and leave the body in place to tell the tale, leaderless and ineffective. Which suits me. One man is easier dealt with than an entire crew and ship,' he said.

'So it seems.' But things were not always as they seemed.

Her gaze held his for a moment longer, looking danger in the eye and seeing its ruthless, dark, infallible strength. She swallowed.

The tiny moment seemed to stretch.

'Reverend Dr Gunner will escort you below to a cabin where you may rest. If you will excuse me, for now.'

She shrugged off his coat and gladly returned it.

A bow of his head and he was gone, moving across the deck to speak to his men.

Kate felt the tension that held her body taut relax, letting out the breath she had not known she was holding.

'Mrs Medhurst…ma'am.' The priest moved forward to her side.

One last glance of hope and longing out across the ocean to where *Coyote* and safety had diminished to little more than a toy ship upon the horizon.

The priest saw the direction of her glance and misconstrued it. 'You really are safe with us.'

'So Captain North reassures me.' But if North were to realise the truth of who she was, of what she was... Captain *Le* Voile, as she always thought of herself. Such a subtle difference from *La* Voile, but one that was important to her. Le Voile or La Voile, it made no odds when it came to North. Either way she was the pirate captain of *Coyote* whom he sought.

*You really are safe with us.*

Kate gave a smile of irony. For what place could be more dangerous than aboard *Raven* with the deadly British pirate hunter who had been sent to capture her?

It was a sobering thought. She forced it from her mind and, with a nod, followed Reverend Dr Gunner below deck.

## Chapter Two

'I put her in my cabin. I'll sleep on the deck with the men—naturally.' Within Kit's day cabin Gunner was lounging in a small wooden chair. The priest pulled a silver hip flask of brandy from his pocket, unstopped it and offered it to Kit as a formality. They both knew that Kit would refuse.

'There's a cot in the corner—you are welcome to sleep there.' Kit was seated in his own chair behind the plain mahogany desk.

'Are you suggesting I could not manage a hammock?' Gunner downed a swig of brandy.

'A man does not forget such things,' said Kit and thought of the past years and all it had entailed for them both.

'He certainly does not.' Gunner grinned. 'They will bury us in those damned hammocks.'

Kit smiled. 'No doubt.' He moved to the large

rectangular window, looking out over the sea. 'How is our guest?'

'Resting. She has a remarkable resilience. Most women would be suffering the vapours at the mere suggestion of the ordeal she has endured. But maybe the shock of it has not hit home yet. Delayed emotional response following trauma—we have both seen it.' Gunner came to stand by his side and met his gaze meaningfully. They both remembered the horrors of the year in that Eastern hellhole.

'Has she any signs of physical hurt?'

'None that I could see. I did explain I was a physician and enquired whether she had need of any assistance, but she declined, saying she was well enough.'

'A lone woman amongst a crew of pirates... How well can she be?' said Kit.

Gunner's mouth twisted with distaste. 'I am rather glad that you killed La Voile.'

'I am not. They would have taken his life just the same in London.' And Kit would have welcomed the extra money that would have paid.

'Always the money,' said Gunner with a smile.

'Always the money,' agreed Kit, and thought of what this one final job would allow him to do. All the waiting and planning and working, and counting every coin until the target was in sight, and the time was almost nigh. He pushed the thought away, for now. 'I will have the day cot set up for you and space cleared for your possessions and clothes. If you will excuse me, I have got work to do.'

'And always work,' said Gunner.

'No rest for the wicked.' There was a truth in that glib phrase that few realised, Kit thought wryly. No rest indeed. Not ever. 'La Voile is dead, the job is done. We go back to England and claim our bounty.'

'And Mrs Medhurst? We cannot touch port in America. We'd be running the gauntlet with the flotilla of French privateers and pirates patrolling their coast. Even with all *Raven's* advantages, she cannot match such numbers.'

Kit smiled. 'We will drop the woman at Antigua when we victual. Fort Berkeley there will organise her return home.'

'A good plan. But it has been so long since we were in the presence of a respectable woman, one cannot help speculate how her presence would have lifted the journey home. It would certainly have kept the men on their best behaviour.'

'You are too long from home, my friend,' said Kit drily.

Gunner gave a smile. 'Perhaps.' He was still smiling as he left the cabin, closing the door behind him.

Kit returned to his desk and the navigational

charts that lay there. But before he focused his attention on studying their detail he thought once more of Kate Medhurst with her cool grey eyes: proud, appraising, wary and with that slight prickly hostility beneath the surface.

*Disharmony between our two countries.* He smiled at that line and wondered how a woman like her had come to be abducted by a shipload of pirates. And even more, how she had fared amongst them. For all the strength of character that emanated from her, she was not a big woman. Physically she would not have stood a chance.

Maybe Gunner had a point when it came to La Voile. Kit thought of his blade slicing through the villain's heart. Maybe it was worth the gold guineas that it had cost him, after all.

He gave a grim smile and finally turned his attention to the charts that waited on the desk.

Kate forced herself to stop pacing within the tiny cabin in which they had housed her. She stopped, sat down at the little desk and stilled the panic roiling in her mind and firing through her body. *Stop. Be still. And think.*

Her eyes ranged over the assortment of medical books, prayer books and the large bible on the shelf fixed to the wall above the desk. On the desk itself were paper, pen and ink and a small penknife. She lifted the knife and very gently touched a thumb to test the sharpness of the blade. The priest kept the little knife razor sharp, potentially a useful weapon, but it was nothing in comparison to her own. The feel of the leather holster and scabbard, and their precious contents, strapped to her legs gave her a measure of confidence.

She would not hesitate to use either the knife or pistol on North if she needed to. Not that she thought it would come to that.

*Coyote* would come for her. It is what she would have done had one of her crew been taken. Regroup, rearm, follow at an unseen distance, then come in fast for the attack. Sunny Jim would do the same. She knew her men—they would not abandon her.

They would come for her and it was vital that Kate be ready. All she had to do was watch, wait and keep her head down. Not today, perhaps not even tomorrow, but soon. It was just a matter of time before she was back once more on her own ship, maybe even with Captain Kit North as her prisoner. She smiled at that thought. The Lafitte brothers, the men who oversaw most of the mercantile, smuggling, privateering and pirate ventures around Louisiana, would pay her well for him. With North off the scene it would be a great deal safer for them all. She smiled again, buoyed by the prospect.

She pleaded fatigue that night so as not to have to join them for dinner, eating instead from the tray he sent to her cabin. *Coyote* would not come tonight, and as for North... An image of him swam in her head and she felt nervousness flutter in her stomach...she would defer facing him until tomorrow.

But of North the next morning there was no sign. It was the priest, Reverend Dr Gunner, who sat with Kate at breakfast and the priest who offered her a tour of *Raven*. She accepted, knowing the information could be useful both to *Coyote* and to all her fellow pirate and privateer brethren.

'I could not help noticing that Captain North was not at breakfast.'

'North does not eat breakfast. He is a man of few needs. He takes but one meal a day.'

'A man of few needs... What else can you tell me of the famous Captain North?'

'What else would you like to know?' He slid her a speculative look that made her realise just how her question had sounded.

'All about this ship,' she said.

Reverend Dr Gunner smiled, only too happy to oblige.

*Raven* was bigger than *Coyote*, but the lower deck

was much the same. There were more cabins and the deck contained not cargo, but long guns. Better gunnery than *Coyote* carried. So much better that it made her blood run cold. Two rows of guns, some carronades, others long nine pounders, and a few bigger, longer eighteen pounders, including two as bow chasers, lined up, all neat on their British grey-painted, rather than the American red-painted, wheeled truck carriages and secured in place by ropes and blocks. There were also sets of long oars neatly stored and ready for use, something that made the hairs on the back of her neck stand up.

'You are oared,' she said weakly.

'They do come in handy at certain times when the wind does not blow. And we are sufficiently crewed to man them easily enough.' The priest smiled. 'We are also carrying extra ballast to make us lie low in the water,' he explained. 'To give the illusion we are heavily laden with cargo.'

'You were deliberately posing as a merchantman.'

'Captain North's idea. He said that when you have a whole ocean to search for La Voile the easiest thing would be to have him come to us. He said it would work.'

'And it did.' A shiver ran through her at North's cold, clever calculation and how easily and naïvely she had stepped into his trap.

'It did, indeed, Mrs Medhurst,' Gunner agreed with an open easy smile as he led her into a room that was lined with wooden and metal hospital instruments.

Her eyes ranged around the room as he spoke, taking it all in, and stopping when they reached the huge sealed butt in the corner. The sudden compassion on Reverend Dr Gunner's face and his abrupt suggestion that they progress to the upper deck confirmed the butt's macabre contents: Tobias. She was relieved to follow the priest up the ladder out into the fresh air and bright sunshine. But the relief was short lived.

North was already out on deck, taking the morning navigational reading, chronometer, sextant and compass clearly visible; a man absorbed in his task. The blue-sheened raven sat hunched on his shoulder, as if it were party to the readings.

His shirt was white this morning, not black, and he was clean shaven and hatless, so that she could see where the sun had lifted something of the darkness from his hair to a burnished mahogany. It rippled like short-cut grass in the wind. In the clarity of the early morning light his golden tanned features had a harsh handsomeness that was hard to deny. But even a rattlesnake could look handsome; it did not mean that she liked it any the more.

North saw her then, cutting those too-perceptive eyes to her in a way that brought a flutter of nerves to her stomach and prickle of clamminess to her palms.

He gave her a small nod of acknowledgement, but he did not smile. Indeed, his expression was serious, stern almost. Nor, to her relief, did he make any movement towards her. Instead he turned his attention back to his measurements and calculations.

'Do not mind North,' said Gunner with good humour. 'It is his manner with everyone. He is a man who takes life too seriously and works too hard.'

As she followed the priest over to the stern of the ship, her eyes scanned the ocean behind them and saw the distant familiar shapes of islands across the water, but nothing else.

She leaned against the rail, feel the cooling kiss of the sea breeze, noticing both its strength and direction as she watched the frothy white wake *Raven* left behind her. Just looking at the ocean, just being on it, never failed to comfort her. Her gaze dropped to the tall lettering that named North's ship, tall and clear and stark white against the rich black paint of the stern. *Raven.*

'There was no name upon this ship when the pirates approached.' She looked at the priest with a question in her eyes. 'I am sure of it, sir.' But was she? Had such a basic mistake brought her to this situation? 'At least, I thought I saw nothing and I sure was looking to see who you were.'

'Do not doubt yourself, madam. There was no name for the pirates to see. Look more closely.'

She walked toward the stern and leaned over it to examine the painted name, and saw exactly the device North had used. 'There is a long black plank, like a frame fixed above the lettering.'

'Largely invisible from elsewhere. It can be flipped down to cover the name.'

'How clever.' So clever that it frightened her.

'It is, is it not? North is clever.'

'How clever?' she asked, needing to know the full measure of the man who was her enemy.

'Do you know anything of ships Mrs Medhurst?'

'I do,' she admitted with a nod. 'Both my father and grandfather were shipwrights and sailors. There have been sailors in my family for as far back as can be remembered.'

He smiled. 'Then look up at *Raven's* sails and rigging.'

She did as he bid and what she saw stole the words from her tongue. Gone was the tatty patched ordinary canvas found on many merchant schooners, and in their place was a large spread of pristine-looking sails. She felt the prickle of cold sweat at the sight.

'And our hull is longer and sleeker than most

ships of this size. North's own design. The combination of the hull design and the sail spread allow us uncommon speed and manoeuvrability, making us faster than most pirate ships.'

'I did not see any gun ports either for the guns below.'

'Optical illusion.' Reverend Dr Gunner smiled again. 'We are carrying eighteen big guns, as well as several small swivel guns.'

*Compared to Coyote's arsenal of eight guns.*

'Our men are drilled to fire one-minute rounds. And—' he could barely contain his excitement '—we have a special powder mix that extends the range of our shot.'

'Oh, my!' she said softly.

'Not to mention our personal weaponry.' He pulled part of the enormous cutlass from the scabbard that hung from his left hip, to expose a small section of the silver shining blade. 'It is a special high-tensile steel from Madagascar. There is nothing to match its combined hardness and flexibility. And we carry an armament that would kit out an army. We are the very best, or, depending on whose point of view one takes, the very worst of what sails upon these seas. We can best any pirate.' He smiled again.

Kate thought of *Coyote* out there somewhere behind, following *Raven*. 'I see.' She forced the curve to her lips, but inside her stomach was clenched with worry and there was a cold realisation spreading through her blood.

'Wonderful, is it not?'

*Wonderful* was not the word Kate was thinking to describe it. The priest was awaiting her reply, but she was saved from having to make one by the arrival of a call that rang out from the crewman in the rigging.

'Ship ahoy!'

It was the words that until only a few minutes ago Kate had been praying to hear. Now, in view of what Reverend Dr Gunner had just told her, they left her with mixed emotions.

'South-south-west.'

Kit scanned the horizon in that direction and saw the tiny spot. Raising his spyglass to his eyes, he trained it hard upon the ship and focused.

He heard the familiar tread of Gunner's boots strolling over towards him. He heard nothing of the woman, but knew she was there from the reassurances Gunner was speaking to her.

They stood there quietly by his side, the woman between him and his shipmate. Gunner, not wanting to interrupt Kit's concentration, stood content and quiet in his own meditations.

The silence stretched.

It was the woman who broke it.

'What do you see, sir?' she asked.

'A schooner.'

'Is it the pirates? The same pirates…?'

He snapped the spyglass shut and turned to look at her. 'It is difficult to say at this distance.'

He felt that same slight prickle of tension and hostility that emanated from her.

'Mrs Medhurst is understandably a little nervous,' Gunner said. 'I have tried to convince her of our superior strength, but…' He smiled and gave a shrug of his shoulders.

'Rest assured, ma'am, if *Coyote* is fool enough to come after us with vengeance in mind, then, as I am sure Reverend Dr Gunner has already pointed out, we will have disabled her before she is within range to fire her own guns. She has only eight small ones, mainly four and six pounders, nine if you include the swivel gun on the rail, to our eighteen larger.'

'How can you know that?' She looked pale in the bright morning sun.

'I have a very good spyglass.' He smiled. 'And I counted.'

She swallowed and did not look reassured.

'Calm your nerves, ma'am, if La Voile's crew threaten violence they will go the same way as their captain.'

He saw the flicker of something in those eyes trained on the distant ship before she masked it, something that looked a lot like fear, there then gone.

'Have I convinced you, Mrs Medhurst?'

'Yes, Captain North, I do believe you have.' Her eyes held his and she smiled, but it was not an easy smile. 'May I?' Her eyes flickered to the spyglass in his hand.

She could not have known what she was asking. A sea captain did not lend his spyglass lightly. But she stood there patiently waiting, with those Atlantic grey eyes fixed on his. There was no sign of any fear now. She seemed all still calmness, but he sensed that slight tension that underlay her. Her hands were steady as she accepted the spyglass and peered through it, adjusting its focus to suit her eyes. She looked and those tiny seconds stretched.

At last she closed the spyglass and returned it to him, their eyes meeting as she did so.

'Thank you.' Her American lilt was soft against his ears. 'If you will excuse me, gentlemen. I think I will retire to my cabin for a little while, if you don't mind.'

They made their devoirs.

His eyes followed her walking away across that deck to the hatch, the gentle sway of her hips, the proud high-held head. Despite the faded black muslin, chip-straw bonnet and bare feet, she had an air about her of poise and confidence.

'She is afraid,' said Gunner softly.

'Yes,' agreed Kit, his gaze still fixed on her retreating figure. She was afraid, but not in the way any other woman would have been afraid. There was a strength about her, an antipathy, and something else that he could not quite work out.

He glanced up to find Gunner watching him.

'Is it *Coyote*?' Gunner asked with just the tiniest raise of his brows.

'Without a doubt,' replied Kit smoothly.

Kate closed the door of the cabin behind her and leaned her spine against it, resting there as if she could block out North and the situation she found herself in.

*If La Voile's crew threaten violence, they will go the same way as their captain.* North's words sounded again in her mind, and she did not doubt them, not for an instant. Not because of rumours or reputations, but because she had seen the evidence with her own eyes.

Her men were coming for her. And they would most definitely threaten violence. *Raven's* sails made her fast. But not faster than *Coyote*.

Sunny Jim was an experienced seaman. He would see the change in *Raven's* sails, but he would not see anything that was designed to stay hidden. Not the long-range guns or their number, or the fact *Coyote* would be hit before she could fire a shot. Not the weaponry aboard, or, worse than any of that, the mind of the man who was a more formidable enemy than any fireside tale foretold.

He would not realise that *Coyote* did not stand a rat's chance against *Raven*.

*Have I convinced you, Mrs Medhurst?*

He had more than convinced her. She had seen the cold promise in those eyes of his, the utter certainty.

Fear and dread squirmed in her stomach. She thought of Sunny Jim and of how much she respected the old man who had been her grandfather's friend. She thought of young John Rishley and how he had his whole life to live in front of him. She thought of each and every man upon *Coyote*. She knew them all and their families, too.

'Sweet Lord, help them,' she whispered the prayer aloud. 'Make them turn back.'

But they wouldn't turn back. She was their captain. They were coming. She knew it and North knew it, too. If her men reached *Raven*, their fate was sealed and the knowledge chilled her to the bone.

She couldn't just let it happen. She couldn't just let them sail unwittingly to their deaths.

So Kate sat down at the priest's little desk and she thought and she prayed, but no answer came. And then she remembered the distant islands and how all of the attention of North and his crew would be on *Coyote* growing steadily bigger. The first tiny hint of an idea whispered in her ear. She knew these waters, all of their layout and what was in them and on them. Any good Louisiana privateer or pirate did. And Sunny Jim was a good Louisiana pirate, too.

It was not the best of plans, she knew that. It was risky. It could go wrong in so many ways. But it was the only plan she could think of, and she would rather take a chance with it than sit here and let her men sail to their doom. Anything was better than allowing their confrontation with North.

Pulling up her skirts, Kate unbuckled the leather straps of her holsters and hid them with her weapons beneath the cot. Then she smoothed her skirts down in place, and, with a deep breath, made her way to the upper deck to wait for the right moment.

'We need to veer to the north,' said Kit. He stood on the quarterdeck with Gunner, the two of them pouring over the navigational chart that covered this area. With one of his men dedicated to watching *Coyote* full time, Kit could get on with navigating *Raven* through these waters. 'Regardless of what the charts say, we do not want to be too close to that cluster of rocky outcrops, or what lies beneath.'

Gunner gave a nod. 'One cannot always trust the charts and it is better to be safe than sorry.'

'Bear to larboard, Mr Briggs,' Kit gave the command to his helmsman. *Raven* began to alter course ever so slightly, taking her in a broader sweep clear of the rocks.

'Clearly visible in daylight, but at night, in the dark...I bet there have been more than a few gone to meet their maker by that means.'

The two of them mulled that truth for a few minutes in silence as they watched those dark, jagged, rocky bases ahead. Kit would not mind meeting his maker. Indeed, over the years part of him had wished for death. But not quite yet.

His gaze wandered to *Raven's* bow, to where Kate Medhurst had stood for so long, staring out at the ocean ahead of them. Now the spot was empty. He scanned the deck and saw no sign of her.

'Where is Mrs Medhurst?' His eyes narrowed with focus.

'She was right there...' Gunner stopped. 'Maybe she wanted some shade from the fierceness of the sun.'

'Some shade...' Kit murmured the words to himself and in his mind's eye saw the dark awning fixed across *Coyote's* quarterdeck. Something about the scene niggled at him, but he could not put his finger on why.

'Probably returned to her cabin.'

'When the cabins are like sweat boxes and there is shade behind us?' Kit raised an eyebrow and met Gunner's gaze. 'How long has she been gone?'

'No idea. Could be two minutes, could be twenty. Some time while we were engaged with the charts.' Gunner was looking at him. 'Call of nature?'

'Perhaps.' But he had a bad feeling. 'Better to take no chances.' They both knew he was responsible for her safety while she was aboard *Raven*.

'Has anyone seen Mrs Medhurst?' Gunner asked of the crew.

'Lady went below some time since,' Smithy answered from where he was holystoning the deck.

Kit and Gunner exchanged a look and went below.

Kit gestured his head towards Gunner's old cabin that, for now, belonged to Mrs Medhurst. Gunner nodded and went to knock on the door.

There was only silence in response. Gunner opened the door, then glanced round at Kit with a shake of the head.

'The head?' suggested Gunner. 'I will let you check that one.' He grinned.

'You are too kind.' But Kit didn't balk from it. He

headed to the bow and knocked on the door that led out onto the ship's head. There was no one outside. But folded neatly and tucked in behind the ledge was black dyed muslin. Kit lifted it out and Kate Medhurst's dress fluttered like the black flag of a pirate within his hand.

'What in heavens...?' Gunner shot him a worried glance.

The two men looked from the dress outside to the open platform of the head.

'She cannot possibly have... Can she?' Gunner whispered in horror.

Kit stepped out first on to the ledge of the head with Gunner following behind.

'Hell!' Kit had not cursed in eighteen months, but one escaped him now. For there in the clear green water a distance from *Raven* was Kate Medhurst, swimming smoothly and efficiently with purpose. Oblivious to the two men that stood watching her, and oblivious, too, to the sinister dark shape beneath the water out near the rocky outcrops.

Kit and Gunner's gazes met and held for a tiny fraction of a second and then they were running full tilt for the upper deck.

# Chapter Three

The water was colder that Kate had anticipated and the distance to the rocks looked further in the water than it had done from up on *Raven*. The cotton of her shift was thin, but it still caught around her legs and swirled in the water enough to slow her progress. But the dive had been seamless and quiet and she was a strong enough swimmer, taught by her father when she was still a girl. He had seen too many people drown and insisted that it might save her life one day. It might save several other lives, too, she thought wryly, if she made it to those rocks unnoticed and was able to flag down *Coyote* when she passed.

Each stroke of her arms, and each kick of her legs, was careful and as smooth as possible, trying to avoid any splashing or noise that would draw a stray glance from *Raven* as she cleared the shadow of the ship.

Quiet and smooth.

Breathe.

Keep going.

The three-line mantra whispered through her head. She did not look up and she did not look back. Instead, she kept her focus fixed firmly on the closest of the group of tiny rocky islands that lay in a direct line ahead. All she had to do was swim to it. North and his crew's attention would all be to the larboard and stern. Kate was starboard and swimming clear. She would have to be real unlucky for them to see her.

Quiet and smooth.

Breathe.

Keep going.

And then she heard the shouts.

Her heart sank.

Keep going. They had what they thought was La Voile's body; it was enough to secure their bounty. They did not need her. And North was an Englishman and a scoundrel to boot. He would not come back for her, but sail right on.

But the shouts grew louder, more frantic, so that she could no longer pretend she did not hear them. She glanced behind and saw what looked like every man on the ship crowded on to the upper deck. And there, at the stern, she could see North, his coat stripped off to expose his white shirt beneath, busy with a rope. The black-robed priest was by his side helping him and she knew in that moment, whatever else North was, he was not a man who sailed away and left a woman in the water.

She stopped swimming and trod water, knowing that to swim on would only make things look worse for her. One last glance at the tiny rocky islands and freedom. A movement flickered at the side of her eye. She shifted her gaze and saw across the beautiful clear green water the tall grey dorsal fin heading directly her way.

Time seemed to stop. For a tiny moment she froze, then turned and swam as fast as she could back towards *Raven* and North and all that she had fled. Her enemy had turned, in one split second, to her only hope. She could feel the beat of her heart and the cold sensation of terror as all of her life flashed before her eyes in a multitude of tiny fast frozen scenes. Ben and little Bea. Wendell. Her mother and father. Sunny Jim. Tobias with his dead unseeing eyes. And North. Why North, she did not know, but he was there with that sharp perceptive gaze of his.

She did not look back. She did not need to. It did not matter if North sent the jolly boat down. In maritime stories people always swam fast and made it to the safety of the boat just in the nick of time before the shark reached them. And she wanted so much to believe those yarns right now. But the truth about sharks was that one moment they were two hundred yards away and the next they were right there in your face. They could swim real fast; faster than any man, and faster than a boat could be rowed. If you were in the water and they wanted you, then your time on this earth was over. Those who survived only did so because the shark let them, so her grandfather said. And he should know since he was one of those that did not taste so good to sharks. They took his foot, but not the rest of him.

Fear was coursing through her body, fatigue burning her muscles like fire. Her breathing was so hard and fast that she could taste blood at the back of her throat. She knew the shark must be right there, but she would not yield, not when she had so much to fight for. Not when Ben and little Bea still needed her.

Something big and hard bumped against her, knocking her off course. She pushed it away, flailing beneath the water, holding her breath, eyes wide open to see the big dark shape. The lazy flick of its tail was so powerful that she felt the vibration of it through the water. Her head broke the surface, her mouth gasping in great lungfuls of air as she watched the enormous white-tipped dorsal fin head towards *Raven's* stern.

Something landed in the water between her and the shark. Something that was swimming towards her. Something that was North. She stared in disbelief.

A few strong strokes of his arms and he was there before her.

'What are you doing?' she gasped.

'Stealing a shark's meal.' He pulled her to him. There was no smile upon his face, but there was something in his eyes that did not match the deadpan voice.

They stared at one another for a tiny moment and she felt as if he could see everything she was, all that she kept hidden from him, from her men, from all the world. As if her very soul was naked and exposed before him. As if he were not North, and she Le Voile. As if he were not British and she American. As if he were just a man and she just a woman with raw honesty and attraction between them. Making her forget about Wendell, making her forget about everything she had sworn, everything she was. All of this revealed, stark and sudden and undeniable in the tiny moments left of their lives. It shocked her, the depth of it, the absurdity of it in this situation.

Someone shouted a warning from *Raven's* deck.

Beyond North, where he could not see, the shark circled and came heading straight for them.

'It is coming back,' she murmured to him. The dorsal fin disappeared as the shark submerged for attack. Her eyes held to North's for her last moment on this earth.

North's arm gripped around her waist. 'Hold on tight,' he whispered into her ear, then turned his head to yell, 'Now!'

She gasped as they were suddenly yanked hard out of the water and suspended in mid-air, swinging precariously. Below them the great jaws of the shark snapped shut as it sank beneath the waves once more.

Only then did she notice the rope around North's waist that was hauling them slow and steady up to *Raven's* deck.

She closed her eyes to the image of the shark and held tight to him, her body pressed to his, her legs wrapped around him in the most intimate way. Nothing mattered other than that they had made it to safety.

She was alive and she could feel the beat of her heart and his. She breathed the freshness of the air and the scent of him where her cheek was tucked beneath his chin. North's arms were strong around her, securing her to him. His body was warm after the coldness of the ocean. He was strength. He was safety. And by holding to him she was holding on to life.

Her breath caressed his neck. Her lips were so close to its pulse point that she could feel the thrum of his blood beneath them, so close that she could taste him. She was alive, and so was he. And she clung all the tighter to him and to the wonder of that realisation.

But at that moment the voices of the men intruded and she felt her and North's merged bodies being guided as one over *Raven's* rail.

They were safe.

The ordeal was over.

Her face was so close to North's that she could feel his breath warm and moist against her skin, their bodies so close as to be lovers. Breast to breast. Heart to heart. Thigh to thigh. In a way no other man had ever been save Wendell. She stared up into his eyes, frozen, unable to move, unable to think.

*Wendell.*

She tried to right herself, but North maintained his grip around her and she was glad because her legs when they touched the solidity of the English oak deck had nothing of strength in them and her head felt dizzy and distant. Somehow the rope was gone and North was sweeping his dry coat around her and lifting her up into his arms, as if she were as light as a child.

'Let me take her from you, Captain. I will carry

her.' Reverend Dr Gunner's voice sounded from close by, but North did not release her.

'I will manage,' he said in his usual cool way. 'It is your other skills that are required.'

She did not understand what North meant, but the faces of the men were crowded all around, staring at her, and exhaustion was pulling at her, and it felt such an uphill struggle to think. Every time her eyes closed she forced them open. She knew she was over North's shoulder as he descended the deck ladder. When she opened her eyes again she was lying on the cot in the cabin they had given her. North was standing over her and Reverend Dr Gunner was there, too, in the background.

North's hair was slicked back, dark as ebony and sodden. Seawater had moulded the cotton of his shirt to the muscular contours of his arms and his broad shoulders, to the hard chest that she had been pressed so snug against. Only then did she see the scarlet stain on his shirt.

'You are bleeding.' Her eyes moved to meet his.

'No,' he said quietly, and gently smoothed the wet strands of hair from her face. 'Rest and let Gunner treat you.'

Before she could say a word he was gone, the door closing behind him with a quiet click.

Gunner opened up a black-leather physician's bag

and stood there patiently. Only then did she understand that the blood was her own.

'You are a physician as well as a priest?'

'Priest, physician, pirate…' He gave an apologetic smile and a little shrug of his shoulders. 'I never could quite decide.' He fell silent, waiting.

Kate gave a nod of permission and laid her head back against the pillow.


Up on the quarterdeck, having changed into dry clothes, Kit stood watching the distant ship creep closer. It was discernible as *Coyote* now without the need for the spyglass.

He thought of Kate Medhurst lying bleeding and half-naked upon the cot. And he thought of her in the water, her body so slender and pale against the large dark silhouette of the shark. And the way that, even as he dived from *Raven's* stern, the scarlet plume had already clouded the clear turquoise water. And more than any of that he thought of that look in her eyes of raw, brutal honesty, exposing the woman beneath with all her strengths and vulnerabilities, and the sensations that had vibrated between them. Desire. Attraction. Connection. Sensations with a force he had not felt before. Sensations that he could not yield to even if what had just happened had not.

As he watched *Coyote*, his eyes narrowed in

speculation. He was still thinking about it when he heard Gunner's approach and glanced round.

'It is an abrasion only.' His heavy leather coat hung over his friend's arm. Gunner chucked it on to the floor and spread it out to dry in the sun. 'The shark's skin has grazed one side of her waist— from beneath her breast to the top of her hip. And the palms of her hands, too, where she must have pushed against it.'

'How deep?'

'Mercifully superficial,' Gunner replied. 'She will be sore for a few days, but she will heal.'

Kit gave a nod.

'What I do not understand is what on earth she was doing in the water.' Gunner shook his head as if he could not understand it.

'Swimming,' answered Kit.

'Surely not?'

'You saw her.'

'Maybe she fell.'

'She did not fall. Her dress was removed and neatly folded.'

'Not necessarily,' countered Gunner.

'She might have removed it for other purposes.'

'Such as?'

'Bathing.'

'With no means to reboard the ship?'

'A woman might not think.'

'Kate Medhurst certainly doesn't strike me as woman who might not think—quite the reverse. I would say, rather, that she has a shrewd intelligence lacking in many a man.'

'I concede you may have point there. She was not bathing,' said Kit. 'She was swimming. With purpose. Away from *Raven*.'

Gunner nodded. 'But there is nothing out there save those rocks. Even if she reached them, what would have been the point?'

'The rocks are not quite the only thing out there.' Kit's gaze shifted pointedly to the horizon and the small dark shape of the pirate ship that followed.

'You cannot seriously be suggesting that she was trying to escape us to wait for them.'

'I am not suggesting anything.'

'But you are thinking.'

'I am always thinking, Gunner.'

'And what are you thinking?'

'I am thinking we need to discover a little more about Mrs Medhurst and her presence upon *Coyote*.'

When Kate woke the next morning she thought for a minute that she was aboard *Coyote* heading back to Tallaholm and Ben and Bea, and her heart lifted with the prospect of seeing those two little faces again and hugging her children to her.

But before her eyes even opened to see the truth, the sound of English voices faint and up on deck brought her crashing back down to the reality of where she was and what had happened. She remembered it all with a sudden blinding panic: *Coyote* and Tobias and North; and the shark; and that North had saved her life by risking his own.

Yesterday seemed like a dream. She might not have believed it had truly happened at all were it not for the ache in her body and the prickle of pain in her side every time she breathed; a dream in which she could not get the image of him appearing in the ocean between her and the shark out of her mind. What kind of man jumped into the water beside a ten-foot shark to rescue a woman he did not know? Not any kind of man that Kate had ever met.

She thought of the way he had pulled her to safety with no concern for himself. She thought of how she had clung to him, in a way she had never been with any other man save Wendell during their lovemaking. But most of all she thought of the gentleness of his fingers stroking the sodden strand of hair away from her cheek. Such a small but significant gesture that made her squeeze her eyes closed in embarrassment and guilt. She thought of Wendell and the memory reminded her that she hated the English and she hated North. She had to remember. Always. She could not afford to let herself soften to him. Because of Wendell and because of who she was.

Yesterday had been an aberration caused by the shock of the shark...and the rescue. This morning she was back to her usual strong self. She was Le Voile. With images of Wendell, little Ben and baby Bea in her mind, she hardened her resolve.

On the hook of the cabin door hung her black dress, her newly dried shift with its faint bloodstain and her pocket. The sight suddenly reminded her of the rest of what she normally wore. Her heart missed a beat. Throwing back the bedcover, and unmindful of her nakedness or the way her newly scabbed side protested, she sprang from the bed and got down on her knees to check her hiding place under the cot, but the holstered weapons were still there just as she had left them. With a sigh of relief she sat down on the bed. And thought.

North was not stupid. He was going to ask questions. About what she was doing in the water. And the thought frightened her. But one of the best forms of defence was attack and so Kate had no intention of just sitting here waiting meekly for the interrogation.

On the washstand in the corner, someone had sat a fresh pitcher of water, brandy and some fresh dressings. Kate wasted no more time. The dressings Gunner had applied had stuck to the dried clotted blood. She eased the mired dressings from her side using the water and dabbed the fresh flow of blood with the brandy, ignoring the sting of it. The wound made wearing her holsters an impossibility. Much as she would have felt more comfortable with them in place she left them where they were. Then, she quickly dressed, tying her pocket in place beneath her skirt, and fixing her hair the best she could with her fingers and the few pins that remained. She stood there, looking into the small peering glass fixed to the wall, for a few moments longer. Calming herself, waxing her courage and determination, readying herself. One final deep breath and she went to face North.

'Come in.' Kit did not raise his eyes from the open ledger before him when the knock sounded at the door. He was expecting Jones the Purser with a list of the supplies needed. It was the silence that alerted him to the fact that it was not Jones that stood before him. He marginally shifted his gaze and caught sight of a pair of feminine bare feet peeping from beneath the hem of the black dress he had hung on the back of Kate Medhurst's cabin door.

'Mrs Medhurst.' He set his pen down, rose to his feet and bowed, as if they were in a polite sitting room of one of London's *ton*. 'Take a seat, please.' He waited until she lowered herself on to one of the chairs on the other side of the desk before resuming his own seat. 'I did not think you would be recovered enough to be out of bed today.'

'I am very well recovered, thank you, sir.' Following yesterday's lapse, her armour was back in place. Her head was held high with that slight underlying hostility that was always there for him. There was the same expression in her clear grey eyes, politeness flecked with strength and defiance, wariness and dislike.

Most women would have still been abed, waiting for Gunner to dress their wounds. Kate Medhurst had not waited for Gunner...or for him and his questions. The grazes on her hands were the only visible evidence of what she had endured the previous day.

'How are your hands?'

'Healing.' She held out her hands before her, palms up for him to see, a gesture of revealing herself to him, a clever tactic given that he suspected that, aside from yesterday, Kate Medhurst had revealed nothing of the truth of herself.

'And the rest?' His eyes held hers.

'The same.' She did not look away.

He let the silence stretch, let that slight tension

that buzzed between them build, until she glanced away with a small cynical smile.

'I came to thank you,' she said, taking control of the situation and looking at him once again.

'For what?' He leaned back in his chair, watching her.

She raised her eyebrows in an exaggerated quizzing. 'For rescuing me.'

'Is that what I did?' he said softly. *Rescuing her... or preventing the escape of a prisoner.*

The ambiguity of the words threw her off kilter for the tiniest moment. He could see it in the *frisson* of doubt and fear that snaked in those cool, unruffled eyes of hers, before she masked it.

'How else would you describe it, Captain?' she asked.

'A lunchtime swim,' he said.

Despite herself she smiled at that and averted her gaze with a tiny disbelieving shake of her head.

He smiled, too. And then hit her with the question. 'What were you doing in the water, Mrs Medhurst?' His voice was soft, but the words were sharp.

Her eyes returned to his. The hint of a smile still played around her lips. 'Swimming. At lunchtime.'

'As I suspected,' he said.

They looked at one another, the amusement masking so much more beneath.

'Tell me about Kate Medhurst.'

'What do you wish to know?'

'How she came to be aboard *Coyote*.'

'In what way do women normally found upon privateer or pirate vessels come to be there?' she countered.

'Were you abducted?'

'Abduction is a delicate question for any woman.'

She was good. 'As is the question of allegiance, I suppose.'

'I do not know what you mean, sir.'

'I am sure that you do.'

She said nothing. Just looked at him with that calm unruffled confidence that hid everything of what was true or untrue about her.

'Where are you from, Mrs Medhurst?'

'Louisiana, America.' She said it with defensive pride, wielding it like a weapon. 'And you?'

'London, England.'

Her eyes narrowed ever so slightly at his answer.

'Why do I get the feeling that I am not your favourite person?' he asked.

'Delusions of persecution?' she suggested, and arched one delicate eyebrow.

He laughed at that. And she smiled, but the tension was still there simmering beneath the surface between them.

'I don't expect you can take me home to Louisiana,' she said.

'No.'

'Too dangerous for you?' she taunted.

'Most definitely.'

'So, Captain North,' she said in a soft voice that belied the steel in her eyes, 'what are you planning to do with me?'

'We are for Antigua to replenish our water and stores before our journey to England. There is a British naval base there, they will arrange your transport home.'

'Thank you.' She gave a single nod of her head.

The conversation had been conducted on her terms. Now she terminated it at will. 'If you will excuse me, sir...' She rose to her feet.

And as manners dictated he did the same. He waited until she reached the door and her fingers had touched to the handle before he spoke again. 'I had presumed you would be happy to travel with us to Antigua. Is that the case?'

'Of course. Why wouldn't I be?'

'Why, indeed?' he asked.

The quiet words hung in the air between them.

Her eyes held his a moment longer and the tension seemed to intensify and rustle between them.

About unanswered questions, implications and the physicality of yesterday.

'Good day, Captain North.'

'Good day, Mrs Medhurst.' Her bare feet were silent upon the floor. The door closed with a click behind her.

He stood where he was, his eyes fixed on the closed door. In his mind he was seeing the one moment when Kate Medhurst had let her mask fall, in the ocean faced with death. Then there had been nothing of poise or polish or clever tricks. Only a pair of dove-grey eyes that had ignited desires he thought long suppressed. Eyes that made him remember too well the press of her half-naked body against his and the soft feel of her, and the scent of her in his nose. Eyes that were almost enough to make a man forget the vow he had sworn...as if he ever could.

He sat back down at the desk and, picking up his pen, curbed the route his thoughts were taking. He wanted her, he acknowledged. But he could not have her, not even were she not hiding something from him. Not even if she were available and she wanted him, too. He thought of that vow, forged in blood and sweat and tears.

A knock sounded at the door, pulling him from

the darkness of the memory. This time it was Jones, and Kit was glad of it.

Kate Medhurst was not being entirely truthful. But whatever it was she was hiding, she and it need have no bearing on his returning La Voile to London.

The afternoon was as beautiful as the morning. Every day was beautiful around this area, except when hurricane season came. Kate did not have to feign that she appreciated the view as she stood at the stern, watching the crystal-clear green waves and the intense warm blue of the sky so expansive and huge…and the distant speck of a ship against its horizon.

North was on the quarterdeck, issuing commands to his men. Her muscles were still tense, her blood still rushing, her skinned palms still clammy from their confrontation in his cabin that morning. Part of her wanted to stay hidden below decks in her cabin, not wanting to face him, but Kate knew she could not do that. *Coyote* was coming. So she stood on the deck, brazening it out, watching Sunny Jim struggle to catch them, and breathed a sigh of relief that Gunner seemed to be right about *Raven* having the superior speed.

As she watched she thought of North's cabin, a

cabin that she would have mistaken for that of an ordinary seaman had it not been for its larger space. Everything in it was functional. There were no crystal decanters of brandy on fancy-worked dining tables, no china plates or ornamentation, no crystal-dropped chandelier as she had expected. Everything was Spartan, functional, austere as the man himself. He did not seem given to indulgences or luxuries. Maybe that was why the men liked him. Or maybe they were just afraid of him. She slid a glance at where he stood with his men, seeing the respect on their listening faces, before returning her gaze to *Coyote*.

There was no tread of footsteps to warn her of his approach, nothing save the shiver that rippled down the length of her spine as North came to stand by her side, his body mirroring her own stance, his gaze sweeping out over the ocean.

'Enjoying the view, Mrs Medhurst?' The Englishness of his accent, cool and deep and dark as chocolate, sent a tingle rippling out over her skin.

'Indeed I am, Captain North.' And she was, now that there seemed little danger of *Coyote* catching *Raven*.

Those dark eyes shifted to look directly into hers. Watchful, appraising, making her feel as though he could see through all of her defences, all of her lies, making her remember who he was, and who she was, making her shiver with awareness that his focus was all on her.

She glanced down, suddenly afraid that he could see the secrets she was hiding, her eyes fixing on his feet that were now as bare as her own and the rest of his crew's. Her mother always said you could tell a lot about a man by his feet. North's were much bigger feet than hers, tanned and unmistakably masculine, with long straight toes and nails that were white and short and clean. Strong-looking feet, grounded and sure as the rest of him. Their feet standing so close together, and bare, looked too intimate, as if they had just climbed from bed. The thought shocked her.

She swiftly raised her eyes and found him still watching her. He smiled, not the arctic smile, or the cynical one, but one that told her he knew something of the direction of her thoughts and shared them. Swallows soared and swooped inside her stomach and her cheeks burned hot. Kate was horrified at her reaction. And North knew it, damn him, for the smile became bigger.

With an angry frosty demeanour she turned her attention back to the horizon and focused her thoughts on Wendell and his sweet kind nature: her husband, her lover, the only man for her. She thought of what men like North had done to him and the weakness was gone. Touching the thin gold wedding band she still wore upon her finger, turning it round and round, she drew strength from it and did not look at North again.

The two of them stood in silence, contemplating the view, watching *Coyote*.

She hoped that he would leave, go back to the work he was normally so busy with, but North showed no sign of moving.

The scene was beautiful and peaceful, but as they stood there seemingly both relaxed it was anything but ease that hummed between them; or maybe the tension was just all in herself.

'She makes for interesting watching,' he said eventually, his gaze not moving from where it was fixed on *Coyote*.

'I wasn't watching her in particular,' she lied.

'No? My mistake. Pardon me.' He flicked a glance at Kate.

'Have you identified her yet?'

'We have.'

Her eyes met his.

'La Voile's pirates.' He paused. 'They are following us.' He waited for her reaction.

'Why would they do that?'

'Why indeed?'

She kept her nerve. 'Vengeance? Or maybe to reclaim their captain's body.'

'Maybe,' he agreed, and shifted his gaze to *Coyote*.

'But they will not catch us, will they? Not with *Raven's* superior speed. I mean…we are quite safe from them…are we not?'

'Oh, rest assured we are safe.' He smiled at her, the small cool dangerous smile. 'But *Coyote* is not.'

She felt the cold wind of fear blow through her bones. 'What do you mean, sir?' She worked hard to appear cool, calm and collected.

He glanced pointedly at *Raven's* sails. Her gaze followed his and she saw to her horror that they were reducing the sail. *Raven's* speed was already dropping.

Her heart missed a beat. Her stomach dropped to meet her shoes.

'You intend to let them catch us!' She stared at him, feeling the horror of what that meant snake through her.

'Not entirely. Just to let them get within range of our guns.'

'Why?' she whispered.

'*Raven* is fast, but not fast enough that *Coyote* will not fathom our direction to Antigua. Better a confrontation out here under our terms than risk her stealing upon us at anchor in the night.'

'She would not…' Antigua was a British naval base, filled with warships that *Coyote* normally avoided. But given the situation she was not sure that North was not right.

'Not when we have finished, she will not,' he said grimly.

She felt the blood drain from her face. When she looked again at the distant horizon *Coyote* was already a little larger. She kept her gaze on her ship rather than look at him, so that he would not see the truth in her eyes.

It took all of her willpower to stand there beside him, watching her men creep slowly closer to their doom, and betray nothing of the feelings of dread and fear, impotence and anger that were pounding through her blood. Instinctively, her hands went to her skirt, reaching for the weapons that were not there. Instead, she forced them to relax by her sides.

Glancing across at North's profile, she saw that he watched *Coyote* with cool, relaxed stillness. Only his dark hair rippled in the wind.

'What is the range of your guns?' she asked, her heart beating fast with the hope that she had overestimated *Raven's* range of fire.

'Our eighteen pounders have an effective penetrating range of five hundred and fifty yards,' he answered without looking round.

Far greater than the two hundred and eighty yards that *Coyote's* six-pounders could manage. She felt sick. Her mind was thrashing, seeking any possible way to stop the impending slaughter. But short of putting a gun to North's head... Her gaze dropped to the large scabbard that hung against his leg, and the leather holster above it...with the pistol cradled within. It was a much larger weapon than her own, but she could manage it all the same...if it was loaded. She glanced up to find his gaze was no longer on *Coyote*, but on her.

'I hope that pistol is loaded,' she said.

He smiled as if he knew it for the question it was. 'Always. But it will not make any difference to *Coyote's* fate. Bigger guns are already aimed and waiting.'

She swallowed, her mouth dry as ash, her heart thudding hard as a horse at full gallop. *Coyote* would see the guns, but she would not realise their size, or the special powder, or their range. She would not know what she was sailing into before it was too late.

*Raven* was barely moving now, making the distance between the two ships diminish fast. Too fast. Even with the naked eye, no one aboard *Raven* could doubt that the identity of the closing ship was anything but *Coyote*. Every second brought her closer.

Kate's fingers found her wedding band again. *Oh, God, please stop them.* But *Coyote* kept on coming.

'Eight hundred yards!' came a shout from the rigging.

She bit her lip, trying to stop herself from crying out. Stood there still and silent as a statue while her mind sought and tunnelled and tried to find a way out for them all.

'Seven hundred yards!'

She thought of Sunny Jim. She thought of young John Rishley. And the rest. All of them men from Tallaholm. Men with wives and children, with mothers and fathers, and brothers and sisters. Men who would lose their lives trying to rescue her.

'You can't just kill them!' The words burst from her mouth.

'Why not?' He turned to look at her, his calmness in such contrast to the rushing fury and fear in her heart.

'For the sake of humanity and Christian charity.'

'You care for the lives of the men who abducted you?'

'Some of them are barely more than boys, for pity's sake. Have mercy.'

'Your compassion is remarkable, Mrs Medhurst.'

'Reverend Dr Gunner is a priest. He will tell you the same as me, I am sure. Where is he?' Her eyes scanned for Gunner.

'He is on the gun deck,' said North, 'making ready to fire.'

She could see the fifteen horizontal red-and-white stripes and the fifteen white stars against the blue canton of the American flag and the skull and smiling cutlass of her own flag.

'Six hundred yards!' the voice called, followed by another from over by the deck hatch, 'Ready below, Captain! We fire on your command.'

'Do not!' Her hand clutched at North's wrist. 'If you sink them, they will all die. And no matter what they have done, they are just men seeking to make a living in difficult times.'

He looked at where she held him so inappropriately. Her fingers tingled and burned with awareness. She loosened her grip, let it fall away completely. 'Please,' she said quietly.

Their eyes locked, their bodies so close that she could feel the heat of his thighs against hers.

'I do not intend to kill them,' he said with equal softness to hers. 'Only to disable them.'

'Five hundred and fifty yards and in range!' the call interrupted.

North turned away and gave the command, 'Fire!'

Her heart contracted to a small tight knot of dread. She heard the echoing boom of a single long gun and watched with horror as the iron shot flew through the air towards its unsuspecting victim.

But the round shot had not been aimed at *Coyote's*

hull. Instead, her foremast was cleaved in two, the top half severed clean to fall into the ocean. Canvas and rigging crumpled all around. The men on deck rushed around in mayhem.

Her hands were balled so tight that her nails cut into her skinned palms. She did not notice that they bled as she braced herself for the echoing cacophony of shots that would follow, standing there knowing that she owed it to *Coyote* and her men not to look away, but to bear witness to their valour. She waited.

But there was only silence.

Kate glanced round at North in confusion.

'She is, no doubt, too small to carry spare spars and canvas, but these waters are busy enough that they should not have too long to wait for help. Either way *Coyote* shall not be following us into port, or anywhere else for that matter.' He paused, holding her gaze. 'If you care to check, you will be relieved to see not a pirate life was lost.' He passed her his spyglass and stood watching her.

She looked at the spyglass, knowing she should not accept it. But she could no more refuse than she could stop breathing. The responsibility of a captain to her ship and men ran deep. So Kate took the spyglass and checked for herself the damage to the men and the ship.

North was right. There were no casualties.

'Let her run with the wind,' he commanded his men.

'Aye-aye, Captain,' came the reply as they ran to increase the sails.

Kate returned the spyglass without either a word or meeting North's eyes. She was aware of how much she had betrayed, but all she felt right now was wrung out and limp with relief for her men. She offered not a single excuse or explanation.

'If you will excuse me, sir.'

He did not stop her, but let her walk away without a word.

Because they both knew that she was not going anywhere other than her cabin. They were on his ship. At sea. He could come and question her anytime he chose. And that there were questions he would ask, she did not doubt.

## Chapter Four

Within his cabin Kit sat at his desk, the paper-work and ledgers and maps upon it forgotten for now. Gunner sat opposite him, leaning his chair back on to its hind two legs and rocking it. The afternoon sunlight was bright. Through the great stern window the ocean was clear and empty, the disabled *Coyote* long since left behind.

There was a silence while Gunner mulled over what Kit had just told him of Kate Medhurst's reaction up on deck earlier that day.

'Women are the gentler sex. Their sensibilities are more finely honed than those of most men,' said Gunner, 'but…' He screwed up his face.

'One might have expected a degree of either fear or animosity towards the boatload of ruffians that took her by force and held her against her will,' Kit finished for him.

Gunner nodded. 'It is possible she has an unusually meek nature.'

*I hope that pistol is loaded?* Kate Medhurst had looked at the weapon like a woman seriously contemplating snatching it from its holster and holding it to his head.

He thought of the essence of forbidden desire that whispered between the two of them, the barely veiled hostility in those eyes of hers and the way her body had responded so readily to his.

He thought of her plunging from *Raven's* head and swimming so purposefully towards those rocks. And of their interaction in his cabin, with her skilful deflection of his questions to reveal nothing of herself.

'I would not describe Kate Medhurst as meek.' Intelligent, determined, formidable, capable, mysterious, courageous and passionate, most definitely passionate. But not meek. 'Would you?'

'No,' Gunner admitted.

'Mrs Medhurst was not so unwilling a guest upon *Coyote.*'

Gunner's gaze met his. 'You think she is lying about being abducted?'

'She never told us she was abducted. We made that assumption. Mrs Medhurst did not correct it.'

'But you saw how the pirates treated her.'

'La Voile would have given her to us easily enough. The rest did not wish to yield her.'

'She was afraid of them.'

'She was afraid, but not of them...*for* them.' He thought of the desperation that had driven her to grab his wrist, to plead for the lives of those men. 'There is someone on *Coyote* that she cares for, very much.'

'A lover.'

Kit thought of the way Kate Medhurst touched so often to the gold wedding band upon her finger. 'Or a husband.'

Gunner looked at him in silence for a moment. 'You think it was not La Voile's body his crew were intent on retrieving. You think it was the woman.'

'It would explain much.'

'But not what we saw between her and La Voile on *Coyote's* deck that morning.'

'Does it not? If we remove our assumptions, what did we see, Gabriel?' Kit asked.

'An argument between two men over a woman,' Gunner said slowly. 'The other pirate...'

'It is a possibility.'

'The only fly in the ointment is her mourning weeds.'

'Are they mourning weeds? A ship that flies a black sail is not in mourning.'

Gunner looked at him and said slowly, 'A pirate's woman might dress as a pirate.'

Kit said nothing.

'And if she is a pirate's woman?' Gunner asked.

'It makes no difference. As long as we have La Voile's body she is not our concern. We offload her in Antigua in the morning. Let them ship her back to Louisiana. We have bigger things to think of.' Like getting La Voile's body back to London. Like returning to face what he had left behind. 'Post a guard on La Voile's body in the meantime.'

'You think she is capable of sabotage?'

'I think we should not underestimate Kate Medhurst. I will breathe easier when she is gone.' And he would. Because every time he thought of her, he felt desire stir through his body. She was temptation, to a life he had long left behind, to a man he no longer was. And that was a road Kit had no intention of revisiting.

The purple-grey-green silhouette of Antigua loomed large before them. The haze of the early morning would burn off as the day progressed, but for now the sun sat behind a shroud that did not mask the brightness from the daylight. Within the rowing boat there was no sound other than the rhythmic creak and dip of the oars and their pull of the water. No one in *Raven's* small party spoke.

The wind that was usually so mercifully cooling seemed unwelcome at this hour with the lack of sun, making Kate's skin goosepimple beneath the thin black muslin. Or maybe it was just the sight of North in his place at the other end of the boat.

His eyes were sharp as the raven's perched upon his shoulder and strayed her way too often, making her remember the lean strength in his body, and the scent of him, and the feel of his skin against hers…and the way he had stroked the hair from her cheek. Making her feel things she had never thought to feel again; things that appalled her to feel for him of all men. And she was gladder than ever that this was the end of her journey with him.

But there was a small traitorous part of her that, now she was safe, wondered what might have happened between them were it not the end. Just the thought turned her cold with shame and guilt. She pushed it away, denying its existence, as much as she denied the tension between them was not all adversarial. And turned her mind to wondering as to her crew and *Coyote's* fate.

North was right, these waters were rife with Baratarian pirates and privateers; one of Jean Lafitte's boys had probably already found and helped the stricken ship. Sunny Jim knew what he was doing and would get them all back safe to Tallaholm, and she felt better at that thought.

\* \* \*

'Something is not right,' Kit said softly to Gunner as they stood before Fort Berkeley on the island not so much later. Jones the Purser and five ordinary seamen who had rowed across with them had stayed in the main town, St John's, to procure water and the list of required victuals. Kate Medhurst stood just in front of him, surveying the yellow-washed walls of the fort that guarded the entrance to English Harbour. She was more relaxed than he had seen her, now that they were about to part company, her secrets intact. He wondered what they were. He wondered too much about her, he thought, as his eyes lingered on the way the wind whipped and fluttered the thin black muslin of her skirt against the long length of her legs. He turned his focus back to the fort and what it was that he did not like about it.

Gunner gave a nod. 'I get that same feeling.'

'No guard outside the gate.' His eyes scanned, taking in every detail.

'And apart from the lookout in the watchtower, not another soul to be seen,' murmured Gunner.

'Silent as a graveyard, and a gate that should be opening, demanding to know our business by now.'

Kate Medhurst glanced round at him, as if she was thinking the same.

'Wait here with the woman, Gunner. If I am not back in fifteen minutes—'

'I'm coming with you,' Kate Medhurst interrupted, as if she did not trust him.

'Maybe Mrs Medhurst has a point,' said Gunner. 'You should have someone at your back.' He touched a hand lightly to his cutlass.

Eventually they were admitted through the fort's gate by a lone marine in a coat faded pink by the sun and taken to see the admiral. The distant dry docks were empty, not a man could be seen working in the repair yards, not a man on the tumbleweed parade ground. Within the yellow-painted building every room was deserted. Not one other person did they pass along those corridors and staircases lined with paintings of maritime battles. And for all of that way there was a faint smell of rancid meat in the air.

'It's like a ghost town,' Kate Medhurst whispered by his side and she was right. 'Is this normal for a British fort?'

'Anything but,' replied Kit softly.

'Something is definitely off.' Gunner's quiet voice held the same suspicion that Kit felt.

He shifted his coat so that his hand would have easier access to both the pistol holstered on his hip and his cutlass and saw Gunner do the same.

The marine eventually led them through a door

mounted with a plaque that read Admiral Sir Ralston.

The office was large and more grandly decorated than many a *ton* drawing room. Ornate, gilded, carved furniture filled it, along with a massive sideboard that looked as though it might have been brought from Admiralty House. There was a large black-marble fireplace, although the hearth was empty save for a pile of scrunched balls of paper which were clearly discarded letters. The windows had roman blinds of indiscriminate colour, pulled halfway up the glass, and were framed by fringed curtains that might once have been dark blue, but were now somewhere between pale blue and grey. From the ceiling in the centre of the room hung a crystal chandelier. But despite all of this faded opulence there was an unkempt feel about the place.

The great desk was littered with a mess of paperwork and documents. A thick layer of dust covered the window sill and every visible wooden surface. It sat on the back of the winged armchair by the fireplace and turned the ringed, empty crystal decanter and silver tray that sat on the nearby drum table opaque. It hung with cobwebs from the chandelier. But the two things that concerned Kit more than any of this were the stench of rum in the room and that the man that sat on the other side of the desk was not Admiral Sir Ralston.

'Acting Admiral John Jenkins, at your service, sir. I am afraid Admiral Sir Ralston died a sennight since.' Jenkins was younger than Kit, no more than five and twenty at the most, with fine fair hair that stuck to a sweaty brow, red-rimmed eyes and thick determined lips.

'I am sorry to hear that, sir. My condolences to you and your men.'

Jenkins gave a nod and gestured to the chairs on the other side of the desk. 'Take a seat. May I offer you a drink?' He produced a bottle of rum from the drawer of his desk.

'There is a lady present, sir,' said Gunner.

'Beg pardon,' Jenkins said and sat the half-empty bottle on top of a book on the desk. 'How are matters in London?'

'I have no idea.' Kit had no intention in wasting time in small talk. 'What has happened here?'

'We are awaiting reinforcements. They are due any day now.'

'You have not answered my question. Why do you need reinforcements?'

'We have lost almost all the men.'

'How?'

There was a silence while Jenkins stared longingly at the rum.

'What happened to the men, Jenkins?'

'Dead,' he said, and did not take his eyes off the

bottle. He reached a hand to it and began to absently pick at the wax near the rim. 'It will have us all in the end. Every last one of us, you know.' He smiled softly to himself.

Cold realisation stroked down Kit's spine. He understood now, not the detail, but the gist. Too late. He was here now, and more importantly so were Gunner and Kate Medhurst.

'Get up,' he snapped the order to them by his side, already on his feet. 'We are leaving.'

'What?' She looked aghast. 'But—'

'I said we are leaving. Now.'

'So soon?' interrupted Jenkins. 'You are welcome to stay and dine with Hammond and me.' He smiled at Kate and walked round to their side of the desk. 'It would be a delight to have the company of a lady at our table.' He offered his hand to Kate.

Kate moved to accept, but Kit grabbed her hand in his and pulled her away from Jenkins, placing himself as a barrier between them.

'Captain North!' she protested and tried to break free.

'They have a pestilence here,' he said harshly to her. 'A pestilence that infects both men and women.'

She ceased her struggle, shock and fear flickering in her eyes.

'Which disease, sir?' Gunner asked Jenkins, the scientist and physician in him coming to the fore.

'Yellow Jack.'

'May God have mercy upon your souls, brother,' whispered Gunner.

'Amen to that,' said Jenkins.

'What were you thinking of, admitting us?' demanded Kit. 'You know the drill when it comes to pestilence.'

Jenkins smiled again and this time it held a bit of a leer. 'Hammond said you had a woman with you. A white woman. An English woman.' His gaze travelled brazenly down Kate Medhurst's body to rest on the small bare toes that peeped out beneath the hem of her dress.

In a prim angry gesture she twitched her skirt to cover them. 'American,' she corrected with a look of disgust that Kit could not tell whether it was due to Jenkins's appetite or the fact he had mistaken her as English.

'How many of you are left?' Kit shot the question at him.

'A handful.'

'How many infected?'

Jenkins gave a shrug.

Gunner slid a look at him. They both knew there was nothing they could do, that it was too late.

'Quarantine the place. Let no one new in and

no one infected out. Burn the bodies of the dead,' said Kit. It was the most he could offer. He pitied Jenkins. He wanted to help and were he alone he would have stayed, for all the difference it would make, but he was not. He had Gunner and a shipful of men to think of. And he had Kate Medhurst.

'It is too late for that.'

Kit met Jenkins's eyes and said nothing. Given his own past he could not condemn any man for a weakness of character, especially not under such circumstances.

'I pity you, sir, but your attitude is despicable,' said Kate Medhurst quietly.

'I suppose that means a mercy shag is out of the question?' Jenkins said.

Kate did not flinch. 'As I said—despicable.'

'And dead,' said Kit as his hand tightened upon the handle of his cutlass. He controlled the urge to pull it from its scabbard and hold it against Jenkins's throat.

Gunner was already on his feet, poised for action.

'But not by our hand,' finished Kit, then, to Kate Medhurst and Gunner, 'Move. We have already spent too long in here.' Not trusting Jenkins not to attempt some last, defiant, contemptuous action, Kit kept his eye on the man until they were out of the office and making their way back down the corridor. Moving quickly, they retraced their earlier steps across the deserted yard and through the gate.

The hired horse and gig still waited where they had left it. In silence Kit picked up the reins and began the drive back to St John's.

'So what happens now?' Kate asked the question after ten minutes of driving during which no one had uttered a word. She was more shaken by what had happened at the fort than she wanted to admit. A whole garrison, wiped out by Yellow Jack.

One summer, when she was a child, Yellow Jack had come to Tallaholm. Some were taken, some were spared. Kate had been lucky enough to recover. She remembered little of it, but her mother still spoke of how terrible that time had been and how she had nursed Kate. *I sat by your side and bathed your body with cold stream water all the nights through to cool the fever.* It made her all the more anxious to get home. But she was very aware that there was no British navy ship here on which she could hitch a ride.

She saw the glance Gunner exchanged with North and a little sliver of apprehension slid into her blood.

'You heard what he said. Your country is sending reinforcements and that will encompass not only the fort, but those frigates that patrol the waters near to Louisiana,' she said.

'No doubt.' North did not look round at her, but just kept on driving, eyes forward, expression uncompromising.

'Indeed, many of the British naval frigates in this area use English Harbour as their base. It's just a matter of time before one comes into port.'

'True. But that time might be weeks or even months.'

'Unlikely,' she countered.

'Very likely, given that word of the pestilence will have passed through the fleet.'

'I'll wait,' she said stubbornly.

'But I will not. *Raven* leaves Antigua tomorrow, Mrs Medhurst.'

'Fine,' she said. 'I am not asking you to delay your journey.' Indeed, the sooner he was gone the safer she would be.

He pulled gently at the leather reins wrapped around his hand and brought the horse to a stop. Only then did he look at her, his gaze meeting hers with that searing strength that always made her shiver inside. 'You are a woman, with no money, no protection and no knowledge of the island. Are you seriously suggesting that you wait here alone?'

That was exactly what she was suggesting, but when he said it like that it made it sound like the most idiotic idea she had ever had in her life; when she knew that honour belonged to her decision to attack an unnamed ship with a raven circling its masts.

'Next you will be telling me you are planning on staying at Fort Berkeley with Jenkins.'

'Don't be absurd!' she snapped. 'I am not a fool.'

'Then do not act like one.'

She glared at him. 'Are you offering to take me home to Louisiana, Captain North?'

'No.' No superfluous explanation.

'So just what is it that you are proposing, Mr Clever?'

'We take you with us to England. Admiralty will put you on a frigate escorting one of the convoys bound for America.'

'England?' She could not believe what she was hearing. 'You expect me to travel all the way to England and hope that I may find my way back from there?'

'There is nothing of hope involved. I will ensure that you obtain safe passage.'

She stared at him with utter incredulity. 'But that will take months.'

'So will waiting here amidst the pestilence for a frigate to drop anchor.'

What he said made sense, yet the thought of sailing thousands of miles to England…and with him of all people… She bit her lip, torn between the devil and the deep blue sea.

His gaze held hers, unwavering and steadfast, cool and perceptive, stroking all of the nerves to tingle in her body. 'And the longer you stay here the greater your risk of contracting Yellow Jack, or carrying it with you when you eventually do find passage back to Louisiana.'

To her children, to those she loved, to a community that was already struggling against hardship and feared the disease more than any other.

'The choice is yours to make, Mrs Medhurst. There is a place for you on *Raven* should you wish to accept it.'

But the reality was that her choice was already made. Kate could not risk either her children or Tallaholm. So she swallowed her pride and quashed the trepidation that gnawed deep in her belly. 'You are right, sir,' she admitted even though it galled her to do so. 'I would be a fool, indeed, if I did not accept your offer.'

He gave a nod and said nothing more. The rest of the journey continued in silence.

Only once they reached the main street of the town did he speak again, addressing his words to Reverend Dr Gunner. 'I will return the gig and do what must be done.' From his pocket he produced a purse that looked heavy with coin and threw it to the priest. 'Find Mrs Medhurst a dressmaker.'

'That will not be necessary, sir!' She felt her cheeks flush with warmth. Only husbands and lovers bought women clothes.

His gaze met hers, then dropped lower from her face to slowly sweep the length of her body before returning to her eyes once more. It was not a leer—a leer she could have handled with a smart put down—but his usual cool, intense, serious appraisal made her blush glow even hotter.

'The Atlantic is a harsh and cold environment. Your attire will not suffice.'

Always so cold and clinical, and yet there was something at the back of his eyes that hinted he was not as devoid of passion and feeling as he would have the world believe. Something dark that made the memory of his strong arms around her and the feel of their bodies pressed tight and close whisper between them, that made her remember the tenderness of his fingers against her face. The butterflies danced in her stomach. Her whole body seemed to quiver.

'And as Gunner is clearly a man of the cloth your reputation should not be so damaged.'

Pulling her gaze from his, she looked at Gunner, who smiled a sheepish smile. She glanced down to her bare toes next to the dusty leather of North's boots.

'Very well. But your money is a loan only. I will pay you back every last coin.'

'If you wish.'

Cool as a business deal to any observer, but what she felt inside was a heat of embarrassment and awareness of a dangerous sensual connection. It made her manner cold almost to the point of rudeness.

'I do, sir.' She climbed down from the gig and walked away without so much as a backward glance.

She did not want to think about being enclosed upon *Raven* for the entirety of a transatlantic journey with him. She did not want to think of the dangers that posed for her. Because if she thought of the enormity of it the fear would overwhelm her. Even now, the seeds of panic stirred in her belly. She stifled them and followed Gunner into the crowded, dusty market square of St John's.

And then, through the mass and press of bodies and woven baskets filled with brightly coloured produce, she saw a face that she recognised and she smiled. Maybe God had heard her prayers, after all.

With one eye on the face she bided her time and, as the crowd pressed closer, she slipped away from Gunner.

* * *

'What do you mean, you lost her?' Kit raised an eyebrow and stared in disbelief at his friend.

'Exactly that,' replied Gunner calmly. 'One minute she was right there behind me, the next she was gone without a sign. It is market day. The square could not get any busier.' He paused before adding, 'You do not think that she might have been abducted?'

'Again?' Kit said the word with heavy scepticism. They both knew that Kate Medhurst's presence aboard *Coyote* had not been through abduction.

'She did not seem so enamoured with accompanying us to England.'

'Hardly surprising.'

'Had she refused, would you really have left her here alone?'

Kit did not answer that one. 'There is another ship newly anchored. She is flying the Stars and Stripes and listing herself as a merchantman, but with a name like *Gator* and the fact that she is here at all, means she is more probably a pirate making the most of the fort's misfortune.'

'There are pirates in town...? We need to find her fast.' Gunner understood what that meant. That American or not, men newly come ashore were always looking for a woman. And Kate Medhurst stood out from the rest of the women in this place.

'You cover the east side, I will take the west.'
Gunner nodded.

Together they set out across the square.

'Bill Linder!' Kate called the name clear and strong before the two men could head into the tavern.

Linder stopped and glanced round at her. 'I thought I heard a home-grown Louisiana voice. Well, if it ain't little Kate Medhurst.'

'You sly old dog, Billy Boy,' the other shorter man, built like a bear, said with a lascivious tone. 'You didn't tell me that you had a girl here.'

'I'm not his girl,' corrected Kate and moved the small distance down the lane towards them. 'I am allied with Jean Lafitte the same as the two of you. Aboard *Coyote*.'

'La Voile sails *Coyote*,' said the bear man.

'True,' she said, and thought it better to keep quiet about Tobias's death for now. 'You still with McGaw on *Gator*?'

'I sure am. She's out in the bay.' He looked at her with a puzzled expression. 'What you doing here, Kate Medhurst?'

'Looking for a ship home to Louisiana. Fast.'

'You sound like you're escaping someone.'

'Maybe,' she conceded. 'Can you help me?'

'Can I help you? Honey, what did I always say

to old Wendell? You have come to the right man, Kate Medhurst.'

She gave a sigh of relief at his words.

He smiled and she saw his gaze meander down over the dusty muslin of her dress, lingering a little too long on the fichu that covered her décolletage, before dropping lower to where the wind had moulded her skirt with a degree of indecency to her legs, all the way down to her dirty bare feet. There was something in that gaze that made her realise that Bill Linder's attitude towards her had changed. Something that was all too obvious when his eyes met hers again.

'How's your wife, Mary, and your two little ones?' she said, trying to keep things a bit safer and casting her mind back across the years to the last time she had seen this man.

'They're good.'

'Please pass on my best wishes to her.'

'I don't think so. She's the jealous type.' The words made her feel uncomfortable and set a warning tattoo beating in her breast.

'She's got nothing to be jealous of. You were a good friend of my husband's, Bill Linder. I thought you were my friend, too.'

'I was. And I am. But you see—' he leaned in closer, as if to share a secret '—I always did have an eye for Wendell's pretty little wife. And Mary knew it.'

She stared at him, shocked at what she was hearing.

His fingers brushed lazily against the tie of her fichu as if he were toying with the idea of loosening it.

'What the heck do you think you are doing?' She slapped his hand away, but in that moment he changed from lazy insolence to fast striking snake, grabbing hold of her wrist and twisting it up behind her back at the same time as the weight of his body barrelled her into the nearby shady alleyway.

'I think I'm doing what I've waited a long time to do, little lady.' His hands moved over her body, his fingers rough against the still-tender wound on her side, searching for her pocket and finding it empty save for a handkerchief.

'She got a purse of money?' his bear companion asked.

'Nope,' said Bill Linder.

'Oh, dear,' said the bear man. 'She's going have to find some other way of paying her passage on *Gator*. I suppose we could pay her coin for her and in return...' He licked his thick dry lips slowly and deliberately.

'In return...' said Bill Linder with a grin that showed his uneven teeth.

The stench of unwashed men was strong. She could see the grime caked upon their sun-baked skin and feel the length of Bill Linder's dirty fingernails cutting into her wrist.

He threw her further into alleyway so that she stumbled against its wall.

A quick glance told her it was blind-ended. No way out other than through the two pirates from *Gator*.

She backed away, giving herself a little distance, and pulled up her skirts.

'That's right, darlin', you get yourself nice and ready for us,' Linder drawled and began to unbuckle the belt of his trousers.

'Oh, I'm ready for you, boys,' she said, pulling the pistol and knife from their leather holsters on her thighs. 'You wait till Lafitte hears about this. He'll hang you both by your scrawny necks.'

'Lafitte ain't going hear nothing. Put the weapons down, darlin', before you get hurt,' Linder sneered.

'You back out of this alleyway right now, or I will shoot.'

'And then what?' Linder asked.

The two men exchanged an amused grin with one another.

'We got you all to ourselves, Kate, honey. Haven't you heard? The navy boys are down with Yellow Jack. Ain't no one going to come and help you.'

Linder's eyes held a nasty glint and the bear man laughed as the two of them closed towards her.

Kate aimed the pistol...

'There you are, Mrs Medhurst. I wondered where you had got to.' North's voice was smooth and quiet and cool, but its authority cut through the situation in the alleyway.

Her finger hesitated upon the trigger.

'She's already taken, friend. You're interfering in something that's got nothing to do with you. Go get your own.' The two men turned with a swagger, ready to chase off the intruder come to spoil their fun, but what they saw checked their cocky attitude.

North was standing there, his faded leather coat pulled back to show one hand resting on the handle of his pistol and the other on his cutlass. In the shade of the alleyway his eyes were black as the devil's. With his dark shirt and his buckskin breeches, his battered tricorne hat and the large black-feathered bird that perched silent and beady-eyed upon his left shoulder, he looked every inch what he was: downright dangerous.

He stood there silent, still, his stance relaxed yet poised for action, and emanating such an air of threat that even Kate felt a shiver of fear go through her.

'You are mistaken, gentlemen. You see, this is everything to do with me…given that this lady is under my protection.'

It was his eyes, she thought; there was something in them, something deadly, like the eyes of a shark. Linder and the bear man could feel it, too. She could sense their sudden discomfort and suspicion and fear and see it in the way they glanced at one another.

'I don't think we've been introduced, sir,' said Linder.

'Think very carefully about what you are asking for,' said North.

The raven cawed as if to mock the men.

*'Merde,'* she heard the bear man whisper as the penny finally dropped and they realised what they should have known straight away from the sight of both him and the raven. 'He's North.'

'Still want that introduction, gentlemen?' North said quietly.

'Begging your pardon, Captain North. We didn't realise that the lady was…in your care.' Linder sounded pathetic.

'We surely did not, sir,' agreed the bear man. 'Our apologies.'

'Not to me,' said North. With a single curt gesture of his head towards her, 'To the lady.'

'Our apologies, ma'am,' they murmured, turning

to her. Then quieter, to her, but not North, 'God help you, Kate Medhurst.'

'Get down before her,' North instructed.

They glanced at one another again, but did as he said, kneeling in the sandy soil of the alleyway.

'Lower,' said North. 'On your bellies.'

She saw them swallow their pride, saw the humiliation in their eyes as they obeyed, to lie face down in the dust.

'Did they hurt you?' he asked her.

She shook her head, not trusting herself to speak.

'Then they get to live,' said North. He bent over, and whispered the words quietly to the prostrate men, 'But if there is ever a next time, gentlemen of the *Gator*…' He let the words hang unfinished, but they all understood too well his promise. 'Now, I think you should leave me and the lady together.'

The two of them got to their feet and ran out of the alleyway as if the devil himself, or North, were on their heels. The raven flew off, following them.

Leaving Kate facing North alone, knife in hand, pistol aimed directly at his heart.

## Chapter Five

His gaze held hers, yet he spoke not a word.

Her heart was pounding hard and fast. Beneath the grip of both the pistol and knife her palms were clammy. Her mouth went dry.

'I had it under control. I can defend myself, sir.'

'So I see,' he said in that quiet sensual voice that made the goosebumps break out across her naked skin. His gaze dropped to the weapons still clutched tight within her fingers, before coming back to her eyes. 'Do you want to put them away now?'

She was not sure that she did. Not because she thought he would hurt her, but because of what might happen when she did. The tension seemed tight enough to break between them. They were standing alone, too close together, in a place shielded from the eyes of others. She could feel the heat of him, sense the dark passion that lurked beneath that cool calm control.

She swallowed. Took a couple of steps back to put some space between them. Turned her back to stow the weapons safely once more.

He was leaning against the wall of the alleyway, waiting, when she faced him once more.

Their gazes held, his with such dark intensity that she feared how much he might have overheard before he stepped into the alleyway.

Neither of them spoke.

Neither of them moved.

She felt like she was trembling inside, from the shock of what Linder had almost done and from the feelings that overwhelmed her when she looked in North's eyes. Of attraction. Of desire. Of a need so raw and guttural she could no longer deny it.

He walked closer.

Kate knew she should move away, but she didn't. She just stood there, knowing what was coming, her eyes never leaving his.

Reaching a hand out, he threaded it through the back of her hair. He hesitated only a moment longer before his mouth met hers and their bodies came together, and he kissed her just as she wanted, exactly how she needed. A kiss that was inviting and passionate and filled with all of the stormy intensity that was in her own soul.

He tasted of something divine, his tongue enticing her own. He was masterful yet not forceful, gentle yet passionate. And his kiss woke other parts of her, parts she had thought long laid to rest. Needs and desires, passions and longing. The feel of him, the touch of him, the scent of clean man and leather and sunshine and sea...and just *North*. And then she caught what she was doing—kissing him. Kissing the first man since Wendell...the only man other than Wendell. And not just any man—North. An Englishman. A man who made his money from killing privateers and pirates.

She broke the kiss, backed away, confused and embarrassed and ashamed, and angry, too, with herself more than him.

'We should go,' he said.

'We should.' Her voice was cool and firm to hide the quiver and flux of conflicting emotions inside.

'But I will have your weapons first.'

'And you think I am just going to hand them over?' She stared at him.

'You will if you do not want the dressmaker to see them. What would she think?' he asked silkily. 'A pirate ship at anchor and a woman with a pistol and a knife strapped to her thighs turning up in her shop.'

*Pirate's moll.* The words whispered unspoken between them.

She gritted her teeth and, sliding her hands into the slits in the seams of her skirt, produced the weapons. She looked at him for a moment, almost tempted to use them, before reluctantly yielding them.

'And the holsters,' he said as she watched her weapons disappear into the pockets of his coat.

*'What?'*

He looked at her.

With an exclamation of disgust, she turned her back, rustled beneath her skirts to unfasten the buckles and finally dropped the leather strapping into his waiting hand.

'Still warm.' He smiled.

She glared at him.

As they walked out of the alleyway together and re-entered the crowded square she felt his hand close firm, but gentle, around her wrist.

'Just in case,' he said softly by her ear. 'I would not want to lose you again.'


Kit was careful not to look at Kate Medhurst again until he had cut a path through the crowd to Gunner.

'Change of plan. You check on the procurement and the men. I will take Mrs Medhurst to the dressmaker.'

He saw the way his friend's eyes moved to Kate Medhurst and Kit's grip upon her, before returning to Kit, and the hint of both curiosity and speculation that was in them, but Gunner was wise enough to say nothing.

Beneath his touch he felt her stiffen and saw the rosy bloom, that had not yet faded from her cheeks since the kiss they had shared, intensify. 'That will not be necessary, Captain North.' Outraged antagonism flashed in her eyes.

'It is entirely necessary.'

Gunner cleared his throat. 'I will see you back on *Raven*.' With a nod, he hurried away, his tall fair frame standing out amongst the shorter dark crowd.

'This way.' Kit directed Kate Medhurst onwards.

'You're not a priest,' she said.

'You noticed,' he replied, but he did not look at her and he did not stop leading her towards the only dressmaker in town.

'Allow me to go in there alone.'

'No.'

He felt the slight resistance in her arm. 'For pity's sake, North, you must be aware of the impression it will give if we enter the shop together.' Her eyes met his, part-appeal, part-indignant anger.

'Fully aware.' He looked at her then—at those beautiful soft grey eyes, and her kiss-swollen lips that tasted like the sweetest thing on earth, and the sensual disarray of her sun-kissed tawny hair from its pins—and felt the urge to take her hand in his own, lead her from this square into the quiet intimacy of an alleyway once more. He wanted to put her against a wall. He wanted to pull up her skirts and make her his own.

'There is a wedding band upon your finger. And we are together, my hand on your arm. What impression do you think it will create?'

'Do you honestly expect me to pretend to be your wife?' Beneath the cover of the frumpy fichu her breasts rose and fell with increasing rapidity.

'I do not expect anything other than you choose your clothes quickly.'

The dark woman at the other side of the counter flashed her gaze between them, taking in Kate's hair that had escaped its pins and the way North stood too close to her, before fixing on North. Her smile was wide and very white in her pretty dusky face.

'You are looking for a dress for your wife, sir?' Her English was smooth with just a trace of an accent, taking them as man and wife just as North had said. Kate could feel the heat in her cheeks, but better this than they thought her his whore, she told herself. And no amount of explaining was going to make it seem anything otherwise. She swallowed and touched at her wedding band for reassurance.

'My lady's wardrobe was lost. We are looking to

replace it. But we are only in port for a few hours. We sail tonight.'

'Such a little time.'

'Not a full wardrobe, just a few items for traversing the Atlantic,' Kate clarified. 'Respectable... and black if possible.' She did not look at North. She was too aware of him and the proximity of his body that proclaimed an intimacy between them beyond the fact that he was buying her a wardrobe of clothes. His kiss still burned upon her lips, her skin still tingled everywhere he had touched. She tried to smooth her hair tidy, tucking the strands behind her ears.

'Fate smiles on you today, ma'am.'

Not with the fort or Bill Linder, she thought. But with North's timely arrival in that alleyway, the little voice in her head whispered, and she knew it spoke the truth. Her pistol was small, its single shot at best only able to cut the attack by fifty per cent. Her knife, to fend off the other barrelled brute of a man, would have been sorely tested. Despite her protestations, and whether she wanted to admit it to herself or not, North had saved her. Again.

'I have the very thing.' The dressmaker smiled again. 'A customer of mine was unable to return to collect her order, a lady of a similar size to yourself. A full wardrobe all finished and ready.' Her gaze dropped to Kate's bare feet. 'Slippers, too.' She looked at Kate with curiosity. 'Dark in colour—a mourning wardrobe, in fact.'

Kate twisted the wedding band harder around her finger and stared down at it, thinking of the man she had lost. 'How appropriate—it will suit my needs perfectly.'

'As would the yellow silk,' said the dressmaker as she saw North glance at a bright yellow dress draped upon a mannequin in the corner.

'No,' said Kate.

'We'll take both,' said North and paid the woman for the clothes and to wrap them.

'After you, my dear,' he said as he tucked the parcels beneath his arms and opened the door for Kate.

'You are too kind to me, sir,' she replied with heavy irony.

He leaned closer as followed her through the door out into the square and said quietly. 'You know very well, Kate Medhurst, that I am not kind at all.'

She felt the shiver ripple through her both at the coldness of the words and the heat in his eyes.

The afternoon was done and the evening begun by the time that the provisions were all aboard. A whole stockroom of sacks of flour and grains, of fruits and vegetables. Livestock, too. The cages containing the hens had yet to be taken below. Kit could hear their soft clucking from where he stood on the quarterdeck.

The cool white-blue of the daytime sky was yielding to the warm orange and glorious red of sunset. The aqua-green of the ocean was silvered in this cobwebbed light of dusk, a swirl of colour bigger and more vivid than anything that could be seen at home in England. Colours there were softer, more muted, like the land and the people. Here, as in the East, life was more immediate, more intense and bold. To be lived all the freer or snatched away in the blink of an eye.

The wind was mellow, but enough to billow in *Raven's* sails and carry her away from Antigua and *Gator*, anchored not so very far away.

'The men are grumbling about missing out on a night in the town's taverns,' said Gunner by his side.

'Tell them they can go back in the jolly boat for their night in the taverns, but Raven shall not be here waiting for them tomorrow morning. Nor will their share of the bounty. And remind them of our trip to the East Indies.'

'Where the local brothels were hotbeds of pestilence even if the women themselves showed nothing of the symptoms,' said Gunner. They both remembered too well what it had done to the crew in the days before they turned hunters.

There was a silence while they both watched the silhouette of the island recede into the distance.

'What happened with Mrs Medhurst…in the square back there?' Gunner asked, without shifting his gaze from the view.

'She had a run in with a couple of *Gator's* boys.'

'You got to her in time?' Gunner's gaze shot to his, his brow creased with concern.

'I got to her as she was about to put a shot through one of them and take her chances against the other with a knife. She is capable, but even so the scoundrels would have had her eventually.'

'Had you not shown up. Where did she get the weapons?'

Kit glanced round at him. 'She was holstered beneath that skirt of hers.' He remembered the flash of those pale legs in the dim shade of the alleyway and was very aware of the leather, within his pockets, that had been strapped so intimately to her thighs.

Gunner's eyebrows rose. 'She really is wife to one of *Coyote's* men.'

Kit thought of the way Kate Medhurst touched so often to her wedding band. He thought, too, of the look of sadness in her eyes following the dressmaker's reference to a mourning wardrobe and of her response— *'How appropriate…'*

'I am not so sure of that,' said Kit.

'She seems too respectable for a pirate's light-skirt.'

'Appearances can be misleading. But I do not think she is a pirate's lightskirt.'

'Then what?'

'A widow.'

There was a silence during which he could feel the weight of his friend's gaze.

'So the dress was mourning weeds, after all.'

'It is now. I am not sure if it was when we first saw her in it aboard *Coyote*.'

'You think she is La Voile's widow?' whispered Gunner.

'That is what I need to discover. I will speak to her after dinner. Until then, I have work to do.'

'Kit.' Gunner's voice stayed him. There was a ripple of embarrassment in Gunner's eyes. 'I think perhaps you should know—her belly bears the signs of having borne a child.'

Kit gave a nod. 'Thank you.'

'Will you not stay and watch the beauty of the sunset? It will be gone within the quarter of the hour.'

Kit was almost tempted. Whilst stood on the deck of a ship he had seen the sun set across the oceans and countries of the world and it truly was a won-drous sight. But to stand here and indulge himself in the pleasure...? He clapped a hand against Gunner's upper arm in a token of their friendship. 'You stay. Enjoy it.' He had work to do. And the problem of what he had overheard in that alleyway to think of.

He left Gunner standing where he was and went to find his desk.


Kate sat on the cot in her cabin, haunted by thoughts of Kit North saving her from Linder, by his hard handsome face and the feel of his mouth on hers.

She touched her fingers to lips that even now still seemed to tingle and burn from his kiss. It seemed she could still smell the scent of him, still feel the strength of his arms around her. Her breasts felt heavy and sensitive, and there was an insistent ache between her legs that could not be denied.

North awoke a longing deep inside her that should not be there, a longing that made her burn with shame and anger and frustration.

She thought of the vow she had sworn. She thought of the love that was in her heart.

Beneath her fingers the gold of her wedding band felt smooth and warm. She looked at the ring on her finger and, pushing North from her mind, filled it instead with Wendell. His presence seemed to surround her, giving her strength. She thought of Ben and Bea and the weakness was gone.

Three-and-a-half-thousand miles of Atlantic Ocean lay ahead of her with North. And given what he had seen he was going to ask questions, a lot of questions. She worried how much he might have overheard in the alleyway. Regardless, he would be more than certain by now that she had not been aboard *Coyote* by abduction. But he had Tobias and that would mean he would not push too hard. She knew it looked bad for her, but shrewd as those dark eyes were, she was confident that they would not guess the truth. No one had ever guessed the truth.

Kate would just have to be very careful how she answered his questions.

Someone knocked at her cabin door and she started.

*North.* His name whispered through her mind, making her heart race, making birds take flight in her stomach, making her afraid that it was not questions he had come to ask.

Taking a deep breath, she composed herself, reminding herself of what men like him had done to Wendell. Opening the door, she was ready to do battle.

But it was not North that stood there. The level of her gaze dropped to the young cabin boy.

'Begging your pardon, ma'am, but Captain North wishes to know if you will join him for dinner.'

Couched in terms of politeness, Kate understood the message for the command it was. It was the summons she had been expecting.

The boy's face and frame were thin. He could barely have been older than nine or ten years of age and his mop of blond hair and freckled cheeks reminded her too much of what she had left behind in Louisiana.

She smiled him. 'What is your name, boy?'

The boy's eyes widened. 'Have I done something wrong, ma'am?' There was fear in his voice.

'You have done nothing wrong.' She reached a hand to his arm to reassure him, but the boy jumped beneath her touch and pulled away as if burned. 'I only ask that I might know what to call you.'

The boy was regarding her with the suspicious wariness of a trapped animal. 'They call me Tom,' he said after a moment.

Heaven only knew what manner of treatment to which the child had been subjected, to warrant such a reaction.

*I am not kind.* North's own admission seemed to echo in her head. All of the stories and rumours she had heard surrounding him came whispering back. Of his cruelty and his temper. Of all those things he was reputed to have done to men doing their best to reclaim the living denied them. It reminded her just who he was, and more importantly who she was. That knowledge and the sight of the child before her fuelled her determination, hardening her will, sharpening it, focusing it with precision.

'Well, Tom,' she said, crouching down to his level, 'please tell Captain North that I accept his invitation.'

'Yes, ma'am.' The boy nodded and, with a tug of his forelock, ran off across the gun deck to where the dining tables were ready and waiting with hungry men.

The usual screens were not in place. North glanced over from where he sat at the head table, his dark eyes meeting hers and sending that shiver of sensual awareness rippling down her spine.

Kate stood there for a tiny second, holding his gaze coolly, bold as a pirate about to wield a cutlass and shield, knowing what was coming and tempted to close her cabin door and make him wait for the skirmish. But the crew were not eating, the dishes sat covered, awaiting her arrival. And she could not be so petty.

Taking a breath, she left the illusion of safety her cabin offered and went to eat with North and his men.

* * *

There was only polite small talk during the meal. She sat in the empty space that had been left for her, close to North and directly opposite Gunner, engaging in the politeness and listening to the surrounding conversations, aware that the men's language was careful on account of both her and their captain's presence at the head of their table. The time passed until, at last, Gunner cleared his throat and, setting down his napkin, got to his feet.

'If you will excuse me, Mrs Medhurst…Captain North?' Gunner's eyes shifted between Kate Medhurst and Kit.

The men eating at all the tables finished their food and, with a respectful nod to their captain, followed Gunner. The men that were serving table also disappeared so that not one soul remained on that gun deck with Kit and Kate Medhurst.

Now that they were alone there was a subtle shift in the atmosphere—a tightening of that multifaceted tension that shimmered between the two of them.

She swallowed, but made no attempt to run. Holding her head up, she faced him calmly across the table, with cool grey eyes and a small defiant curve to those honey-sweet lips.

'I'm getting the impression that there is something that you wish to discuss with me in private, Captain North.'

'Am I so obvious?'

'Just a little.'

He smiled and so did she.

'Do you wish something to drink?' he asked.

'I will take a brandy, thank you,' she said, no doubt to shock him.

He poured her one and himself a lemonade, acknowledging her derisory glance at the lemonade with a smile.

She sipped the brandy. 'You wasted your money, and mine, on that dress. I do not wear yellow.'

'Why not?'

'It does not suit.'

'On the contrary, I think it would suit very well.'

The silence stretched.

She met his gaze directly and dispensed with the small talk. 'So what exactly is it that you wish to ask me?'

He smiled at her tactic and then supposed with her he should always expect the unexpected. He studied her face closely and saw a mask of beautiful composure. She was cooler under pressure than any man he had known. She revealed nothing, not a flicker of a tense muscle, not a swallow in a dry throat. Not the slightest tremor of her voice.

'Those men in the alley today. You knew them.'

She did not miss a beat, held his eyes with confidence. 'I recognised them as being from Louisiana.'

'They were pirates.'

'Really?'

'Really. How do you know them in Louisiana? Friends of yours, were they?'

She smiled again. 'We're all friends in Louisiana.'

'Or perhaps of your husband's.'

The mask slipped for a tiny second. Something flickered in her eyes, something raw, before she glanced away to hide it, her fingers rotating the thin gold wedding band on her finger. 'My husband is dead, Captain North.'

'Tell me of him.'

She looked at him again, the emotion gone, her cool composed self once more. 'I would rather not,' she said in a voice that beneath the soft velvet held a hint of steely strength.

The silence hissed between them. She held his gaze, bold and stubborn in her defiance. They could sit there all night and she would say not one word. He tried a different tactic.

'You know Lafitte.'

'Everybody in Louisiana knows Jean Lafitte and his older half-brother Pierre.'

'Pirate overlords.'

'I would describe them more as trade facilitators.'

'They are French corsairs.'

'They might have been French born, but they are of New Orleans and everything they do is for the good of Louisiana. And I am sure you are well aware that Louisiana is now a part of the United States of America.' Anger and pride flashed in her eyes. 'They are not violent men, not murderers.'

'And are these non-violent trade facilitators La Voile's overlords?'

'How would I know?'

'Because you knew La Voile. Because you were with him, willingly, on his ship.'

She did not deny it.

'What manner of man was La Voile?' he asked.

'Not the manner of man most would expect, that's for sure.'

'Did he treat you badly?'

'He did not.' There was confidence in her eyes and wariness.

'And yet that morning *Coyote* attacked *Raven*, there was a disagreement between you and him.'

'Was there?' She arched an eyebrow, brazen and cool.

He let a small silence stretch between them before the important question. 'Were you La Voile's wife, Kate?' he asked softly.

The shock in her eyes was real. She blinked for

a moment and then she gave a little laugh, half-incredulity, half-amusement. 'His wife?' She glanced away and shook her head.

'Are you telling me that there was nothing between you and La Voile?'

Her eyes shifted to his once more. 'On the contrary, I am not telling you anything, Captain North.'

'You certainly are not,' he agreed. 'I wonder why.'

'I wonder,' she said.

The silence seemed to hiss between them.

She looked beautiful and pale and proud.

Their gazes held, and for all their stab and fish and parry of words there was the whisper of that other underlying tension between them. That same thing that had made him take her in his arms in the alleyway and kiss her. She could feel it, too. He could tell by the look in her eyes. In the flicker of the candlelight they looked not dove-grey, but charcoal-dark and serious and sensual.

He slid his hand across the table and took her fingers gently in his.

She did not snatch it away, just looked at where their hands lay there together.

The tension pulsed strong between them in the silence.

She swallowed. 'I am a respectable and loyal widow,' she said slowly before she raised her gaze to meet his. 'So you may ask your questions, all you will, but you will hear no answers.' Her hand withdrew from his, but her fingers were soft as a caress in their parting.

He did not doubt it for a minute.

'For all you are English and a bounty hunter, you seem an honourable man, Captain North.'

His smile was small and tight and cynical. 'Do I?' But appearances could be deceptive.

'So I am sure you will understand when I tell you I will not compromise mine.'

'Perfectly,' he said. He knew what it was she was saying. That she would not betray anything of her connection with La Voile…and that she wanted nothing to come of the passion that was smouldering between her and Kit.

The latter suited Kit perfectly well. The desire was there, palpable and thick and real between them, but he wanted nothing to come of it, either. Kit Northcote would have, but Kit North did not. And North had business in London to think of and a vow to honour.

'You offered me safe passage, Captain North. Do you rescind it?'

'The offer remains unchanged.' Whoever she was, and whatever she was hiding, did not matter. He had La Voile pickled in a butt at the other end of the deck. And that was all he needed to return to London and do what was required.

'Thank you.' She gave a small nod of acknowledgement. 'If you will excuse me, sir, it has been a long day and I would like very much to retire for the night.'

He rose, his eyes holding hers. 'Goodnight, Mrs Medhurst.'

'Goodnight, Captain North.' Her bare feet made no sound as she walked across the deck to her cabin.

Whoever she was, and whatever she was hiding, did not matter, he thought again.

But whoever's widow she was, it was not La Voile's.

# Chapter Six

Kate awoke to the morning bell ringing up on deck. The warmth and comfort of the dream was still upon her, of her children and her home back in Tallaholm. She clung to its soft remnants, pressing her lips to Bea's plump baby cheeks and breathing in the scent of Ben's tousled mop of golden blond hair as she ruffled it and told him to be a good boy for Grandma. But the images faded too soon and she was left lying alone in the tiny cabin aboard Kit North's ship.

How long would it be before she saw them again? Weeks, maybe even months, stretched ahead—weeks in which she was trapped here with Kit North. A dangerous man in more ways than one.

She thought of last night's encounter, of questions asked and unanswered, of the louder unspoken tension between them. She had more or less blatantly told him she would not sleep with him and that he should stay away from her. She could scarcely believe her own audacity.

Would he honour her request? She touched against the fingers that his had held, seeing again the cool cynicism of his smile at her admission of his honour despite being English and a bounty hunter.

She thought of the way he ate with his men, not apart on some high captain's fancy table, sharing the same plain food, not fine fare prepared by a personal chef, as she had believed all British captains did.

*I am not kind.* The words sounded again in her mind, with their brutal ring of honesty.

He was North the Pirate Hunter. He was not kind. But he had not hesitated to dive into the water with a ten-foot white-tip shark to save her. And she was under no illusion as to what would have happened in that alleyway with Bill Linder and his sleazy companion had North not arrived.

He was not kind. But the caress of his fingers and the touch of his lips were all gentleness.

He would honour her request, she thought. And that, more than anything else, was the one thing that would make the three-and-a-half-thousand-mile journey that lay ahead easier.

\* \* \*

In those first few days, as their journey got properly underway, she was proved right in her estimation of his honour, for North kept his distance just as much as she had hoped he would. And Kate was relieved. For the sake of her children, for the sake of her mama, and for all who waited in Tallaholm. And for the sake of the vow she had sworn to Wendell.

It was Gunner who sat with her at meals and Gunner who came on occasion to speak to her when she stood at the rail, looking out over the endless ocean and all she was leaving behind.

In the evenings, when the work was done and the daylight gone, the azure-blue of the sky curtained with midnight velvet and diamond stars, *Raven's* crew got together in the dining room, screened off from the rest of the deck, and drank a little grog and talked and laughed and sang old songs of love and loss, of drink and women, and the sea. Gunner played the fiddle and an older man, called Pete, played a little flageolet. They did not seem English. In those evenings she forgot they were her enemies. They were just men the same as those from Tallaholm that crewed *Coyote*.

But North was not there, not on any of those first evenings of *Raven's* journey. Not at dinner time, when he ate at the opposite end of the table to her, their seats too far apart to allow conversation. Nor later for the singing and the music and camaraderie.

On the fifth evening when she came from her cabin to join the social he was over talking to Gunner, but when he saw her approach he left the gun deck, giving her a small but cool nod of acknowledgement as he did so.

Her eyes lingered on the deck ladder up which he had disappeared, realising that his absence from the leisure time was because of her presence. She should have been glad of it, but instead all she felt was a curious empty kind of sadness.

Aware that she had been staring too long after him, she glanced round to find Gunner watching her.

'Maybe I will just spend the evening in my cabin reading one of those books you were kind enough to lend me, sir,' she said.

'You will do no such thing, Mrs Medhurst,' he countered, lowering his voice a notch before adding, 'North never joins us in the evenings.'

'Not ever?'

Gunner shook his head and poured her a small glass of grog. 'He prefers to work.'

'But he cannot always work. There must be times when he—'

'There are not,' Gunner cut off her words gently. His brow furrowed in worry and there was a far-off look in his eyes as he stared at the table between them. 'North is a hard man, Mrs Medhurst, but hardest of all with himself. He is…driven, relentlessly, without rest, without mercy.'

'What brings a man to such a place?'

'His past.' Gunner looked into her eyes.

'What happened in his past?' she asked quietly.

'Things you could not imagine, Mrs Medhurst.'

She stared at him.

'Where's that fiddle of yours, Reverend Dr Gunner?' one of the men called.

Another was starting up the first notes of another traditional folk song.

Gunner's confidences were over. Lifting his fiddle from its battered case, he began to play.

The men joined in, singing and stamping their feet in time to the rhythm, smiling and laughing, enjoying the jolly tune.

Kate watched them, her tankard of grog sitting on the long scrubbed wooden table before her. Just the same as the previous nights, but this night was different. Gunner's words seemed to ring in her head, sending a discomfort through her.

All of this camaraderie and bonhomie while North was elsewhere, alone, working. She should be glad he was not present. He was dangerous. This was what she wanted, for him to stay away from her, wasn't it?

*What happened in his past?*
*Things you could not imagine.*

She was still pondering on it when Gunner sat down beside her an hour later.

'Reverend Dr Gunner, are you feeling all right?' Even in the mellow soft light of the lanterns the priest looked too pale around his eyes, but with the telltale flush of cheeks that boded ill. It was warm on the gun deck, but not enough to account for the sheen of sweat that glistened upon his face. The hour of playing seemed to have drained all of his energy.

He shook his head as if to shake away her concern and set his fiddle on the table surface, something he never did; he always was careful to keep it in its case. 'I do feel a little under the weather,' he admitted, and with that his eyes rolled up into their sockets and he slid from the bench to collapse on to the deck.

The dancing and the singing stopped abruptly. The flageolet, too.

Kate got down on her knees, laying her hand against his forehead and feeling how hot he was.

'Go fetch Captain North,' she instructed the nearest man, then turned Gunner on his side in case he should be sick and choke upon it. The men were all crowded around, worried but not knowing what to do, Gunner was the physician, after all; he was the one who normally dealt with such occurrences.

North came immediately. The men cleared a path for him as he made his way to where she knelt by Gunner.

They carried the priest to his cot in North's day cabin and Kate followed.

'Go back to your cabin, Mrs Medhurst. The matter is in hand,' North instructed.

'If you do not mind, Captain, I'll stay.' Her eyes met his meaningfully. 'I think you're going to need my help.'

She waited until his crew were gone before she spoke. 'He is burning up with fever.'

They looked at one another, both realising the awful possibility—that what had wiped out the naval fort and yard on Antigua was now here on *Raven*.

'It might be a coincidence,' she said.

'Unlikely.'

'Either way he has a fever that needs to be cooled.'

'This is not work for you.'

'I had Yellow Jack as a child. I will not contract it again.'

He just looked at her.

'For goodness' sake, I was a married woman. I have seen a man's body before.'

'He is a priest.'

'And a friend to us both. I am not going to sit in my cabin doing nothing. We need a basin of cold water and clean rags. And some boiled water that we can leave to cool.'

For a moment his eyes held locked to hers, the expression them unreadable.

She did not back down, just held his gaze steady. Gunner had been kind to her.

'Do you know what you are doing, Kate Medhurst?' he asked.

She swallowed, understanding the layers of meaning in the question.

'I do,' she said, still holding his eyes. 'I have seen fever before.'

But they both understood that was not what he was asking.

After a long moment, North gave a nod. 'I will fetch what is needed.'

*Did she know what she was doing?*

There was no time to think about it. A man's life was at stake.

Kate moved to Gunner's side and began to roll up her sleeves.

The night seemed very long.

Kit held the small cup to Gunner's mouth and

tried to pour a few drops of the cooled boiled water between his friend's cracked dry lips, but most of it just spilled down the side of his face. He sat the cup down on the surface of his nearby desk.

'A little is better than nothing,' Kate Medhurst said from his side.

'But not enough.'

'Drop by drop,' she said.

His eyes moved over the thin sheet that covered Gunner's naked body and was already drenched with sweat although they had not long changed it.

'I will mop his brow and sit with him, while you go get some rest,' she said, her American twang soft and lilting in the room.

'I am staying.' Gunner was his friend, his ship-mate and the man who had saved his life. And even if he were not, it would not matter. He held out his hand for the wrung-out rag she was holding, ready to wipe away the rivulets of sweat that ran down Gunner's brow and cool the fever that burned beneath the pallor of his skin. 'You rest.'

'I do not have a ship to captain in the morning,' she pointed out.

'This is my responsibility.'

She stood there silent for a moment and he could feel the weight of her gaze upon him, even though he kept his focus fixed on Gunner.

She passed him the cloth. 'You are a stubborn

man, Captain North.' The words, uttered soft as a caress, felt like a compliment rather than a criticism. She walked quietly away then, pausing when she reached his door. 'I will be back at dawn.'

His eyes met hers across the cabin, glad of her words, and her strength and her capable practicality.

He nodded his acknowledgement and turned his attention back to Gunner.

But what neither of them knew in that moment was that by dawn hell would have come to *Raven*.

Kate Medhurst came back long before that hour.

Eighteen of his fifty men were struck down with the same fever that held Gunner.

Kit North had not slept. His eyes held their same steady resolve and determination, but also an unmistakable fatigue, and beneath them was the smudge of smoky shadows. He looked bone weary beneath that rigid backbone of his.

She told herself she was not doing this for North, that it was purely selfish interest. For if *Raven* did not complete her journey safely, how was she going to get back to her children and to Tallaholm?

'Eighteen of your men are affected so far, not including Reverend Dr Gunner. It could go higher. You are undermanned with them down and, on top of that, the ill need nursing and you've still got to sail *Raven*. You cannot do all of that alone.'

He did not shoot her down, just let her speak. 'I get the feeling you are about to offer me a solution.'

'Let me take charge of nursing the ill. I'll need six men who will do what they are told.'

She waited for him to refuse. Most men that didn't know her always did. They judged her on the fact she was a woman, not on the strength that was inside.

But he did not refuse.

'And Gunner?' he asked.

'I will nurse Reverend Dr Gunner myself.'

He gave a nod of acknowledgement.

They worked together.

Those men without symptoms were massed on the lower deck. North informed them of the situation and how it would be managed, while Kate watched on. A captain to his men, a commander, a natural leader, his men hung on his every word, their faces grim with worry, yet eyes that spoke of a deep-seated trust in him. Unlike most captains he ruled with a firm hand of fair justice rather than through undeserved or unending lashings and beatings, and the difference was clear. His leadership was instinctive, easy and unquestioned.

'Move the hammocks of those afflicted to the

aft. Those who are clear bunk to the fore. Keep a clear boundary between. We are fortunate to have Mrs Medhurst amongst us as she has much experience of nursing the ill.' A deal less experience than North's words implied.

The crew's gaze turned to rest on her as he spoke and she looked at them with the confidence of a woman who had had nursed a shipload of men with Yellow Jack a hundred times before. They needed to believe in her as much as North. They needed to believe they could beat this and sail on and not panic and give up or bail for their lives.

'Riley, Horse, Sandbatch, Gilley, Henhead and Scrobe,' North instructed, 'you are assigned to assist Mrs Medhurst. Do as she commands. For the rest of us it is business as usual.'

His eyes met hers fleetingly and alongside the usual complex dark feelings of attraction was respect and the knowledge that the fate of *Raven* rested in both their hands.

Kate Medhurst was still on her feet, wiping down Gunner's face when Kit finally made it back to his cabin. Through the big stern windows the night sky was tinged with a beautiful deep azure. Stars big and bright and numerous as a sprinkled bag of diamonds twinkled in the sky. The ocean was dark, a deep pitch-black that made men think of the darkness of their own souls and the monsters that lay hidden in the realms beneath.

A single lantern burned on the table. Beside it Gunner lay naked on the cot that had been stripped of all sheets. Only a cloth draped across his hips preserved his modesty; his thin pale body looked so corpse-like that it made Kit fear the worst.

'How is he?' he asked as he came to stand by her side.

'He was sick again earlier, hence the lack of sheets. We have no clean ones left.'

'That, I can do something about.' He passed her the fresh linen he had brought with him.

'Thank you.' She smiled a small smile.

For three days she had nursed his friend and organised and run an operation of caring for the rest of his crew, who were afflicted with the pestilence, with the efficiency and expertise of a captain running his ship. And in all of those three days and nights he had not seen her sleep, not once.

Her face was shadowed with exhaustion and worry, the same worry he felt twist deep in his gut over Gunner's fate.

'Is he going to make it?' He glanced at the man to whom he owed so much before looking into Kate Medhurst's eyes for the truth that words might hide.

'I do not know,' she said with bare honesty. There was no attempt to deceive, whether through kindness or otherwise, nothing of that edge of conflict that was usually there between them. Fatigue had blunted it, exposing something of the woman beneath the armour. It felt like, in this at least, they were fighting on the same side.

'When will we know?'

'Probably by the end of this night.' She set the linen down on table.

He swallowed down the bile that rose at the thought of Gunner dying. Turned away so that she would not see how much the prospect affected him. 'I will stay with him. You get some sleep.' His voice was gruff. He did not look at her.

'We'll both stay with him,' she said quietly, and he heard the movement and glanced round to see her sit down in her chair.

He should have insisted. But he was too tired to argue and, in truth, he was not sure that he wanted to face the dark hours ahead alone. He sat down on the chair beside hers.

'How long have you been friends?' she asked.

'Three years. It does not sound long, does it— three years out of a whole lifetime?'

'Long enough,' she said. 'There is much that can happen in three years.' There was something about the way she said it, something sad and reflective, that made him think that she was talking not only about him, but about herself, too.

'Very much.' His eyes lingered on Gunner, remembering all that they had been through together—the worst of times, and the best.

'He means a lot to you.' Her voice was gentle.

'He saved my life,' he admitted.

'Saved you from a shark, did he?' *Like you did me.*

He glanced round at her, his eyes holding hers, remembering that moment between them.

'Threw me to them, more like,' he said.

'And that saved you?'

'Without a doubt.'

She said nothing, but her silence, like her presence, seemed comforting in a way he did not understand. It seemed to reach out to him. It seemed to connect them as much as the way that she held his gaze and did not look away.

'I would have destroyed myself otherwise.' He smiled, but the bitterness of shame and guilt was still there. 'Along with everyone else I cared about.' And the anger, too, even through the tiredness.

'The dreaded drink,' she said, misinterpreting his abstinence from brandy and other spirits.

'Amongst other things.' He looked at Gunner in silence for a while, at the way the tremors still shivered through his friend's body and the labour of his breath. Death seemed to hover close in that cabin. Even Bob the raven, sitting on his perch in the corner, was silent and brooding.

Kit felt helpless and too aware there was nothing he could do to help. He got to his feet, needing to do something, so tired he could not think straight and yet knowing he could not rest, that this was his friend, his ship, his responsibility, his duty.

'In many cultures the raven is associated with battle and death,' he said.

'Is that why you captured and trained your raven—as a symbol of such?'

He gave a small soft laugh. 'The raven I trained when I was in prison. Bob came to the bars of my cell one day. We became friends.'

'Bob?' she said with a teasing arch of her eyebrows that, despite everything, made him smile.

'What is wrong with the name Bob?'

'Nothing. I guess I was expecting something a little darker or more Gothic or mystical.'

'I think he is more of a Bob.'

'I think you are probably right.' She glanced across at where Bob sat hunched and watching. 'And your boat is named for him?'

'My boat was a black sail, built to fly fast and to scavenge.' Wringing out the cloth in the clean cold water, he held it to Gunner's forehead, trying to cool the fever that raged beneath the flush on that pallid skin. 'He is going to die, isn't he?'

The question was not really for her, was not really a question at all, more a trying to come to terms with the hard fact himself.

He felt gentle hands take the cloth from him and place it once more in its basin.

'Sit down, Kit North,' she said softly. 'There is nothing more we can do except wait. And pray.'

'I do not pray.'

'Why not?' she asked.

'I have no right to pray.'

'Everyone has a right to pray.'

'Not everyone.'

'You are very hard on yourself.'

'Not hard enough,' he said, his eyes holding hers, daring her to argue or question.

She did neither. She sat down in her chair and reached her hand to his, taking it in her own. It was a small hand, slender and soft, but a practical hand, a hand that worked rather than frittered away time in leisure. A hand that was gentle yet firm. No woman had touched him like that. Even in the old days, when he had bedded the best of whores with the worst of rakes, it had all been about selfish gratification. This felt like something very different. He knew he should remove his hand from hers, but he did not; he could not.

With his eyes on Gunner he sat down beside her.

The long hours of the night stretched ahead, the

time when men's lives were weighed in the balance and taken or given. But for the first time in such a long time, he was not alone. Kate Medhurst, with her strength and her calm practicality, was by his side. He threaded his fingers through hers, and was glad of it.

'Why in heaven's name am I lying here naked as the day I was born?'

The imperious demand dragged Kit from deep slumber to the cabin aboard *Raven* once more. Kate Medhurst's head rested on his shoulder, her soft breath warm and moist against his cheek. His arm was curled protectively about her, while her hand rested against his chest. Their legs were entwined like lovers. There was an ache in his back as though someone had kicked him with an iron-clad boot, where the wooden chair frame had pressed against his spine for hours. And, worse than any of that, he had an erection that would have dwarfed Mount Olympus.

She woke when he tried to move, her eyes soft at first, her mouth smiling, then, as reality intruded, that changed. She hastily disentangled herself, springing to her feet, her cheeks blushing red, as if caught *in flagrante* while he adjusted his coat to disguise his awkward predicament.

\* \* \*

'Gunner?' North's voice sounded hoarse as if he had not used it in eons. She forgot her embarrassment as she watched him. 'Gunner!' He smiled. A proper smile, a real smile. Full of joy and relief and gladness. It was the first time she had seen it and the man it exposed beneath. It changed his face from one of hard determination to one that she could not take her eyes from. He looked in that instant like the weight of the world had been lifted from his shoulders. He looked happy. Like a man who could have swept her off her feet with laughter and made the world all right again. She watched the transformation in amazement.

'Thank God,' he whispered. A man that did not pray, but she remembered the soft murmur of his words in the night and felt his strength surround her.

'I am naked before Mrs Medhurst, Kit!' Gunner complained. 'Grant a priest some dignity.'

'You have been ill, old friend.'

'Not any more.' Gunner's voice was weak, his face skull-like and just as pale. But the fever had passed and he was still with them. 'My apologies, ma'am, for my state of presentation,' he said to her. Then smiled. '*Quid pro quo* for my treatment following your encounter with the shark.'

'We are even,' she joked. 'Welcome back, Reverend Dr Gunner. You had us scared for a while.'

'I had myself scared for a while.'

She smiled. 'We were waiting for the fever to pass before replacing your bedsheets.' She could feel the heat flush her cheeks and did not look over at North, knowing how they had awoken together. 'I am glad you are returned to us, sir.'

Gunner smiled weakly with dry cracked lips.

'I will leave you in Captain North's capable hands.' Then, to North, 'I must go and check on the others.'

The smile was gone, the hard, determined, emotionless pirate hunter back once more. But something had changed between them. Something small and yet important, something in the depths of those dark eyes that made the blush heat her cheeks all the more. He gave a nod and turned back to Gunner.

She slipped away and left the two friends together.

Six of Kit's men were not as lucky as Gunner. He buried them the next day in the traditional maritime way that they would have wanted, their bodies sewn up in their hammocks. Those of the crew well enough to walk collected on the upper deck for the funeral. Men, even pirates and sinners, deserved dignity in being laid to rest, especially when there had been nothing of dignity in the manner with which the pestilence had taken their lives.

Kit stood there before the assembled crew, feeling, as did all of his men, the loss of those who had been taken. The leather-bound book of prayer was alien in his hand, shaped and used to the touch of another. He could feel the slight dents worn by the press of Gunner's fingers. This was a priest's territory, but Gunner was still too weak to climb from his cot.

Across the deck, some little distance behind the crowd, Kate Medhurst stood. The shabby black muslin she had worn all of the past days and nights was gone. In its place she had donned a fresh dress, one of those from the wardrobe bought in Antigua. A black silk and matching bonnet with her own familiar black fichu fitted in place to cover her décolletage. The colour intended to mourn another now a mark of respect for the men she had nursed and lost.

He opened the book and the men fell silent before him, bowing their heads, hats and caps clutched in hands.

*All we can do is wait and pray.* Her soft words sounded again from the previous night. And his own reply, *I do not pray.*

Yet here he was with the prayer book. The irony

was not lost on him. He wondered if she was thinking the same. She had every right to. But when his eyes met hers it was not mockery that he saw there, but understanding—that this was a captain's duty to his men.

She gave a small nod. Of acknowledgement, of encouragement, of support. Her face was etched with fatigue, the shadows beneath her eyes blue in the brightness of the daylight—from working to help his men, from being there to help him. All those nights without sleep and yet her shoulders were squared and her head held high as ever it was, with strength and dignity and unwavering steadfastness. In all of his life, Kit had never seen a more beautiful woman.

He put aside his own discomfort and spoke the words from the prayer book.

There were tears in the eyes of some of the men as the canvas-shrouded bodies slid into the clear green ocean, sinking down to disappear beneath the waves.

When it was done and over, he looked again for Kate Medhurst, but the place on the deck where she had stood was empty.

## Chapter Seven

In the few days that it had taken Gunner to regain something of his strength *Raven* had long left behind the balmy climes of the Caribbean. The waters of the mid-Atlantic were not aqua-green but darker, deeper, a grey-blue that did not invite swimmers. The wind was stronger, colder, biting even, but for today, at least, the sun still shone and she could understand Gunner's insistence in coming up on deck to lean against the rail and look out over the vast endless surround of ocean.

'Only for a little while,' she reminded him. 'And then you should rest again.'

'I do nothing but rest.'

'You can work on your scientific papers.'

'You nursed me well, Mrs Medhurst.'

'Captain North did more.'

He smiled.

'I guess there is a bond between men who have saved each other's lives.'

Gunner glanced round at her with a quizzical expression. 'What makes you think I saved Kit's life?'

'He told me so. "By throwing him to the sharks," I believe was the precise expression.'

Gunner chuckled at that.

'What happened?'

'So much,' said Gunner, and looked away over the ocean again.

'How did you meet him?'

'In a tavern in Portsmouth three years ago. My ship was in port and I was making the most of the last of my land leave. He was not North then.'

'Who was he?'

'A different man altogether.'

'In what way?'

'In ways he would not wish me to divulge.'

She said nothing, knowing better than to persuade any man, let alone a priest, to break a confidence, no matter how much she wanted to know the answer to the question.

'I did not trust to leave him there. So I took him with me. And threw him to the sharks.'

'I do not understand.'

He smiled again as he glanced round at her. The wind fluttered through his short blond locks, the bright clarity of the sunlight revealing in his face the ravages of his fight with the Yellow Jack. 'Priest, physician, *pirate*...' Those same words he had said to her once before.

'I did not think you were being serious.'

'Entirely serious, my dear Mrs Medhurst. I was a pirate, part of a black-sailed cutthroat crew and I suppose you might say that I press-ganged Kit into joining us with the help of more than a few bottles of brandy. He did not know what he was signing up for. And by the time he realised, it was too late. We were well on our way, heading for the riches of the East. Superb plunder. A fine living for almost a year.'

'What happened?'

'We intercepted a jewel load belonging to the Sultan of Johor. The Sultan, quite rightly, took exception and sent his navy after us. Our captain was hanged, drawn and quartered while we watched. The rest of us were imprisoned in the Sultan's gaol, death by labour. In this case the labour was ship-building for his navy.

'Kit had changed by then, his body grown strong from the hard work on the ship. He stood up against the tyrant guards, for the older men of the crew, for the injured and the sick. And in return they punished him, with solitary confinement and more.'

She felt her stomach twist in horror at the word punished and all that it suggested.

She closed her eyes, remembering what North had told her of Bob the raven coming to him when he was in prison.

'More than any other man could have endured. He survived. Not as he was. He became the man he is today. All those months alone, all that time to explore his own mind. He designed *Raven*, in that cell, and an escape plan. When they let him out eventually, we built her. Right beneath the noses of the guards, as if she was just the same as every other ship we worked upon. After she was completed and taken to the harbour, Kit broke us out of there. We took the ship. It was not stealing, you understand. We had built it. It was Kit's.'

'And the pirates became pirate hunters.'

'Kit's idea. As I said, he was a changed man. He did not drink, did not game, did not so much as look at a woman. He said we would earn our money honestly. You might take comfort in the fact that La Voile is our last job. A special commission. Once Admiralty pay the bounty on him Kit will hunt pirates no more.'

'What will he do?'

'I do not know. You will have to ask him that question.'

Her thoughts swirled around Kit North, what Gunner had just told her turning all of what she had believed on its head. Glancing up, she saw that the priest was studying her face.

'I do not know your story, Kate, nor will I ask you, but I believe you suffer as much as he does, in your own way.'

'I do not—' she began.

But he shook his head and pressed a finger to his own lips to stop her denial.

She looked into the truth in his pale-blue eyes.

'Now, I think you were right.' He took a deep lungful of air. 'I have ignored my scientific papers for too long.'

She nodded and took his arm in hers while he leaned on his walking stick with the other. Slowly they made their way across to North's cabin.

She helped Gunner inside, settling him in his chair, before her eyes met North's where he sat working behind his desk. Met and held.

So much that she had not known about him. Her heart seemed to swell with the newfound knowledge.

'Mrs Medhurst.' He got to his feet, all formal in front of Gunner, but what was between them, what had always been between them, seemed to whisper louder than ever.

'Captain North.'

Their eyes held for that moment too long before she dipped a curtsy and departed the cabin.

\* \* \*

Kit watched while Gunner leaned back in his chair and, fitting his spectacles on to his face, lifted the small pile of papers from the occasional table by his side.

'How are you feeling?'

'All the better for some fresh sea air…' Gunner smiled. He still looked tired and thin, but the colour of his skin was healthier and his eyes were his old self. 'And the company of Mrs Medhurst.'

Kit moved his focus back to the log book that lay open before him. 'It seems she is good for you.'

'Even if she is the widow of La Voile,' said Gunner.

'She is not the widow of La Voile.' Kit did not look up.

'You are sure?'

'When it comes to Kate Medhurst I am not sure of anything. But whoever she was wed to, I do not believe it to have been La Voile.'

There was a small silence before Gunner said, 'I told her how we met, something of how *Raven* and Kit North came into being, and that La Voile is our last job.'

'And what did she tell you?'

'Nothing.'

Kit gave a hard smile and kept on writing.

'You are attracted to her.'

'Because of the other morning? You may be a priest, Gunner, but even you know better than that.'

'And she is attracted to you, too.'

Kit's hand paused midword, only a tiny pause, but enough for the ink to blob.

'I may be a priest, but I have eyes in my head. And even had I not, the atmosphere between the two of you is thick enough with passion to cut a knife through it.'

'You are imagining things, Gunner. It is the after-effects of the fever.'

Gunner laughed in his usual good-humoured way and, looking down at his scientific paper, began to read.

Kit stared at the page before him without seeing anything of it. He was thinking of Kate Medhurst by his side through the long hours of the night; a woman who refused to explain anything of herself to him, not her presence on La Voile's ship or her acquaintance with *Gator's* men, not the fact she knew Jean Lafitte, and especially not anything of the man to whom she had been married. What did he really know of her? Nothing.

But that was not entirely true. He knew that she had eyes that made a man forget the darkness in himself and lips that were the sweetest he had ever tasted. He knew that she was more courageous than most men he had met and that her mind was sharp and clear and intelligent. He knew that she had a sense of honour and had borne a child. And that something niggled in his mind about the very first time he had seen her, standing beneath that black awning with La Voile and the other pirate.

But most of all he knew that Gunner was right—he was attracted to her, all of her, despite everything of his situation and hers. He was attracted to her with a desire that seemed to be escalating. And she was attracted to him, too.

And that was why it was more important than ever that they stay well apart.

The wind had dropped, and *Raven's* progress slowed. The last of the Yellow Jack had left the ship and all of those Kate had spent her time nursing were recovered enough to return to their normal quarters and duties. What had been her infirmary vanished into storage deck once more.

Kate sat on the edge of her cot, staring at the wood of the cabin door when she should have been readying herself for dinner. Everything had returned to normal, although not for Bowes and Ashton, Lyle and Smithy, or Rimmer and Caxley. She thought of the young men whose bodies lay somewhere at the bottom of the clear green waters near the Caribbean. Nothing would ever be normal for them again. Maybe not for herself, either.

Only now that the emergency was over, and her role in it done, did it hit her. She was so tired, so very tired. And she could not get what Gunner had told her yesterday of Kit North out of her head. He had been press-ganged to a pirate against his will. He had endured months of solitary confinement. He had designed *Raven* in his prison and built her. He had got his men out of there and back home against all the odds. No other man could have done such a thing. Kate knew that with all of her heart and soul.

He was not the man she had thought him, but one that had risen from conditions that would have crushed others: one with integrity, trying to do what he believed was right as much as all of those who worked in the trade with the Lafittes did. As much as Wendell had done and herself after he was gone. She had to admire that and his strength and his care for his men. She had been misled by her own prejudices. Because he was English. Because he did not understand their cause or why they were forced to go about it as they did. The plain truth was that Kit North, the pirate hunter reviled across the Gulf of Mexico and the Caribbean, was a fine man.

She rested her head in her hands; the knowledge gnawing at her because it didn't change the fact of who they both were. Nothing was ever going to get round that one. He was a very fine man, indeed. A man she wanted as a friend…and a whole lot more than that if she were being entirely honest. But if she let down her barriers, if she let him get close, there was every chance that a man as intelligent and shrewd as Kit North would see exactly who she was. And right now, that was something she could not risk.

This was not about her. This was about her children waiting for her back in Tallaholm. This was about being there to guide and guard them into adulthood. And it did not even start to go anywhere near Wendell.

She thought of Ben and baby Bea, and her heart ached for them.

And she thought, too, of Kit North. And the ache in her heart seemed to intensify.

A knock sounded on her cabin door.

*North.* Her pulse leapt at the thought.

'They are waiting for you at the dining tables, ma'am,' came one of the crew's voice.

'Thank you, sir. Please tell the Captain that I'll be right there.'

The sound of footsteps receded across the deck.

She pulled the black evening silk that he had paid for from the little wardrobe and changed, fitted the fichu carefully in place, before combing, winding and pinning her hair tight into its pins.

She wrapped a long dark shawl around her shoulders against the evening chill. Then, slipping on a pair of long black evening gloves, she took a deep breath and went to dinner.

Kit tried hard to keep his eyes from where Kate Medhurst sat at the other end of the dinner table.

She was quieter than normal during the meal, probably worn out by the days that she had worked so hard to save his men, to save Gunner. Yet too often her eyes moved to meet his across that small distance.

She was in his mind, with the strength of the passion that, tonight, seemed stronger than ever between them, despite that she was allied in some way with Lafitte and La Voile and the rest of the Baratarian pirates. Despite the fact she was keeping her dark secrets as much as he was keeping his.

'How is your scientific paper coming along, Reverend Dr Gunner?' she asked. And Gunner was only too happy to tell them all. It relieved something of the slight tension that seemed to hover about the table.

Young Tom was playing footman, bringing a dish of sweet potatoes to the table when the dish slipped from the boy's hands, and crashed to the floor. The china smashed into pieces, its mashed orange contents splattering far and wide.

'Daft lad!' Wilson, who was also serving table, uttered without malice.

But Tom being Tom froze, a look of terror on his face, cringing before Wilson. 'Please don't beat me, sir. I'm sorry, sir.'

'Come here, Tom,' Kit commanded.

The boy crept to stand before him.

'You forget where you are, boy,' he said.

The lad nodded.

'Remember, as I told you the last time.'

Tom took a breath and looked around him. 'I am on *Raven* and I am one of her crew.'

'And what do you know of *Raven*?'

'That no one is beaten without just cause here. That it is safe.'

'It is safe,' confirmed Kit. 'So hear what else it is that Mr Wilson has to say to you.'

'Yes, Captain.' Tom nodded and went dutifully to stand before Wilson.

'Best get a shovel and a cloth, and clear it up, lad,' said Wilson.

The boy bobbed his head, 'Yes, sir, Mr Wilson, sir.' Flashing Kit a toothy grin, he rushed off to do as he was bid.

Kate Medhurst seemed frozen at the other end of the table, her face filled with compassion for the boy.

'The boy requires uncommon gentle treatment

on account of his rather traumatic past. We found him being cruelly treated in the Johor prison—the lone survivor from his family, all of which had been killed. North rescued him and is equipping him with the means to survive. I have it on good authority he will make a fine sailor one day,' he heard Gunner say.

The men round the table all grinned and raised their glasses with murmurs of, 'Aye, sir, he will that.' But Kate Medhurst just made a choking sound. Her eyes were filled with tears when they met his across the table.

'Please excuse me, gentlemen,' she managed in a strangled voice and, with her face averted so that it could not be seen, she fled the dining room.

The men all glanced around, awkward, uncomfortable, tough, strong, leathered men who had sailed through the worst of storms and could cleave a man in two and think nothing of it, helpless before the tears of a woman. They wanted to aid her, but did not know what to do. They all looked at him. Gunner's eyes, too, met his down the length of the table.

A single nod of his head and he went after her.

Kate was mortified. She didn't even know why she was crying, just that the tears would not stop. She needed to pull herself together, up by her bootstraps as her mama always said. She had never shown weakness in front of her own crew. Now here she was making a fool of herself before those against whom she should remain strongest and keep up all her defences.

A knock sounded against her door and she knew it was North even before he spoke.

'Mrs Medhurst.'

'Go away.' She did not even glance at the door, just scrubbed the tears from her eyes. She didn't want him to see her like this—weak and vulnerable. She could not let him see her like this—not when her guard was down and when she couldn't think straight, let alone protect her secrets.

But he did not go away. The door opened and Kit North stepped into her cabin, his eyes taking in her and her damnable tears. She turned her back to him that he wouldn't see them.

'Kate.' His voice was quiet.

She sniffed, tried to get a rein on herself. 'I will be all right in a minute. Go back to your dinner, Captain North.' Her voice was husky and on the verge of breaking. She wanted him just to turn around and leave. The only sound was the quiet click of the door being closed. But he had not left. She could sense his presence standing there.

His hands were gentle as they turned her to him, so that she could not hide from him any more.

'It's nothing,' she said, although he had not asked the question. She did not meet his eyes.

'It would take a great deal more than nothing to make a woman like you cry.'

She kept her gaze on the wood of the door behind him, willing herself to be strong.

'Something of the boy, Tom, upset you,' he said, as perceptive as ever.

She swallowed. 'Was what Gunner said of him true?'

He nodded. 'Unfortunately so. He was a passenger aboard one of the ships the Sultan of Johor's men captured.'

She squeezed her eyes shut, trying to stop the tears, but they welled and leaked to roll down her cheeks just the same.

'Do not let it distress you. Tom will always have a place with me. He is safe and well cared for. And always will be. I promise you.'

And she believed him. She truly did. The sob escaped her.

'Kate,' he said softly, He pulled her against him, wrapping her in his embrace.

He passed her his handkerchief while she cried in earnest, for the boy Tom, and for her own little Ben and Bea, and for the man before her.

He held her, just held her, in his warmth and support and strength. Held her until the tears were all cried and the shudder of the sobs echoed though her body, and the terrible twisting, gnawing tension that had been tight in her all these days since that morning of *Coyote's* capture had loosened its grip upon her. Until she felt empty. And calm.

Standing there in North's arms. It felt like a safe harbour from the storm. She knew that was all wrong and that he was the storm who could destroy her. But in that moment the knowledge seemed small and inconsequential. What she felt, what pulsed through her heart, what filled her every pore, what was deep inside the marrow of her bones, that was all that mattered.

'This is about more than Tom,' he said. Not a question, just a fact.

Her cheek was pressed against his shirt, against the hard muscle of his chest, against the beat of his heart. She nodded.

'He reminds you of another.'

She pulled back, and looked up into his eyes. 'How do you know?'

'Gunner told me that your body bears the marks that you have carried a child.'

'Two children,' she said. 'Ben is six years old. Bea is four. Both are as blond as young Tom and as their father was. Both the cutest little pumpkins you ever could meet.'

'Where are they now?'

'Back home in Tallaholm. My mama looks after them while I'm away. It is a good arrangement. It gives her purpose since my papa died a few years back.' She took a breath. 'I miss them so much. They are the reason I was in such a hurry to get back to Louisiana, the main reason at least.'

'You should have told me.'

'Why? It would not have made any difference. I knew you could not go into Louisiana waters.'

'I would have found a way.'

She looked up into his eyes, so dark and intense. 'I believe you would have, Kit North,' she said in a voice that was barely more than a whisper. 'You are not the man I thought you were.'

Their gazes held and locked.

The next step was inevitable and unstoppable. She knew it was coming and she wanted it. She needed it.

His mouth lowered to hers and she met his lips with all the tenderness and feeling that throbbed in her heart.

She gave herself up to him. She gave herself up to all that her body had been deprived of these past three years. All that her heart missed and craved.

He kissed her with tenderness and gentleness and, beneath it, the same fierceness of passion that she felt; their lips igniting those sparks to flames that could not be doused. She was lost in its heat and so was he.

And when he snuffed out the lantern light and unlaced the black silk from her, stripping it off... when his hands caressed her naked skin with reverence and tenderness and desire...when his mouth closed upon her breast to pleasure them both... when she pulled the shirt from him and ran her hands over the toned hard muscle of his body, feeling bumps and ridges and welts on his skin, feeling his strength, feeling the power that was in him... it was more than want, more than desire. It was a need so guttural and raw that she could no more deny it than wilfully stop herself from breathing.

Everything in him mirrored what she felt. As though he understood, as though he was just the same as her. As though his strength could feed her and mend her and make everything all right again when it hadn't been all right for such a long time despite all of her pretences.

Their bodies spliced together as if they had been made to fit that way.

There was only Kit North, only this healing that was happening between them as their bodies merged. They moved together, their rhythms perfectly in tune, reaching, striving, needing what only the other could give. A journey together. A journey that faded everything else to oblivion.

'Kit.' She called out his name as they finally reached their destination and she exploded in a surge of white light and stardust and sunbeams and a pulsing pleasure that overcame the entirety of her being as he pulled out just in time to keep her safe.

And afterwards, when the urgency and madness had passed, when their bodies parted and they both realised what they had done, awkwardness and embarrassment replaced passion. She clutched the covers to her, hiding her nakedness even though it was dark.

'I should go.' She felt him leave the cot, felt the dip of the mattress as he sat on its edge and pulled on his drawers and breeches, quickly dressing himself. Then rose to leave. There was a small hesitation, as if he had turned to say something, then thought better of it. He did not say another word, just left, closing the door quietly behind him.

She lay there, her body warm and sated, while a cold wind of horror blew through her heart at what she had just done. Lying there, naked beneath the sheets, his scent strong upon her, her skin still flushed from his touch, she stared up through the darkness towards the low wooden planks of the ceiling above. Everything she believed of herself was shaken. All of her values and her standards. If someone had told her two weeks ago that she would have behaved like a wanton, forgetting everything that was important to her, forgetting the vow she had sworn, so driven by the need to couple with Captain Kit North that she would lay herself down before him and go at it like a barnyard animal, she would have laughed in their face at the utter absurdity.

*What have I done?*

Betrayed the memory of her husband. Betrayed her children. Betrayed her own self.

She was Le Voile. He was the man the British establishment had sent to capture her.

*Lord help me, what have I done?* The question whispered again and again through her mind as the full horror of it sank in.

Her anger was not at him, but herself. For her weakness.

But she knew the answer, and worse than that was the fear that, despite that knowledge, if he were to kiss her again and whisper her name with such tenderness, she would do it all again.

In the darkness of the tiny cabin Kate shivered and, wrapping her arms around herself, curled on her side. She did not weep, there were no more tears left to cry.

She just stared into the black night and wondered how on earth she was going to get through the rest of this journey with what lay between her and Kit North.

* * *

Kit did not return to the dining tables. He did not want any of the others to guess what had just happened between him and Kate Medhurst, both for her sake and his own. Instead, he climbed the ladder that led to the upper deck and sought the sanctuary of the open night sky.

Briggs was at the helm, Collier on watch, but neither would bother him. Through the darkness that submerged him they would see nothing of the truth. He stood by the rail, feeling the whip of the wind against his face and through his hair and staring out into the dark roar of the ocean.

He thought he was a man who had righted his course. He had sailed so far and never felt temptation to veer from that course, not once, until he met Kate Medhurst. And now he had faltered, fallen. So close to home.

'There you are.' Gunner's voice was quiet as he came to stand by his side, handing Kit his lantern so that he could lean between his stick and the bulwark to look out over the side at the dark night seascape.

'You should not be up here. You will exhaust yourself,' Kit said.

'I thought I was the physician here,' Gunner said, and he could hear the smile in his friend's voice.

They stood in silence for a little while, with only

the creak of the timber and the flap of canvas and the ever-present roar of the ocean.

'Is she all right?' Gunner asked softly after a few moments.

'I hope so.' He hoped, but he feared what he had done had only made matters worse.

Another silence before Gunner spoke again. 'Are *you* all right?'

'Why would I not be?' He would not lie, deception went too close to the tear in his soul that could not be mended, but he would do all that he could to protect Kate Medhurst's reputation; he owed her that, at least.

'No particular reason,' said his friend. But he had the sensation that Gunner knew something had happened between them, maybe not the full extent of it, but something that should not have happened all the same. He should not have bedded her. He should not have loved her. It whispered of dishonour, in more ways than one. He would have put his head in his hands were there no one to witness it.

'Seeing the boy, Tom, upset her.'

'You were right. She is a mother, with two young children back in Louisiana—a son and a daughter. She misses them.'

'I am sorry for her. It cannot be easy.'

'More difficult I would guess than either of us can imagine.'

'Did she tell you anything else of herself or her circumstances?'

'A few things,' he said, staring out at the blackness. 'But nothing that changes my thinking on her.' He could still feel the softness of her skin, he could still smell the clean womanly scent of her and feel her in his blood. What had happened in that cabin felt like a lot more than just sex. It felt like something he had no damn right to experience.

'Well, I suppose we should be glad of that.' Beside him he could feel the weight of Gunner's gaze upon him.

'Yes, I suppose we should,' he said, but supposing and being were two different things.

'Come on, old man, best get this old crock back down below,' said Gunner.

Kit took hold of his friend's arm to help guide him through the darkness.

Slowly the two men moved together across the deck towards the ladder.

She could not hide from him for ever. She had to face him sooner or later, and the sooner it was done, the better. Kate rinsed her face in the cold water and stared at her reflection in the small looking glass that hung over the cabin's washstand.

The night spent sleepless with regret and remorse, with guilt and shame, with anger and all sorts of other confusing emotions, had left its mark on her face. Her eyes were ringed with shadows, her complexion too pale and ashen.

The soap and water had washed North's scent from her body easily enough. But no amount of scrubbing could erase the knowledge of what they had shared together. It felt like that was engraved on her soul.

Lord, help her, she cringed at the thought of seeing him again.

But not once in her adult life had she hidden from what had to be done. Fear was a thing that lurked behind you, in shadows and round corners, the only way to deal with it was to turn round and confront it. She did not know any other way. So she dried her face and dressed in her own black muslin and fichu and the black shawl, and tidied her hair all neat and respectable. And with her head held high she went to face the crew of *Raven* and its captain, too.

Gone was the bright sunshine of home. In its place were grey skies and a churning charcoal ocean beneath, both of which matched the sombre mood that hung about the ship this morning.

North was in his usual place on the quarter-deck, peering into the distance through his spyglass when she emerged from the deck hatch. There was no sign of Gunner, although the rest of his crew seemed at busy industry. Bob the raven sat perched on North's left shoulder.

Her heart was beating harder than normal with the illogical fear that somehow what had happened between her and North was branded there on her face for all to see, almost making her turn right around and hurry back to her cabin.

But none of the men treated her with anything other than their normal respect.

North's eyes met hers across the deck. She gave him a small polite nod of acknowledgement, as if nothing had happened last night, then walked to stand by *Raven's* larboard rail, not too close that might be construed she was angling after him, but not far enough away that might be thought avoidance.

A few moments later and she heard his footsteps. Her heart began to race in earnest, part of her praying he would walk on by.

All her blood rushed and tumbled, and she felt her cheeks blush rosy as any green girl's at the sight of her lover, as his footsteps came to a halt by her side.

She did not trust herself to look round at him, not until she could be sure of her composure.

'Last night—' he began to murmur quietly.

'Should not have happened,' she said, finishing

the sentence, taking control of the situation. She knew what she was going to say, had rehearsed the words a hundred times through the night, but still her throat was dry. 'We were both tired and our sensibilities were running high.' She said it quietly, but with a firmness of confidence that brooked no disagreement. 'It will not happen again.'

'It will not,' he agreed. It was what she wanted to hear, but those words upon his lips made her feel strangely bleak. 'I hope you do not feel that I took advantage of you. It was not my intention.'

She met his eyes then, seeing that there was a gravity in them that matched the darkness of the daytime sky. 'You know you did not,' she said, angry that he could think such a thing. 'Do you honestly think me so weak as to be so easily coerced against my will?'

'No, Kate,' he said. 'I do not think any such thing.'

She gave a tiny nod. 'Please do not let me keep you from your duties, Captain North,' she said, effectively dismissing him.

'You know I could not allow such a thing, even were I to wish it otherwise, Kate Medhurst,' he said softly, and there was such a look in those dark eyes of his that made her feel as though she had just had a glimpse of some deep personal truth in him—a look that held both intimacy and pain.

He walked away, returning to his charts and his spyglass.

She wanted to retreat to her cabin, but she stayed where she was, looking out over the grey swell of the ocean, for the sake of appearances and pride.

*You know I could not allow such a thing, even were I to wish it otherwise, Kate Medhurst.* It was not so much the words that haunted her as that look in his eyes.

Her bonnet's black ribbons fluttered wildly in the wind. Her skirts moulded themselves to her legs and beneath the dark shawl she shivered from the cold and from other things, too. But still she stood there, and would do so for the next half-hour until, with her pride intact, she could go below. She shivered again, the shiver bone deep and cold as ice this time, as though someone or something had walked over her grave. And then she saw it—the ship that sailed out of the bank of clouds in the distance, the ship on which Kit North had trained his spyglass. And her mouth went dry and her stomach gave a somersault and she understood the reason for the men's mood and intensity of focus. And her heart leapt at the same time as there was something sad beneath it.

For the ship heading straight for *Raven* was one that Kate recognised. Although it was sailing under French colours and flew neither black sails nor any flag to proclaim its privateer status, she was under no doubt as to the identity of the schooner—*La Diligent*. Only one man commanded that vessel: Captain Jean Lafitte. And there could only be one reason why Lafitte was this far across the Atlantic and flying not the bloody flag but the white one of *parlez*.

The ship heading straight for *Raven* was coming for Kate—to save Le Voile from North the Pirate Hunter and take her home to Louisiana.

## Chapter Eight

Kit watched Lafitte's ship, judging the distance with an expert eye, aware that there could only be one reason big enough and important enough to bring Lafitte chasing all this way across the Atlantic.

'Continue to hold our current course and speed, and ready the guns,' he commanded.

'Aye, aye, Captain.' The men moved smooth and efficient as cogs in a clock. Everything timed to precision. They all knew who was coming and that Lafitte had not carved a name for himself amongst the Baratarian pirates for nothing. They all knew that *La Diligent* was a match for *Raven*. They knew, too, that her long guns were big enough to come close to the range of those that *Raven* carried.

Kate Medhurst stood statue still, her hands gripping the rail, her focus fixed all on the pursuing ship.

He moved to stand by her side. 'Go below, Kate.'

She glanced round at him, meeting his gaze briefly, but with an intensity that mirrored what he was feeling himself. 'You know who that is, right?'

'I know,' he said. Then, to Briggs, 'Escort Mrs Medhurst to her cabin.'

'No.' She turned to where Briggs was advancing towards her, stopping him in his tracks with a look before returning her gaze to Kit. 'That will not be necessary, sir.'

Briggs looked at Kit.

'As the lady wishes,' he murmured, knowing that short of slinging her over his shoulder and carrying her down that deck ladder by force she was going nowhere.

Briggs hurriedly returned to his station.

'Six hundred yards!' shouted Collier from the crow's nest, whose eyes were trained on the approaching ship.

'Stand ready with the guns,' Kit ordered.

Kate stared round at him with a look of incredulity. 'Do you not see the white flag of *parlez*?'

'I see it.'

'And yet you mean to shoot at him?'

'Just as he means to shoot at us.'

'You are mistaken!'

'I do not believe so.'

'He wishes to *parlez*,' she said, not understanding what it was Lafitte had come to do.

'He wishes anything but to *parlez*. He knows who I am. And the cargo I carry. He intends to stop me reaching London with La Voile.'

'You don't know what he wants until you listen to what he has to say,' she implored. 'Jean Lafitte is an honourable man. I give you my word on it.' Desperation made her careless.

'Men are not always as honourable as they might seem, Kate.'

But she still did not understand what was happening here and no amount of words would ever convince her. But she would see soon enough, *La Diligent* was already within penetrating range for her own guns.

'Kit, please...' Her hand touched his arm and stayed there, betraying them both.

He did not look at her, just kept his gaze fixed on the closing ship, gauging distances and direction with finesse, knowing that although *Raven* had the advantage of being on the windward side, with less hull exposed and more manoeuvrability, this was still a very dangerous situation.

'You should brace yourself, Kate.' Lafitte would fire; Kit was convinced of it.

'Have you no honour?' she demanded.

He froze at the words that stabbed with stiletto

precision into his weakness, his darkness, his Achilles heel. He turned to her, meeting her eyes directly, forgetting in that tiny sliver of a moment about *Raven* and *La Diligent*, about where they were, or how much he was revealing of himself.

'No,' he said in a cool quiet voice. 'My honour is lost and cannot be redeemed.'

She looked at him with disbelief and disgust and contempt and he took it, accepting that judgement unflinchingly because it was completely warranted.

'God have mercy on your soul, Kit North.'

'I sold my soul a long time ago. For me there can be no mercy, Kate.'

Their eyes locked in the moment of painful truth and revelation before with a measure of disgust and disbelief she turned and walked away from him. He watched her go, knowing that whatever she might have felt for him was no more. And rightly so. He returned his focus to *La Diligent*, now much closer.

Something glinted in her rigging, tiny and brief, and Kit realised that he had misjudged Lafitte's plan by one small important point. The sudden truth of it became clear as he identified the glint as a sharpshooter, the long-barrelled rifle in the man's hands, so carefully taking aim.

'Get down, Kate! Now!' he yelled, but it would be too late, he knew that even as he sprinted the distance to reach her. The shot rang out, like the clear snap of a branch in a silent wood.

She was turning towards him, her face looking to his.

With all the force he could muster he threw himself forward, shielding her, taking her down, twisting as he clutched her to him and they fell together. He landed heavily, the pain like a hard heavy punch to his shoulder pinning him there when he would have got up.

She lay on top of him, like they were making love. Her face inches from his own, her eyes wide and staring with shock.

'Kit...?' she whispered, her breath warm against his cheek. 'Kit...!' as the realisation began to hit her.

He tightened his arm around her. She was safe.

'Three hundred yards,' he heard Briggs's voice shout from somewhere far in the distance.

'Fire the guns!' he instructed. The echo of his command ran down the line. *Raven* roared as her guns let loose on *La Diligent*.

The dizziness and darkness roiled in his head. He fought to clear it.

The guns were sounding and the stench of smoke and saltpetre had drifted up from the gun ports to sting her eyes and fill her nose, but Kate barely noticed. She stared with horror at the pool of blood spreading out so dark and wet on the pale scrubbed wood where Kit lay.

'Lafitte's fleeing, heading back from where he came.' The voice seemed so faint she barely registered it.

She could not take her eyes off Kit as she trembled from shock and horror and the need to help him, to save him. She did not remember getting to her knees by his side or bunching her shawl to form a pad. The fine cotton of his black shirt was sodden where she pressed the pad firm against the white-and-red flesh that gaped at his shoulder.

His face was pale, his eyes dark as jet as they looked into hers. 'I am fine,' he said. 'I just need a little assistance to reach my cabin.'

By the time Gunner arrived Kit's men had laid him out on the cot within his night cabin. They stood in the background, caps in hands, afraid to leave, their faces, usually so strong and merciless, haunted with the same gut-wrenching, blood-chilling fear that was trembling through her own body.

'Maybe we should we move you below to the surgical room,' she said quietly, seeing the never-ending leak of blood that was spreading over the sheets.

'No.' His tone was adamant.

'It is just a flesh wound that needs to be cleaned and bound,' said Gunner as he stood by Kit's side. Then, to the men, 'We need basins of water—cold and fresh boiled—and the packets of linens from the cabinet in my medical room.'

They nodded and hurried away, easier in activity than idleness. The door clicked shut behind them.

'If you would be so kind as to assist me in stripping off his coat and shirt,' said Gunner.

'Your strength is not yet fully recovered. I will call one of the men back to help me.' She moved towards the door, but Kit's quiet voice stopped her.

'No, Kate.'

He exchanged a glance with Gunner before Gunner said, 'We cannot let them see how bad it is.'

Her stomach dropped, her blood froze. She stared at the priest. 'You said it was just a flesh wound.' But she understood even before he answered the unspoken question.

'I am afraid I lied,' Gunner said softly.

'They are men with pasts, Kate,' said Kit. 'They need a strong leader. Without it, *Raven* would be a very different place for you and Gunner.'

A ship of leaderless ex-pirates in the middle of the Atlantic would be no place for a priest who had not yet regained his strength, or a woman. 'How bad is it really?' she asked.

He glanced at Gunner for the answer.

'We will not know until I get a proper look at him.'

She nodded.

Between the three of them they prised the thick leather coat from him, cut the shirt from his blood-smeared body and pulled off his boots and stockings, covering him with a blanket so that when the men returned they would see nothing. But even that exertion brought an ashen sheen of perspiration to Gunner's face and left him breathless.

Once the water and the linens had arrived and the door was safely shut once more, Gunner closed his eyes and leaned against the bed, catching his breath. When he opened them again he met her gaze, holding out his hands before him, revealing openly for the first time the extent of the tremor that beset them.

'It is a delicate operation to probe the wound and one that requires precision if it is to be successful.'

'I will do it myself,' said Kit.

'You will do no such thing,' she said firmly and stepped forward. 'I will be your hands, Reverend Dr Gunner.' Although she spoke to Gunner her eyes never left Kit's, holding them with determination until, at last, he gave a tiny nod of assent.

Gunner's pale-blue eyes looked into hers. They both knew Kit's life hung in the balance.

'Tell me what to do,' she said.

And he did.

As she washed the red smear of blood from Kit's chest and shoulder, she saw for the first time what her fingers had felt the night they made love—his body was a lattice of raised and ragged scars. And she understood at last that solitary confinement had not been the only way the prison guards had punished Kit North.

The sight made her throat feel thick and tight with emotion, almost broke her heart, but she hid it from him, refusing to meet those dark eyes lest they saw the truth in her own. She swallowed down the rock in her throat, stowed away the deluge of tears that would have fallen, silenced the sobs that crammed tight in her chest for release, for none of those would help him. But strength, practicality and caring hands—they would. Summoning up all of her strength and self-control, she got on with the task, doing what must be done.

He lay there not saying a word, not flinching from either the pain or the past revealed so clearly all over his body. The blood welled and leaked from the wound constantly. She cleansed it as best she could, moving the basin and cloth aside when she was done, before standing ready before him.

'Now for the real fun,' said Kit, cool and calm as ever. As if his life blood were not dripping all over the floor. As if a bullet had not torn its way through half his shoulder.

'Are you sure you want to do this, Kate Medhurst?' he asked and there was an undertone there that made her understand something she did not want to.

'Are you sure you want to let me, Kit North?' she replied, never shifting her gaze from his.

He laughed, but the laugh became a cough, laboured and painful so that she felt the cold fear for him spasm again and caught hold of his hand in her own, squeezing it tight as if she could give him something of her strength.

When the coughing stopped he laid his head back on the pillow, his eyes holding hers. 'Do it,' he said, then glanced across at Gunner with a nod of his head.

Gunner passed her one of the horrible hooked metal devices she had seen in the glass cupboards down in his surgical room. Such an instrument of torture that she quailed within at the thought of what she was going to have to do with it.

'Having second thoughts?' Kit's voice taunted.

'Are you?' She parried his too perceptive question with one of her own.

'No,' he said. 'Not over you. Not any more.'

Their eyes clung together. She wanted to weep, she wanted to tremble, she wanted both to hold him to her and to flee this room, this situation and him. She did neither of them.

Instead, she took a deep breath and glanced over at Gunner. 'I am ready.'

Gunner moved to insert a piece of wood between Kit's teeth so that he might bite down on it and not his own tongue when the pain got too bad. But Kit refused it with a shake of his head.

So Gunner stood behind her and spoke the instructions in a slow, clear, calm voice.

Taking a deep breath, she moved the metal probe to the wound and then closed off a part of herself to follow Gunner's every command.

She probed the raw pulp inside Kit's body, with one instrument and then another, and he made not one sound. Deeper, further, harder, she probed and probed, until, at last, after what seemed an intolerable lifetime, she saw the dark, misshapen lead ball.

'I found it,' she said.

Gunner passed her a pair of small pointed tongs. 'Prise it out.'

Her eyes flicked up to meet Kit's. 'How are you managing there?' she asked softly.

'Have you started yet?' He smiled, but his face was devoid of colour, leaving him powder white, as if the wound had indeed bled every last drop of blood from him, and the sheen of sweat upon his skin glistened in the daylight that flooded through the porthole.

She returned her focus to the wound, blanking out everything, save Gunner's voice, and listened carefully to what he was telling her to do.

With steady hands she dug out the bullet that Jean Lafitte's sharpshooter had put in him, dropping it with a clatter into the waiting metal dish. Then with the merciless care and the relentless tenacity that Gunner demanded, and Kit deserved, she began examining the wound, removing every tiny fibre of cotton and leather that she could find.

Every time she thought she was done, Gunner had her go back in with that sharp metal probe, poking and prodding in that bloodied, raw, gaping hole of flesh until it looked like a piece of butcher meat. And she did it. Like the men in Johor who had tortured him, she tortured both him and herself in doing so. And she did it willingly because she would have done anything to save his life.

The pain must have been unbearable, but not once did he flinch. Not once did he cry out, or groan or even murmur. She could see the knotted muscles and strained tendons tight beneath the skin of that shoulder and could feel the strain that gripped his whole body and the sweat that trickled in rivulets. She prayed that he would know the mercy of passing out, but he did not take what mercy offered.

With what must have been utter relentless determination, he stayed right there, aware and awake the whole time.

It was the longest wait. An agony of suffering that was like nothing she had ever known. Not like birthing her two children. Not like hearing the news that Wendell had been killed. Because here with this was the terrible weighty burden of guilt. For she knew that Kit North had taken that bullet for her.

At last Gunner pronounced the probing finished. At last she placed the probe down into the dish and he passed her the black-threaded needle, and she sewed him up as if she were sat back in the homestead in Tallaholm, stitching curtains for the windows.

'No.' Gunner touched a hand to her arm, stopping her when she would have fetched a dressing for the wound. 'No dressing. The air will heal it better than anything. Keep the bedcovers clear.

'There is nothing more we can do,' Gunner said. 'Except pray.' Practically the same words she had said to Kit when they sat by Gunner's side that night.

'You know that would be wasted on me, Doc,' murmured Kit. He managed a smile. His face was grey. Sweat was beaded on his forehead and upper lip. His voice was weak, but the look in his eyes was strong and dark and determined as ever.

'One of these days, my friend,' teased Gunner, but she could see the toll just being on his feet all that time, watching carefully over her shoulder, had taken on the priest–physician. He was almost as pale as Kit.

'Go, get some rest, Reverend Dr Gunner. I will look after our captain.'

Gunner gave no argument, only staggered through to the day cabin to collapse on to his own cot.

The water in every basin was scarlet. The pile of stained rags on the floor was too large. Her hands were stained and wet with Kit's blood. She stared at them. So much blood. Surely too much for a man to lose and still live? The fear squirmed in her stomach.

'So, you are going to look after me, are you?' he said.

She forced herself to swallow the fear down before she let herself look up at him.

He was watching her, his eyes on hers.

'Shouldn't you have passed out from the pain by now?' she asked softly.

'Sorry to disappoint, Kate. Pain is my friend.'

'So it seems.' She smiled.

And so did he.

'Sit down,' he said.

But she was afraid to face him. 'When I have cleared up and washed up.' She moved to gather up the rags.

'No,' he said, his voice quiet, but still with command.

She stopped, leaving the rags where they were.

Her eyes moved to his face, scanning his eyes, fearing what she might see there.

'Sit down now, Kate, before you fall down.'

'I'm fine, really, I am,' she insisted, but she sat down on the little wooden chair by his bedside all the same. Her eyes scanned the cabin, moving over the pile of scarlet-soaked rags, over the blood that had run down his arm to drip from his fingertips to pool on the bare deck planks below the cot. And the marks of everywhere her bare feet had trodden. The deep dark stain of the blood pool and her own bloody footsteps would be preserved in the wood for the rest of *Raven's* life, she thought as her gaze travelled over her bare toes smeared red with his blood. So much blood that she feared there could be none left in his veins. So much blood that she feared…

'Are you?' His voice was soft, but held a timbre that seemed to reach into her chest and stroke a finger against her heart. He had just endured what would have sent most men out of their minds. Pain that was beyond imagining. Blood loss to drain a body dry. And his concern was not for himself, but for her…the woman who was the cause of it all!

She looked up into his dark, dark eyes, eyes that were intelligent and perceptive and tender. 'You need to rest, Kit.' Her voice was hoarse in her struggle to stop herself breaking down. He needed her strength, her care, her reassurance, nothing else, not right at this moment in time. That would all come later…if he survived.

'We both need to rest, Kate.'

She looked at where his bloodstained hand lay loose and open, palm up on the cot's sheet. She reached her own hand to gently close around it. Their fingers, so engrained with blood, entwined. 'Maybe you are right,' she admitted.

Only then did he close his eyes and take the rest his body must have been screaming for.

She sat there, exhausted physically, emotionally and spiritually; her eyes on his face, knowing in that moment that she was bound there by much more than their linked hands, or the stain of his blood that marked half her body.

His face was ashen, his breathing shallow. The bullet was out, but the danger was far from over. A cliff edge stretched ahead, for them both.

Gunner was right—all they could do was pray.

\* \* \*

The shaft of cool silver moonlight behind his eyelids woke Kit in the solitary cell of the Johor prison. The press of the poker in his shoulder was white-hot, bringing a sweat to prickle and run over his skin, holding his breath hostage in his throat, clouding the thoughts from his brain, obscuring the other pain ever present and mammoth in comparison to anything they could do to him.

He embraced it. Suffered all that they could do to his body. All their paltry efforts. All their taunts, their threats, their promises of how they would make him suffer, what they would take from him before they took his life. They were supposed to terrify him. They were supposed to make him cower and beg. They were meant to break him. But nothing of it touched him.

*Take it*, he could have said to them. *Take it all.* It meant nothing to him. Not what they could do. Not when it went nowhere near the real torture. He did not fear death, but welcomed it and the relief it would bring from the real torment that churned in his soul.

Regret. Remorse. Guilt. He could not forget. Not for a minute. Not even for a second. What he had done.

It had taken those long days and nights locked alone in the tiny cramped cell for him to look into his soul and see what he really was. Only then had he finally realised the man he had been and fully appreciated that the fault was all his own and no one else's. Enlightenment. And a vow sworn. Kit Northcote had died in Johor and Captain Kit North been born.

He thought again of what he had done and the shame of it was excruciating in a way none of their knives or pokers or whips ever could be.

Devlin, Hunter and all the rest of the men who had been there that night to witness it were present there in the cell with him, their mouths silent, but their eyes speaking volumes. And present, too, were those he had brought to their knees—his own father and mother, his own sister…

That pain was unbearable. He cried out against it and in the midst of the torment he prayed for the poker to touch again that it might distract him from that real pain, prayed for the stench of burning flesh that would follow, but the only smell was that of the sea and the wind and dampness of night. There was no clank of metal or rake of hot coals, only the quiet roar of the ocean; no dripping damp wall at his back or hard press of manacles, but a soft mattress and the comforting rock of the waves. There was no relief, only the pain, and the one thing that sustained him through it was the vow he had sworn.

\* \* \*

The moonlight through the porthole shone its gentle silver light into the cabin. The bloody rags were gone, the red-water basins, too. Not one of Gunner's instruments of life and torture remained. The only evidence of what had taken place all those hours earlier were the stained planks beneath her feet and the half-naked man lying on his back upon the cot.

Kate could not sleep despite the exhaustion that pulled at her body. There were so many thoughts crowding in her head, so much confused emotion vying in her breast, so much fear and guilt, so much she did not understand—about that sharpshooter's shot; about the man who had saved her from its bullet...and the way she felt about him. If he died... Something contracted in her chest at the thought and there was an ache there, dull but persistent.

A man so unlike any other. A man she had expected to hate; a man she should hate. He represented everything she despised—the British, a hunter whose prey was honest, hardworking, American citizens who had been driven to justifiable forms of privateering and piracy; he was ruthless, hard, emotionless, someone who put money and a bounty above all else. There was no denying he was all of those things. And he was everything that she respected and admired, too—a man of integrity, a man who had risked his life to save hers, be it to dive into an ocean to snatch her from the jaws of a shark, or to use his own body to shield her from a bullet—a bullet from a privateer she had defended and for whom she had pled. A man of initiative and intelligence, who had not left his crew to rot in an Eastern prison, but had broken them out and got them home. A man who had rescued a small boy to whom he owed nothing.

A tear escaped as her eyes moved over his torso. What had they done to him in that prison? Too much pain and suffering for any one man to endure.

Her gaze travelled higher to his hard handsome face. There was nothing of peace in his slumber. The place that it took him was not a good one. And little wonder given the scars that marked him. Kate watched the troubled dreams and saw the pain that etched his face, sleep revealing the truth he hid so well in waking. He hurt, she realised. He hurt the same as her, just as Gunner had said.

'Emma…Devlin…' The garbled murmurs escaped his lips, fast, troubled, his level of distress so evident that it shook her.

'Hush, I am here,' she whispered the words softly and soothed a hand against his troubled brow, as she did to little Ben when a nightmare struck.

And in his dark place of sleep Kit seemed to

hear her and calmed beneath the gentle brush of her fingers.

He was the man she should hate, but what she felt for him was very far from hate. What she felt for him…

'Hush, my love,' she whispered, soft as a summer breeze through palm leaves and pressed a butterfly kiss to his forehead.

And she wept, for him and for her children, for Wendell and for the damnable mess she was in.


It was Gunner who woke her, with his light knock on the door before he entered the night cabin.

She woke with a start, her dreams confused and troubled. Images of Ben and Bea and Wendell, of Jean Lafitte and Bill Linder…and Kit all too clear in her mind and her heart beating too hard with raw emotion, and her chest too tight with the knowledge of what had changed between them.

The moonlight had long gone, replaced instead with the bright light of day, harsh and unforgiving.

She was slumped in the chair, her head resting on the edge of the cot near Kit's legs. As she righted herself she took a breath, preparing herself, screwing her courage to the post before she moved her eyes to Kit.

He was awake, his gaze fixed on hers. His face

was still pale, but not grey as it had been the day before. Something fluttered inside her heart.

'So, you are still with us, Captain North.' Her voice was soft and husky from sleep and the tears she had shed in the night.

'For my sins,' he replied softly, but there was something in the way he said it that made her think the words were not in jest and brought the memory of what she had seen etched upon his face flooding back.

'How is our patient this morning?' asked Gunner with his usual cheeriness. He did not wait for an answer. 'I brought you breakfast.' He set a bowl of blood-soaked oatmeal on the little bedside table. 'You should eat while it is still warm.'

She could smell the metallic stench of the pig's blood, the tingle of it hitting the back of her throat, making her head swim and her stomach revolt. Ironic, for what was a little pig blood in comparison to the crimson tide that had washed the floors of this cabin?

Gunner leaned closer, peering at the ragged wound with its blood-encrusted black stitches and the newly appeared surrounding bruising. 'No discolouration, no pustulation. Healing nicely.'

'I had a good surgeon,' she heard Kit say, and when her eyes moved to his it was to find them on hers. Their gaze lingered, so many words unspoken between them.

'I will take over from here,' Gunner said.

She did not argue, but gladly left.

## Chapter Nine

'I did not mean to interrupt,' said Gunner once the door closed behind Kate.

Kit eased himself up to a sitting position. 'You did not interrupt.'

'She saved your life, Kit. I could not have got the bullet out.'

'I know.'

'And she has not left your side.'

He knew that, too. He thought of the fatigue shadowed beneath her eyes. He thought of the sight of her there, sleeping, overcome by exhaustion. He thought of the feel of her hand within his own. Of all that she was and all that she made him feel.

There was a silence while Kit ate, the pig blood replacing some of his own which had been lost.

'That shot Lafitte's man fired. His aim was true. The bullet was meant for Kate Medhurst.'

'It was.'

'It does not make any sense.'

'Quite the reverse,' said Kit. It made perfect sense, once one rid oneself of the blinkers. The truth was glaringly obvious and had been right from the start.

'Care to enlighten me?'

'Not yet.' Not until he had got his own head around it.

He finished the oatmeal and the grog, then, ignoring the protests his body made, swung his legs over the side of the bed.

Kate poured the water from the jug into the little basin in the washstand and sponged away the rusty stains from her naked skin. Her face, her neck and décolletage, her hands and forearms. Her feet and shins. Even her thighs where the blood had soaked through the layers of black muslin. She washed her hair, too. At the end of it, her skin was white again and the water in the basin crimson. She rolled the muslin to a tight ball and stowed it beneath the bunk where her holsters and weapons had been hidden, remembering that it had once been her intention to put a bullet in Kit North's chest herself. Now everything, and nothing, had changed.

He was still North the Pirate Hunter. She was still Le Voile. And he knew. Even though he had not spoken the words. It was there in his eyes when he looked at her. She could feel it in the very air between them.

He knew. And he had still taken that bullet for her. Jean Lafitte had come, but not to rescue her.

She was confused, so confused. Everything in her life had been so simple before. Everything made perfect sense. But not now. Now, she did not know what to think any more. All that she had believed had been turned on its head. Friend and foe. Betrayal and loyalty. Love and hate.

She lay down on the cot and closed her eyes. But no matter how long she lay there she could not sleep. And she could not stop the thoughts that twisted and spun in her head. So, after a while, she rose and dressed herself in the black silk from the Antiguan wardrobe. Black stockings tied in place with black tapes. The matching black slippers upon her feet. She combed out her wet hair, leaving it long and loose to dry. Then ate the light breakfast Gunner had left before eventually heading up on to the upper deck.

She stood there, looking out over the grey Atlantic Ocean, the rhythmic roll and spray of the waves lending her some sense of relief.

The tap of Gunner's stick sounded as he came to stand by her side

'Here you are,' he said quietly.

'Here I am,' she said, without looking round. 'How is he?'

'He is typical North,' said Gunner in a voice that made her smile despite everything else that was in her chest.

They stood in companionable silence for a while.

'It was my fault that he was shot,' she said.

'Men make their own choices, Kate.'

'He told me to go below. He told me Lafitte meant to fire. But I would not listen. I...' She could not tell Gunner the truth of her words in those final moments. No doubt Kit would tell him soon enough. 'I thought I knew better,' she finished instead. Then looked round, meeting his eyes for the first time, saying what every man on *Raven* already knew, 'He took that bullet for me.'

Gunner's silence was an agreement.

She sighed and returned her gaze to the grey roll of waves, watching them in silence for a few minutes. 'Does Captain North have a woman?'

'No. I have already told you the way it is with him and all the usual vices of a man at sea. Why do you ask?'

*Emma... Devlin...* 'No reason.'

Voices sounded. Men moving to the quarterdeck. She glanced over and saw Kit standing there in his faded leather coat and his hat, and Bob the raven on his shoulder. As if his shoulder were not torn apart. As if he had not been hovering so close to death's door all through the night.

'What is he doing?!'

'Taking the morning briefing,' said Gunner quietly.

She shot a look of accusation at the priest. 'You should have stopped him. He is not well enough—'

'He is the captain. And these men need to be led.'

She made to move past him, but he stopped her by the lightest touch upon her arm. 'If it is any consolation, I have seen him rise the next day after a lot worse.'

'What could be worse than yesterday?'

'Much more than you could imagine, Kate,' said Gunner softly so that she remembered the scars upon Kit's body.

Her eyes moved to where Kit stood, at the helm of his ship. Those dark eyes met hers for the briefest of moments, before he turned away and got on with giving his orders.

'If you will excuse me, Reverend Dr Gunner.' She left and headed back down to her cabin, needing to be alone, needing time away from the man who affected her too much.

In the days that followed Kate Medhurst steadfastly avoided him. She did not come to the dining tables. She spent too much time in her cabin, and the minutes during which she did surface on deck was when it was busy, overrun with crew, and she kept well clear of wherever he was to be found.

Part of him was relieved by it. But it was just putting off the inevitable. She knew it every inch as much as him. His eyes traced her silhouette against the prow, the black silk dark and sheened as Bob's wings in the dying sun.

'Take over, Reverend Dr Gunner,' he instructed. 'Carry on, Mr Briggs.' He made his way up the length of the ship to her, aware that the eyes of his crew were watching.

'Mrs Medhurst.' He stopped by the rail only a few feet away from her, sharing the same view.

'Captain North.' She did not look round at him. 'I was just leaving.' She began to turn away.

'You cannot hide in your cabin for ever, Kate,' he said quietly.

The words stopped her in his tracks. She did not flee. Just stood there very still for a moment before resuming her position at the rail. 'No, I suppose I cannot.' She closed her eyes for a moment, then opened them again, and took a deep breath before she glanced at him.

'Tell me about your husband,' he said softly.

Their gaze held for a long second until at last she

gave a nod and looked out once more to the vast grey expanse of the ocean.

'His name was Wendell Medhurst. He was born and raised in Tallaholm, the same as me. We married when I was twenty-two years old and had our son, Ben, a year later and our daughter, Beatrice, Bea for short, a couple of years after Ben. He was a good man—a kind husband, a loving father. We owned a small general store. It earned us a good living. And then with all the political trade blocks—first the French, then the British, and finally our own government. So many blocks as to be a stranglehold—we could not make ends meet. Could not put food on the table for our children. It was the same for all of Tallaholm, as much as New Orleans. So Wendell did something about it.' She glanced round at him, something of the old light of defiance in her eyes. 'He stood up to you British.'

'He became a pirate,' he said.

'He became a privateer, with a letter of marque from the French consul. He might have flown French colours, but everything he did was to benefit Louisiana.'

'He plundered British merchant vessels.'

'He stood up for his family and his country against tyranny.'

'He became one of the Lafittes' men.'

'He worked for himself, not Jean or Pierre Lafitte.

The Lafittes helped with the set-up, the storage and distribution of goods, and offered a measure of protection. They know people in high places, powerful people.'

'The overlords.'

'In a manner of speaking I suppose they are.' She nodded.

'What happened to Wendell?'

'He was murdered by the British.' She met his gaze. 'A naval captain boarded his ship and slit his throat in front of his crew.'

Just as he had feigned with the boy on *Coyote*. Only then did he realise how much it must have affected her to see his blade held to the boy's throat. The threat had been an empty one, but she could not have known that.

'I am sorry, Kate. That never should have happened.'

'It should not. But it did.'

There was a silence.

She met his gaze. 'So you will understand something of my feelings towards the British.'

He said nothing. He did understand. Too much.

'I loved him,' she said, and looked down to where her fingers twisted the plain gold wedding band on her finger. 'I still do.' She swallowed. 'I always will.'

Her eyes met his again and he saw her pain and her grief, and the strength that had driven her.

'I know,' he said.

'How many days until England?'

'A week at most.'

She nodded and looked out again at the ocean.

They stood in silence together.

He felt her pain as keenly as he felt his own.

He understood, but understanding changed nothing. He walked away, left her standing there and returned to his duty.

At the dining table a few evenings later Gunner was sitting opposite her and little Tom beside her, keeping her company at the dinner table, now that she had given up hiding in her cabin. It made her heart swell to see how much the boy had come out of his shell.

'If you're not wanting that...' Tom eyed the chicken pieces in gravy sauce that she was poking round her plate, like a starving dog staring at a food-laden table.

'Take it.' She pushed the plate towards him. 'A growing boy needs to keep his strength up and I am not hungry tonight.'

'You weren't hungry last night, neither. Nor any of the nights since the captain got shot.' He looked at her with concern creasing between his brows.

'Eat the chicken, Tom,' Gunner said.

She forced a small smile to her face. 'My appetite does seem to have deserted me these days. I cannot think why.' But she knew why.

She glanced down the length of the table to where Kit sat with Briggs, Collier and Hastings. On the surface he was his usual self. Cool, strong, remote almost. A captain in every sense. And yet she noticed he looked pale and there was still a slight stiffness in the way he moved.

As if sensing her gaze, Kit moved his eyes to hers. Across the small distance the tension vibrated between them. So much unspoken. So much he had not asked her. Not one question on Jean Lafitte. No mention of Le Voile.

She returned her attention to Tom and to Gunner, to find the priest watching her.

'You cannot go on like this,' Gunner said softly.

'I cannot,' she agreed. It was time to take matters into her own hands.

Kit was alone when he came into the day cabin, just as she had known he would be. From the shadows that obscured her she watched him close the door behind him and lean back heavily against it, closing his eyes, his shoulders slumping as if he carried the weight of the world upon them. The sunset that blazed through the huge stern windows washed the pallor of his face rosy and revealed the darkness of the shadows that smudged beneath his eyes. It touched mahogany streaks to the darkness of his hair and showed the full extent of the vulnerability only revealed now he thought himself alone. The sight of it touched raw against her heart. She swallowed.

He must have heard it for she made no move or any other sound, yet his right hand slid quickly to the handle of his cutlass and his posture changed.

And then his eyes were open and trained on her standing there in her black dress in the shadows where the sunset did not reach. She stepped out into the rosy glow of light.

His hand dropped away from the cutlass but he did not revert to leaning against the door.

They looked at one another in the silence.

'You know, don't you?' she said. 'Who I am.'

'Captain La Voile,' he said softly.

She gave a smile that had nothing of mirth in it. 'I have dreaded this moment, since first you brought me aboard *Raven*. But now that it is finally here, it is almost a relief.' She took a breath. 'Does Gunner know?'

'Only me.'

She gave a sigh. 'You already know why. I guess I should tell you the rest of it.'

He said nothing. But she wanted him to know, this part of it, at least.

'*Coyote* was always mine, built by my grandfather. I had sailed her in those waters from the time I was a little girl. I knew them better than anyone else. When Wendell died I had my children to provide for and a very good reason to hate the British. I wanted to sail under American rather than French colours, but as our countries are not officially at war I could not obtain an American letter of marque. So, officially, I became a pirate. Unofficially, Mr William Claiborne, the Governor of Louisiana, gave me his blessing. I had the knowledge and the ship. But no self-respecting privateer or pirate would have crewed for a woman, so I gave them the captain they expected.'

'A player.'

She nodded. 'All he had to do was look the part and do what I told him.'

'I should have known the very first time I saw you on *Coyote*, with the dark awning above the quarterdeck, a screen for the woman who habitually stood in a captain's place.'

'In my defence the sun is very fierce in our Louisiana waters. I did not want to burn.'

'Who have I got pickled in my medical room?'

'Tobias Malhone.'

'I would not have killed him had he not been fool enough to attack.'

'I know.' She nodded. 'He was a violent and brutal man. It was not supposed to be about killing, but about trade and honour. Tobias was starting to believe he really was La Voile. He was trying to cut me out. Even if you had not come along I was closing down the operation, so that he could not destroy my good name.'

He came to stand before her, the toes of his boots touching the dark hem of her skirt.

'How did you know?' she asked.

'You are a widow who still wears her wedding ring and dresses in mourning. You told me that your children were both fair-haired like their father, your husband. The man in the butt is not fair-haired. And Jean Lafitte would not have got in his ship and sailed halfway across the Atlantic to stop me reaching London with a dead La Voile. Imagine what it would do to his reputation if it was revealed that the prime operator amidst the Baratarian pirates was a woman with two children at her skirts.'

'It took me a while to work that one out. I thought he had come to rescue me.'

'I underestimated him, too. I thought he meant to "lose" La Voile in a skirmish.'

Neither of them mentioned the bullet. They did not need to. It was there thick in the atmosphere

between them, mixed with the passion and everything else.

'I am Le Voile.' The admission was finally out
there in the open between them. Now she just had
to ask the question they had both spent the last days
avoiding. 'What are you going to do about it, Kit?'

He took her gently in his arms, and he leaned his
forehead against hers, his eyelashes brushing hers
as they shuttered. 'I do not know, Kate. I honestly
do not know.'

It was cool and grey the day they landed at
Plymouth.

For all it was summer it did not seem so. England
was a place so alien to her. She missed the bound-
less blue skies of Louisiana. She missed the sunshine and even the stifling humid heat that she so
often complained about. But most of all she missed
her children and her mama and her friends; and
all of her life that was wrapped up in Tallaholm.
Devon, England seemed every single one of those
three-and-a-half-thousand miles away.

She climbed from the little rowing boat and stood
there in the harbour's yard, looking around her.
Men hurried here and there over the damp ground.
Carts, coaches and gigs crowded the road leading
in and out—both delivering and collecting from the
boats and ships waiting to leave and just arrived.

Officers in the dark-blue uniforms of the British royal navy, their men in dark jackets and the wide trousers and striped tops of seafarers.

'So many of your King's men,' she said, and felt a shiver ripple down her spine to be standing there in their midst, like a spy who had infiltrated the garrison of her enemy.

'This is the Royal Navy's dock. Merchantmen use the harbour just a little along the coast,' Gunner explained.

'*Raven* is not a Royal Navy vessel.'

'We have special dispensation given that we sail on Admiralty business.'

She understood now why the ensign had been hoisted before they approached the harbour. 'Who would have thought that the American pirate Le Voile was so important to the British Admiralty?'

'So important that they'll hang him by his scrawny pickled neck and pay us handsomely for the privilege,' said Briggs from behind her.

Collier and the others nodded and smiled, practically rubbing their hands at the prospect. 'Very handsomely indeed. When North says he'll deliver he does. Ain't it so, Captain?'

She swallowed.

A muscle tightened in Kit's jaw, but he said nothing in reply.

The men turned their attention to shifting

sea chests and the great oak butt that contained Tobias's body. But their words remained.

The ground seemed unsteady beneath her, the way it always was after so many days at sea. Except that it was not only sea legs on dry land making her feel like her world was tilting. The men's words stripped everything else away, paring it down to the danger she was in.

*Run.* The word whispered in her head. *Escape.* Kate watched Tobias's coffin no longer, but turned away. And found her nose practically touching Kit North's chest. She made to sidestep, but his hand captured her elbow fast and firm, preventing her flight.

She looked up into his eyes, knowing that whatever else he might do, he was not going to let her go.

They made it as far as the end of Dartmoor. Kit stopped short of heading into Exeter, choosing, instead, to spend the night in the small market town of Chudleigh at the edge of the moor. The quieter location of the Courtenay Arms Inn meant there would be fewer problems in securing stabling for both the cargo and horses.

The first hint of trouble came once they had booked in for the night and were sitting in the tap-room, and the landlord and his wife brought them their plates of mutton pie and potatoes they had ordered.

Kate was sitting by his side.

'Thank you,' she said as the woman set the plate down on the stained and pitted table surface.

'American?' the landlady asked, her dark brows drawing together.

'Yes, I am, ma'am.' Kate held her head high and proclaimed it loud.

A hush seemed to spread across the tap room.

The landlady's fingers fixed upon Kate's plate, lifting it back on to the great wooden tray she carried. 'I don't rightly know that we serve Americans in here. Not with them causing our boys such a trouble across the sea.'

Suddenly there was a dangerous atmosphere in the inn. *Raven's* crew's hands let go their tankards of ale to close upon the handles of their muskets and knives.

Kit got to his feet and spoke not to the landlady, but across the room to her husband behind the bar. 'If you do not serve the lady, you do not serve any of us.' His fingers rested lightly against the handle of his cutlass.

'It's late and you'll be hard pushed to find accommodation elsewhere at this hour,' the man answered.

'We will,' agreed North. His eyes held the landlord's. 'As pushed as you to find others to fill your empty rooms and stables.'

The landlord seemed to understand that the threat was not idle. He gave a nod to his wife. 'Serve her. I don't suppose there's much harm in having her under our roof for one night.'

The woman nodded and banged the plate down before Kate with a surly expression.

The standoff passed.

The locals drinking at the bar and through in the snug glanced their way too often, but Kate showed not one sign of intimidation.

His men grew rowdy, the earlier threat diluted by ale.

A serving wench came to clear the empty plates from the long wooden table. Beneath her apron the girl's bodice was tight and low cut, her grubby chemise laced so low and loose that her huge soft breasts were in danger of spilling free. With a sly glance at Kit's face she leaned over, presenting him with a full view. She leaned closer, deliberately brushing them against his arm, offering herself to him. The men sniggered, their gazes locked on those breasts, licking their lips. His gaze moved beyond the girl to another woman, whose eyes, the colour of the ocean they had just crossed, were watching him.

The girl's gaze followed his before returning to his face.

'A fine man like you…' Her fingers reached to toy against the lapel of his coat. 'You want to get yourself a nice English whore instead of an American.'

'I am not his whore.' Kate's voice cut like a blade through the jollity and laughter.

Silence descended upon the table.

'What are you, then?' the girl demanded, turning to her with narrowed eyes. 'His prisoner?'

'She is my betrothed,' said Kit coldly and removed the girl's hand from his coat.

'I beg your pardon, sir,' the girl said coolly and, lifting her tray, left in a hurry.

Silence hissed. The whole of the crew was looking at him and Kate.

Gunner raised his tankard. 'It seems congratulations are in order.'

Kit said nothing.

'To the Captain and his lady,' said Gunner.

'The Captain and his lady,' the men all chorused and toasted them with their tankards of ale, stamping their feet and cheering.

'Calls for a celebration, I reckon,' said Briggs.

'I will leave you to celebrate, gentlemen,' Kate said, getting to her feet. 'It has been a long day. I think I'll turn in for the night.'

The men all stood, as if they were gentlemen and she their captain's lady in truth.

Kate's expression revealed nothing, but when her eyes met Kit's he saw the flash of resentment in them.

'Gentlemen.' Kit rose and followed close behind her, so that all of those locals who watched her too much left well alone.

Kate was very aware of Kit walking behind her. All the way up that rickety staircase. All the way along that long narrow corridor. They walked in silence past closed doors until they found the one they sought. When he opened the bedchamber door for her and she saw the sea chest sitting there on the floor she thought it was his, she thought…

'Your wardrobe,' he said from where he still stood out in the narrow corridor of the landing.

She glanced round at him, relieved that he had no intention of coming in, the atmosphere thick and cagey between them with so much that remained unclear. 'Thank you.'

The wardrobe he had bought for her in Antigua. The words pulled all that was unspoken into the little distance between where they each stood. All they had shared: the shark, the alleyway, their bodies united in lovemaking, the bullet in his shoulder and the biggest of all, the thing that neither of them was mentioning and that was there, huge and obvious as a mountain—*I am Le Voile... What are you going to do about it, Kit?*

The question still whispered without answer, growing more insistent and louder and tenser with each passing day, twisting tighter in the pit of her stomach now that they were on British soil.

She would not beg. She would not plead. She had her pride and her integrity. And so did he. But it did not make all those dark long hours of not knowing any easier. She turned her mind from that and thought of her vow.

'You should not have told her we were betrothed.' The sight of the serving wench touching him had made her throat tighten and her fingernails cut into her palms. *A fine man like you...* She swallowed down the memory and fidgeted with the wedding band on her finger, reassuring herself. It was not as if it was a real betrothal.

'What would you rather I had told her?' *The truth?* He did not say the words, but they were there just the same.

She glanced away, knowing what that would mean. Her fate would be sealed. The crew of men downstairs would not stand so ready to defend her honour. There would be nothing of friendship or respect.

'Lock the door behind me. And do not open it

again until morning.' His voice was unemotional, instructional, cool almost, as if the enormity of the dilemma did not rage between them. As if he did not hold her life in his hands. He made to close the door and leave.

'Why do you have a care for my safety?' Her words stopped him in his tracks, but he did not turn round. 'Oh,' she said softly. 'I forgot. You get a bigger bounty if I am alive.'

He turned to her then, his face all cool, hard dispassion, but those dark eyes fixed on hers held a conflict so deep and serious and tortured that it resonated right through to her core.

The silence hissed loud.

He did not say a word to break it, just looked at her and then closed the door and she heard his booted steps recede along that narrow passageway.

She locked the door just as he had said, then leaned her spine against it and stood there, with her eyes on that sea chest, knowing full well that a bigger bounty was not the reason he was safeguarding her.

Moving to the bed, she eased off her slippers, blew out the candle and crept beneath the thin blanket.

The smoke from the extinguished candle drifted in the darkness, lit grey and curling by the moonlight that showed through the small dirt-hazed window. The flimsy curtains that framed it on either side stirred in the draught. From the taproom below came laughter and the rowdiness of men's voices. From outside came the creak of the heavy wooden inn sign swaying, and the wind's low howling from across the moor.

Kate lay there in the darkness, until the taproom downstairs emptied and voices and hooves faded across the moor. Lay there unmoving and silent for so long, until the men had ceased their singing and the footsteps had faded and internal doors had opened and closed again. Until there was only the creak of the sign and the moan of the wind. And only then did she let herself think of Ben and Bea back home in Tallaholm so far across the ocean and what would happen to them if she did not return. Only then did she close her eyes and silently weep.

All that he was. All that he had become. All that made it possible to live with the knowledge of what he had done. All of it hinged on integrity...on honesty. On a vow he had sworn in a prison on the other side of the world, the words of which were seared upon his heart, as raw and meaningful as if he had spoken them only yesterday. He would never be Kit Northcote again. He would not lie. He would not cheat, not in the smallest of things...or in the largest.

He had signed a contract with the Admiralty and taken half the payment up front. There was no getting out if it. He was promised to deliver them the pirate La Voile. He could give them Tobias; all of his crew would stand witness that the man in the butt was La Voile. And the Admiralty would pay the money. But Kit would know the truth—that he was lying, that he had conned them. That he had *cheated* them. Just the thought made him feel sick.

But if he delivered them what they had paid for... He swallowed. The fact that she was a woman would not save her. They would hang her, privately, if not publically. The most courageous woman he knew. A woman of integrity and strength. The woman to whom he had made love. The woman who had dug a bullet from his shoulder. He balled his fists. How could that be right? Where was the integrity in leaving two children motherless? Where was the honesty in a man betraying his lover?

She was La Voile. And she was also the woman he cared for.

So he was damned if he did, and damned if he did not. He either cheated Admiralty or he sent Kate Medhurst to her death.

That was the crux of the decision before him. Stark and brutal, no matter how many ways he might try to disguise it and name it otherwise.

## Chapter Ten

'Briggs is watching the door that leads up to the bedchambers as you instructed. You really think that the anti-American feeling is so strong as to be a risk to her?' Within the stables Gunner leaned back against the wooden partition and watched Kit strapping the saddle on to his horse.

'I do not wish to take the risk. Hostility is in the air, stoked, it seems, by a series of sensationalised stories of what La Voile and his pirate friends have been doing to the British merchant vessels in their waters.' He did not like the way she had been treated over her nationality. And no matter the risk to her safety Kate would refuse to keep quiet or pretend she was anything other. But protecting her from attack was not the only reason he was keeping a close eye on her.

He could not trust that she would not try and make a run for it. No other woman would risk it, but Kate Medhurst was not any other woman. She would not balk at the dangers for a woman alone and penniless in a foreign country. Just the thought of her alone out there, at the mercy of men who would hurt her... He tightened the buckle and moved on to the next strap around the horse's girth.

'This betrothal—' Gunner began.

'Feigned. To save her reputation,' he interrupted in a harsh voice.

'That is a shame,' said Gunner. 'When the two of you are such a good match for each other.'

Kit ignored the words and kept his focus on the strap he was buckling

Gunner got the message and turned to leave.

'Gunner,' Kit said, his fingers stilled against the horse's belly.

His friend stopped and glanced back.

'The vows you swore as a priest... The vows that define a man...'

Gunner waited.

'Is there any way you could break them and live with yourself?'

The morning sunlight spilled across the straw-strewn floor. Outside a blackbird was singing.

The two men looked at each other.

'No,' said Gunner softly. 'I could not. Why do you ask?'

But Kit just shook his head and turned his attention once more to the horse before him.

The little column of men and horses and the carts wound their way across those narrow bumpy highways, creeping slowly but surely towards London. Kit rode out in front, keeping his distance from Kate, checking on her welfare, but leaving her to ride beside Gunner. But too many times during that long day that took them out of Devon and halfway across the south coast of England, she glanced at him to find those dark eyes upon her.

The Cardinal's Cap Inn in Milbourne was busier than the one at Dartmoor had been, and its guests, a little more mannerly. But she was still very aware of the looks her accent drew. And of the slightly threatening message that Kit's protective presence sent them. He paid extra money that she did not have to share a bedchamber with other women travellers and walked her there after they had eaten. But whether it was as a man protecting the woman he cared for or a guard escorting his prisoner, she did not know.

Neither of them spoke.

The tension seemed more strained than ever.

There was not a single word. Only the sound of that door closing. Only the sound of his booted steps walking away to leave her there alone. Only the knowledge, as she made her way through the candlelight to lie on the bed, that in two days they would be in London.

Would Kit really give her up to hang? A man who had made love to her body with such tenderness, a man who had saved her life and who looked into her eyes as if he felt things for her. Part of her could not really believe he would do it. And part knew him a man who would not flinch from doing the hardest thing. It was not about the bounty, for Tobias's body would secure him that easily enough. It was about integrity. And whatever else she knew, or did not know, about him, she knew that he was a man of integrity. It was the thing she admired most in him. And the thing she most feared, for it was his integrity that could hang her.

There had to be a way out of this. But no matter how many times she turned the problem round, no matter how many different angles she looked at it from, she could find no solution. There was no rest to be found on that lumpy over-warm bed. With a sigh she abandoned the elusive quarry of sleep and moved silently to stand by the small window.

The moonlight shone across the coaching yard, bleaching the gaudy inn sign to more muted hues and showing the empty dark carriage bodies lined up there like beasts crouched ready to pounce. Over by the stone wall a lone figure stood looking out over the nocturnal English countryside. The silhouette of a man in a shabby leather coat, wearing an old-fashioned tricorne hat—a pirate's hat, or more accurately a pirate hunter's hat, for upon the man's left shoulder sat the dark shape of a raven. Sleep eluded Kit North as much as it did her.

For a few minutes she stood there and watched his familiar figure so still and silent. And then, lifting her dark shawl from the chair on her side of the bed and slipping her feet into her shoes, she unlocked the door and crept from the bedchamber.

At the sound of her footsteps Bob flew up to perch on the inn's sign and watch them.

She came to stand beside Kit where he stood overlooking road and field and hedgerow, but seeing nothing of them.

'You should not be here, Kate.'

'Probably not,' she agreed, but she made no move to leave, nor did he want her to.

She stood by his side, watching out over that same view, just as they had stood together on *Raven*, looking out over the ocean.

'A man has got to sleep some time,' she said.

'Not always.' He could not remember the last time he had slept.

The wind howled across the fields, blowing a

rustle through the hedgerows that lined the road and divided the fields.

'Who is Emma?' she asked.

He shifted his gaze to her, to study her profile.

'My sister.' He wondered what else of his secrets he must have spilled in his nightmares.

She gave a nod and asked no more.

They stood in silence a little while longer, contemplating the view, before she spoke again. 'We will be in London the day after tomorrow.' She did not glance round, nor ask the question. That she could be so cool, so controlled, was a measure of her strength and made him realise that he was making the right decision. It had to be tearing her up inside; it was certainly doing as much to him and she was the one whose life hung in the balance.

He swallowed. 'We will.'

She turned to him then, her eyes moving over his face, down over his open coat, down over his shirt as if she could see the scars beneath, down to his holsters and his weapons before coming back up to his face.

They stood so close, facing one another, in that deserted dark coaching yard, arms loose by their sides.

'Integrity,' she said.

'Integrity,' he echoed.

'Such a difficult decision to make…whether to compromise it.'

'It was.' More difficult than she could ever imagine.

'Maybe I should have made it easier for us both. Maybe I should have taken the decision out of your hands. Since you are the only one who knows the truth of who I am.' Her gaze dropped to his holsters again, to his pistol, just as it had done that day on *Raven*, before coming back up to meet his eyes again.

'You know it is always loaded,' he said quietly.

'Yes.' All that had happened on *Raven* seemed to whisper in the quiet breeze of the night around them.

He took the pistol from its holster, turning it in his hand so that he was holding the barrel as he offered her the handle.

She inhaled a deep steadying breath, staring at it for a moment before she accepted it from him.

He opened his coat, exposing his chest.

He saw her swallow as she removed the safety catch, saw the slight tremor that ran through the pistol as she aimed it at him.

'Close your eyes if it makes it easier.' He guided the muzzle to press against his heart. 'One squeeze of the trigger and it is done.'

She stared at his heart with determination in her

eyes, but he could feel how much the pistol's muzzle trembled against his chest.

The moment stretched between them.

'Do it, Kate,' he urged.

She glanced at his eyes, then looked at where the pistol pressed to his heart and, giving a sigh, let it drop away before making it safe. Stepping closer, she slid the pistol back into its holster, before meeting his gaze once more.

They stood there and those short dark seconds of the night stretched longer.

They stood there and there was the thud of his heart and of hers.

'Tell me,' she said.

'I will cheat Admiralty and give them Tobias. Kate Medhurst was just another of his victims. They will send you home with the next convoy.'

Her eyes closed tight as the relief flooded through her. 'Thank God,' she whispered.

'I cannot deprive children of their mother.'

'And were I not a mother?'

'My decision would be the same.'

They stared at one another.

'Go back inside, Kate. It is late and we have many miles to cover tomorrow.'

But still she stood there.

'You might be giving them Tobias but the seas are free of Le Voile. I have already told you that her piracy days are over. I give you my word on that. So you are not cheating them. Not really.'

He smiled a bitter ironic smile at that because it did not change what was written upon the contract he had signed. And it was not La Voile he was delivering.

'Go,' he said with quiet command.

She nodded and walked away.

He watched until he saw her face appear at the small lead-latticed window and knew she was safe.

Bob swooped down to resume his perch on his shoulder. And Kit turned his gaze once more to the dark roll of fields.

Kate breakfasted with Gunner the next morning in the Cardinal's Cap Inn's dining room.

The bread was fresh baked and soft, the warmth it still held from the oven melting the fresh pale-yellow churned butter that she spread thick upon it. The tables had been wiped down of last night's spills and tankard rings of dried ale. The worn and uneven stone-flagged floor had been swept and washed, and the windows opened to let the morning air chase away the stale odours of pipe smoke and soured ale and lend a brisk chill to the dining room. A maid was sweeping out the ashes from the great hearth on the other side of the room. The landlady was busy in the kitchen, and the landlord, with a drying towel in his hand, could be seen in the doorway that separated the two rooms.

*Raven's* crew occupied the other tables, their normally robust manner subdued this morning, but whether it was due to a surplus of ale the night before or another cause she could not tell. Of Kit there was no sign.

'Does Kit sleep late this morning?' she asked Gunner quietly, wondering at what hour he had finally gone to bed.

Gunner shook his head. 'He is in the stables, checking over the horses and the cargo. He was already out there when I came down at five.'

She wondered if he had slept at all.

Something of last night's overwhelming relief had faded. This morning what she could not seem to get out of her head was that look in his eyes when he had pressed the muzzle of his pistol to his heart. And those soft words.

*And were I not a mother?*

*My decision would be the same.*

'Mrs Medhurst…Kate…' Gunner lowered his voice. 'Please do not think me impertinent…Kit seems… Did something happen between the two of you? A disagreement, perhaps…?'

She shook her head, knowing that what was between the two of them would remain that way. She could not tell him. 'Why do you ask?'

'Because there is something in his eyes this morning that I had not thought to see there again.'

'What do you mean?'

But Gunner just gave a little sad smile and shook his head in reply.

Her appetite waned, but she finished her bread and butter, and drained her coffee cup, not knowing when they would next get to eat.

The big wooden door banged as Kit came through it. 'We need to get moving. Now.'

'Aye-aye, Captain.' The men did as he bid, finishing up their food and making their way out to the yard.

'Gunner…Mrs Medhurst.' He did not look at her. His manner was cool, hard, efficient. Almost like the very first time they had met. Almost. But something was different, something she could feel the essence of, but not quite define. 'The bill has been paid. I will wait for you outside.'

The door banged again and he was gone.

She shot a glance at Gunner, but he was already on his feet and waiting for her. His pale blue eyes met hers and she felt a chill of unease stroke against her heart where there should only have been relief.

Ignoring the feeling, she fastened her bonnet on her head, slipped her gloves on to her hands and followed Gunner towards the front door.

* * *

Kit urged his horse onward. Now that the Cardinal's Cap and Milbourne were far behind the sun slipped from behind the clouds to brighten the day. Early morning had turned to late, but still his train of horses and men and carts pressed on, knowing they had Whitchurch to reach tonight.

He led from the front, keeping his distance and his eyes from Kate.

They rode for another hour before they stopped to water and feed both the horses and men, eating the great chunks of bread and cold ham and cheese for which he had paid the Cardinal's Cap landlord handsomely.

He studied his map, checking the roads that lay ahead, eating the bread, keeping his mind fully engaged on the task in hand so that he did not have to think of the other darker things that lay ahead in London.

'When is the wedding to be, sir?' Briggs asked.

'The wedding?' He glanced up from the map.

'Between you and Mrs Medhurst. What other wedding could there be?' Briggs teased with a grin.

Kit had glanced across at Kate before he could stop himself. Her eyes met his and held so that the secrets they were hiding seemed to vibrate in the air between them.

Only the two of them and Gunner knew there was never going to be a wedding.

Only the two of them knew the truth.

He should say the words, *When we get to London*. Or some other lie. Once an oath was broken the floodgates were opened to release lie upon lie, cheat upon cheat, until a man had no hope of saving his soul, or living with the deeds he had done. But he could not. The weight of his own darkness pressed down heavy upon him. He would damn himself to save her a thousand times over, he thought, and wondered that the decision had taken him so long.

'Captain North and I have yet to make that decision.' It was Kate who answered, with neither a lie nor the truth.

'Are we invited, ma'am?' little Tom asked. '*Raven's* crew, that is.'

Kit was glad the question was not directed at him. He saw the way the little boy looked at her. When she left it would break the lad's heart as much as his, had he a heart to break.

'At any wedding of mine and the Captain's I am sure that all of *Raven's* crew would be very welcome guests.' Again, no lie. Her clever use of words ensured it, cleverer than his had ever been.

He was glad when the time came to put away the map and ride on.

\* \* \*

All day he rode out ahead alone, apart from the rest of them.

All day she could feel the wedge that was between them.

She should have been glad of it. She should have been willing the hours to pass all the quicker, for the sooner they reached London and she was aboard a frigate bound for America the better. She would be safe, heading home to her children and her family. And she would leave him behind, never to see him again.

He was British. She was American.

He was a pirate hunter and she the pirate he had been paid to capture.

And he was a man who had compromised his integrity to save her.

She had known that it would cost him to compromise himself, but to see it, to feel it, this difference in him... She thought of how she would feel had she to stand up and renounce all that she believed in, her cause and country, to save him.

Being closer to London, the White Hart Inn at Whitchurch was much busier than those of their previous stops. No one accosted or challenged her on her accent, but she saw the glances that were shot her way when she spoke and heard the dark murmurs. There was an air of threat about the place and no locks upon the doors, so that when Kit escorted her to her bedchamber that night and did not leave, she was glad of it.

'There is a bad feeling about this place. You should not be alone.' He did not say anything of her nationality.

He jammed a wooden chair beneath the handle of the door so that it could not be opened from outside. She watched the care he still took in private over his weakened shoulder as he removed his heavy leather coat and laid it down on the floor before the chair. She knew what he was doing as he unsheathed his cutlass and positioned it on one side of the coat.

'Planning on undoing all my hard work with your shoulder?' she said, walking over to stand before him.

'It is healed.' His expression was cool and dispassionate, his eyes did not meet hers. He laid the pistol at the other edge of the coat.

'Even so, there is a perfectly good bed over there. You can sleep above the covers, I can sleep below. I promise I will not ravish you.'

He glanced at her then. But he did not smile. Just gave a nod of his head.

And so that is what they did. She, fully clothed beneath the blankets, he, wearing his coat above them. Lying on that bed together, a thousand miles apart in the darkness.

There was a two-foot gap between them. At no point did they touch, but she could feel the tension that hung about his body, as if it were her own, feel the darkness of his turmoil.

She tossed and turned.

He lay still and unmoving, but awake. She could sense it, hear it, feel it, all through the long slow stretch of those hours until at last, when he thought her asleep, he gave up the pretence and walked quietly to stand by the moonlit window, staring out into the darkness. She watched him standing there for a few moments, like a man who had sold his soul, like a man who was haunted. And then she rose from the bed and went to stand beside him.

'I did not mean to wake you,' he said.

'I was not asleep,' she admitted.

He glanced round at her then and there was something so tortured in those dark eyes of his that it was as if a hand had taken hold of her heart and squeezed.

She slid her fingers to cover his. 'In all the time I have been Le Voile I have never regretted it, not once. Indeed, it has been my salvation. But only now, only when I see you, do I wish with all my heart that it were not so.'

She felt the caress of his thumb against hers.

'La Voile Noire—the black sail,' he said quietly.

'Not quite,' she said. '*Le* Voile Noir—the black veil. My little joke. I was a grieving widow and a pirate captain, and I was obscuring what was there in plain sight before all the world.'

He stared at her, a hard look of shock on his face.

'Please do not feel bad, Kit, everyone made the same assumption. No one looked beyond the black sail.'

'And when they referred to *La* Voile…'

'I did not correct them. It is what they wanted, what they needed to believe. Part of the illusion.'

'The illusion of Tobias.'

The silence echoed between them. She could feel the change in him, feel the stillness and sudden increase in tension, feel intense heavy weight of his gaze.

She looked up into his eyes. 'It started out right and justified, but…' She bit her lip. 'Things are not so clearly delineated any more. Who is friend and who is foe. What is right and what wrong.'

'So all these three years you have been *Le* Voile,' he said very carefully. He stepped up close to her, staring down into her face with sharp urgent eyes.

'You know I have.'

'And Tobias, La Voile.'

'I guess.'

He rummaged in an inner pocket of his coat,

pulling out a folded document that was pale in the moonlight, and crossed the room quickly.

With fast efficient fingers he lit the candle stub using the tinderbox. She saw him swallow before he opened out the document, and, in the flickering candlelight, carefully scan the neat penned black lines.

His eyes shuttered. His body relaxed. He gave a sigh of relief.

'What is it, Kit?' she asked, her eyes staring into his.

'My salvation,' he said, and he smiled as he passed the document into her hands.

Her gaze moved over the rusty stain that marked the paper, the same stain that was preserved upon the deck of Kit's night cabin on *Raven*, before she read the words written there.

And then she smiled, too. His salvation, indeed.

For the document was his contract with the British Admiralty. And the name of the pirate he had been contracted to capture and rid the seas of, written clear and without ambiguity in every single instance throughout, was *La* Voile.

He smiled, that same smile she had once seen him give on *Raven*, of happiness and relief, a smile that lit her soul and made her heart swell for him. It was as if he had stepped out of the darkness of a terrible oppressive shadow into the light. She was so glad for him, so relieved. She knew how much this meant to him.

Reaching a hand to cup his cheek, she felt the roughness of the beard stubble that shadowed and darkened his cheek, his chin and above his lips. She slid her fingers against it, caressing the harshness and masculinity that made him the man he was. Anchoring that man now he had returned, never wanting him to leave lest the darkness of that unfathomable torture swallow him up again.

He smiled and, reaching a hand round her waist, pulled her to him, stroked the long loose strands of hair and stared down into her eyes.

Tomorrow they would reach London. Tomorrow they would go before the Admiralty. And she would start her journey home to Louisiana. She longed for it and she dreaded it, too. Because of this man standing before her.

After tomorrow it would be as if she had never met him and everything would go back to the way it should be. Her heart belonging to Wendell. Her life devoted to raising Ben and Bea and caring for her mama. She would be the person she had always been. Strong and loyal and true—to her children, to her country and the memory of the man she had sworn she would always love.

All of that came tomorrow. But tonight…she was

here and looking into those dark, dark eyes with all their secrets and integrity and her heart was filled with tenderness for him and her body alive with desire for him. Tomorrow she would step back into her old life. But tonight…tonight she followed her heart and the longing in her soul.

He blew out the candle and they kissed and stripped off their clothes, and they loved together beneath the light of the silver moon.

The hour was still early, too early to wake Kate.

Kit thought of their lovemaking of the night. She had loved him, giving herself and her heart with an intensity of meaning that matched what was within his own body and mind and soul.

Today she would go home across the seas and he would face what it was he had spent the past three years both running from and to. It had to be this way. He could not weaken. Not now. Not when he was so close, in the home straight. And besides, he had nothing he could offer her. If she knew the man he really was, she would not look at him the way she did now. She would revile him. She would lock her door and her heart against him, not open her soft arms and hold him to her breast. He did not deserve a woman like her. And more importantly she did not deserve a man like him.

Last night was a dream that would sustain him

for the rest of his life. This morning, life was there again, waiting with all its harsh reality.

He slipped quietly from the bed and, taking care not to wake her, washed in the basin of cold water and shaved the last of the blue-shadowed bristle from his face. Splashing the water through his hair, he smoothed it back from his face and stared at the man reflected in the looking glass. Always his life was a battle against the weakness within. It always would be. But today he would go to the Admiralty and deliver them La Voile in truth. Le Voile would never sail again. And he would let her walk away and turn his face to London and all that he had worked the last years to do. He stared at the man and knew he would always be glad he had known Kate Medhurst.

He smiled to himself and with a deep breath rolled down his shirt sleeves, tied his neckcloth into place and pulled on his coat.

Out on the window ledge, Bob gave a caw and Kate stirred to waking, looking over at Kit with sleep-misted eyes and a shy smile.

Kit walked over to the bed. 'Bar the door behind me,' he whispered as he dropped one final kiss to her lips.

She nodded.

Kit walked out of her bedchamber for the last time.

* * *

Gunner was sitting alone at a small table in the corner of the White Hart's dining room when Kit entered. Those of the crew who were up and ready sat together at a larger table in the centre of the room, largely in silence and looking dog-eared as seamen always did on those first few days ashore.

Gunner's normal calm expression was gone. In its place was a tense worry that stroked foreboding through Kit.

With a nod at his men he sauntered over to Gunner's table and sat down opposite him. He ordered only coffee from the serving wench who appeared from the kitchen doorway in her apron. When she was gone he asked, 'Something wrong?' He wondered if Gunner knew that he had stayed with Kate last night and disapproved. He would not let a slur be cast on her.

'We have a problem,' Gunner said quietly.

'What kind of a problem?'

In reply Gunner handed him a newspaper folded over to reveal half a page, and pointed halfway down a column of print. 'That kind of a problem.'

Kit's eyes read the words with quick precision and all of his assertions about cursing were forgotten. 'Hell!'

'Not good.'

'And with such impeccable timing,' he said sardonically and set the newspaper aside.

'What time are we due at Admiralty?'

'Three o'clock.'

A silence stretched while they both contemplated the magnitude of the development and how it changed everything for Kate.

'You could plead her case. Admiralty might make an exception given that you are delivering them La Voile.'

'They will not,' said Kit. 'You have had dealings with them before. You know they will not.'

'If you turn up with Mrs Medhurst at Admiralty this afternoon…'

'It is not Louisiana to which she will be sent,' finished Kit.

'It is not,' agreed Gunner quietly. 'She will not be going home anytime soon.'

'She has two children waiting for her there. Six and four years old.'

Gunner shook his head and glanced away, the compassion clear in his eyes. They both knew Kate's children would not remember her by the time she returned to Louisiana…*if* she ever returned. 'We need her as a witness. And even if we did not, we could not leave her here. She would not be safe. The government have probably already started rounding up all the stray Americans.'

'Not all,' Kit said softly. 'They will not be arresting Lady Haslett.'

'Lady Haslett is not an ordinary American woman. She is a member of London's *ton*. Her husband is from one of the oldest and most powerful families in England.'

'My point precisely,' said Kit softly.

Gunner stared at him. 'Are you suggesting what I think?'

'It is seven o'clock. We have eight hours before we must be at Admiralty. Could it be done in time?'

'We passed a church on the way into town. A little gentle persuasion may be required...' Gunner's long bony fingers caressed the handle of his cutlass. 'But, yes, it could be done in time.'

They fell silent while the serving wench delivered Kit's coffee and left again.

'I will explain the situation to Kate. And ascertain whether she wishes to do what is necessary.'

Gunner gave a nod. 'God works in mysterious ways. I cannot pretend that America declaring war on Britain is in any way desirable, but marriage between you and Kate Medhurst might be no bad thing for either of you.'

But Gunner did not understand, not Kate and not him.

Kit's face was grim. He sipped his coffee and waited for Kate to come downstairs.

## *Chapter Eleven*

Kate's first indication that something might be wrong was that there was not one man of *Raven's* crew in the inn's dining room. The second was the fact that Kit had secured them a private parlour for breakfast. The third was the look on his face—a dark intensity and tension so different to the man who had left her not so long since in the bedchamber.

She felt her cheeks grow warm at the memory of the intimacies that they had shared in the night. She had done things with him, given a part of herself she had sworn never to give again. It had seemed so right in the dark privacy of the night when all that had existed was him and her and their relief. Now in the stark clear daylight, with responsibility and respectability back in place, the wild abandon and tenderness of their bonding seemed to belong to another place and time.

Last night had been a different Kate Medhurst. This morning she was herself once again, but the echoes of the night still whispered between them.

'That coffee sure smells good,' she said with a smile, feigning a normality she did not feel as she sat down at the table.

But Kit gave no reply.

The serving wench delivered her a breakfast of warm bread rolls, a dish of strawberry jam and a fresh pot of coffee. Kit poured her coffee, adding a splash of cream and a tiny lump of sugar just the way she liked. And in all that time he did not say a word so that the skin on the nape of her neck began to prickle and a chill of foreboding seemed to spread across her skin and she was seized by the certainty that something was badly wrong.

She took a sip of coffee, but did not touch the bread.

Only when the door of the parlour closed behind the serving wench did he speak.

'There is something you need to know, Kate. Something that changes everything.'

A cold draught blew gentle across her heart, sending a chill through her blood. 'What do you mean? How much can have happened since last night?'

'A lot more than either of us could have anticipated.' From the table by his side he lifted a folded newspaper and passed it to her.

The cup of coffee sat untouched on the table as the printed words hit her. 'America has declared war on Britain!' Her heart stuttered. She stared at him, her mind stumbling over the implications of the headline.

*Something that changes everything.*

She wanted to deny it, to hope that all would be as they had planned. But she knew in her heart that he was right.

'The Admiralty are not going put me on a ship and deliver me home, are they?'

He shook his head, his eyes holding hers.

'What will they do?'

'Intern you with the other Americans who are here. For the duration of the war most likely. It is what happened during the War of Independence.'

A war that could last for years. Years locked in a prison camp in England while her widowed mother struggled alone to bring up Kate's two children.

She was so close, so close, and now at this eleventh hour, it was all being snatched away. She wanted to shout out in anger at the injustice. She wanted to weep and cover her face with her hands. She wanted to rail against what was happening. But she knew if she let herself weaken then the floodgates would open and Lord only knew what would come out tumbling out then. So she kept herself together and took a steadying breath.

'There is a way around it, Kate.'

She looked at him. 'What way?'

'They would not intern you if you were married to a British citizen.'

Only the beat of her own heart sounded.

'A gentleman. Someone whose family was one of the oldest and most distinguished in England, and who could stand as your guarantor.'

'Where would I find such a man?' Her eyes held his. She held her breath, afraid that she had misunderstood what he was suggesting and even more afraid that she had not.

'Here, before you.'

Silence.

'Marry me,' he said.

She glanced away. Marriage, to another man. *Marriage.* She thought of all that she had done to avoid it. Becoming Le Voile and all that it had cost her. She thought of what marriage would mean to the memory of Wendell; of what it would say about her and her lack of loyalty. It would make a mockery of everything she had sworn—that she would stay true to him and only him. How could she then marry another? And not just any other, an Englishman, a man who hunted pirates and privateers— a man like those responsible for Wendell's death. And worse than that, a man for whom her feelings already invoked a sense of guilt when it came to the memory of her husband.

'There has to be another way,' she said quietly and saw something flicker deep in those dark eyes before he masked it.

'Believe me, there is no other way.' His voice was cool, clipped, focused. 'It would, of course, be a marriage in name only. As your husband, they would entrust me with your keeping. I have business to deal with in London, but I would arrange for Gunner to return you to Louisiana as soon as it was safe and have the marriage annulled.'

'Could it be so easily done?' A marriage dissolved as if it had never been? As if it counted for nothing.

'As long as it is not consummated.'

She could not meet his eyes. 'Is it not too late for that given we have already...?' She swallowed and tried again. 'That we have...' She rubbed a hand against the back of her neck, knowing that what she had done with Kit North, sleeping with him, loving him, would earn her the condemnation of every respectable citizen in Tallaholm. She knew what she had done was wrong, but when it came to Kit North it seemed all of what she thought she knew about herself and her morals and beliefs went out of the window.

'I believe the church and law consider only those relations that have occurred, or not, after the marriage ceremony.'

She nodded and finally met his eyes. 'You would be marrying a woman who is now officially an enemy of your King and country.' And more than that, much, much more than that.

'I brought you here. And, as I told you before, I have enough on my conscience without adding making your children motherless to it.' His voice was quiet and cool, the look in his dark eyes unreadable. 'I have no preference in the matter. The choice is yours to make.'

But there was no choice. Not as far as Kate could see. Without him, she stood no chance. She would be England's prisoner. But as his wife… She told herself that she was only doing this for her children, to get home to her country, for her freedom; that the marriage would be meaningless because it would be annulled.

And were all those things true she would have agreed to the plan without so much as a second thought. But she knew there was much more to it than that, maybe not for him, but for herself. Things that frightened her to admit. Things that she did not want to feel. Things that made guilt weigh heavy upon her shoulders.

She closed her eyes, swallowing down the guilt, feeling all those forbidden feelings whisper and smile their victory in that part of herself she would deny.

*Forgive me, Wendell.*

And when she opened them again she said, 'Then I choose you, Kit North. I will be your wife.'

He was silent for a moment, his dark eyes on hers. 'I will make the necessary arrangements.' Cool. Impassive. As if it truly were just a marriage name. As if they had not lain together and shared their bodies and shared their souls by the light of the moon over ocean and land. 'Be ready in an hour.'

So soon? Inside her guilt scraped at her again. She took a breath. Nodded. 'An hour,' she said with a calmness that belied all that was vying and fighting beneath.

'Remember to remove your wedding band.'

Her eyes met his in horror at the realisation. Her hand clutched to it to keep it there, the thought of taking it from her finger too much to bear.

He rose from his chair and walked away, closing the parlour door behind him.

She stared at the cup of cold coffee, scarcely able to believe how much her world had just turned upside down. She felt as though she had been standing in the middle of a quiet dusty street on a lazy sunny afternoon only to be hit, without the slightest whisper of warning, by a speeding mail coach.

In an hour she would marry the pirate hunter Kit North. The man for whom her body thrilled and longed, and her heart ached, and the man for whom she would betray the memory of Wendell and all she had sworn.

The scene was like something from a comedy. In the small country church of All Hallows the early summer sun flooded through the stained-glass windows to bathe the worn and ancient flagstones of the floor in a rainbow of heavenly light. Wooden carved statues of beatified martyrs and the Holy Virgin looked down with gentle expressions. Kit wondered how gentle their expressions would be if they could see the congregation that lined the pews of their church.

*Raven's* crew looked like the motley bunch of ex-pirates they were. Every one of them was armed to the teeth with pistols and knives. But they had smoothed their hair and wiped the dirt from their faces. Their jackets had been brushed and the dust washed from their feet. Most were even wearing shoes. Kit felt both proud and humbled by the sight of them standing there with their backs straight and their heads bowed in a house of God.

By his side Gunner was calm and serene, his

expression so gentle, yet the way the priest before them in his black robes was sweating and the slight tremor in the Common Book of Prayer gripped so tightly between his fat white fingers told Kit that some degree of persuasion had indeed been required. Whatever Gunner had done, the sweating priest had found a way to overcome the not-inconsiderable obstacles of no banns being read and neither the bride or groom, nor a single one of the guests, being of his parish. Old Pete Pinksy was standing at the side with the flageolet on his lips, playing hymns softly.

'Had I known he knew such music aboard *Raven*...' Gunner whispered with a smile.

And then Old Pete stopped, and started playing 'The Queen of Love.' And Kit knew without Gunner's whisper that Kate had arrived.

He resisted the urge to look round, just kept his face pointed forward and tried not to think of her expression of horror when she had realised that she was going to have to marry him. He did not want this any more than she did, but he had brought her here and promised her safe passage home, and it was true that he did not need anything else on his conscience.

Marry her. Face Admiralty. Send her back to Louisiana. Then he could draw a line under all that had happened with her and return to his life in London. It was simple. It was the right thing to do. For the sake of two innocent children. Nothing else. He gritted his teeth and closed his ears to the other things that whispered within, the things to which he could not allow himself to listen, would not allow himself to listen.

The music was coming to a close. He should not have looked round, but he did, seeing her walking those last few paces that would bring her to stand by his side. Her face was pale. She was wearing the black silk dress from her Antiguan wardrobe and her black fichu, clothes for a funeral, not a wedding.

Her only concession to the occasion was the small posy of wild pink briar roses that she clutched between her hands, their sweet perfume subtle and fresh in the mustiness and polish of the old church. Her tawny hair glowed golden in the sunlight, but her eyes were a resolute grey and they were filled with a determination and courage that no bride should have to wear as she walked down the aisle.

She was not alone. Young Tom walked in her father's place by her side. Kit saw the way the boy held his head up and the thin shoulders squared with pride at the honour of being chosen out of all the crew to perform this task of a man. The lad's eye caught Kit's and he grinned, his pleasure like a fountain flowing out of him to spread all around, such a stark contrast to the guarded look in Kate's eyes. Difficult though this time was for her, she had thought of the boy. Hers was the strongest of hearts, but it was gentle, too. There was not another woman in the world like Kate Medhurst. Had he not been the man he was... Had this marriage been in earnest... Had she not still been in love with her dead husband...

Her eyes met his, and he felt something tighten in his chest. The dust motes drifted between them like it was an otherworld scene. Kit called on his strongest reserves and with a will of iron turned his face forward once more. His gaze, cold and hard, moved to the fat priest.

'Marry us,' he commanded.

And the man did.

Kit went through the ceremony. Her fingers were cold within his, Wendell Medhurst's ring gone in material, but its presence still symbolised by the thin pale band of skin its absence had left beneath. He slid on his own ring to cover it.

Her eyes welled. Her lip trembled. She caught it between her teeth, biting on it to control the emotion, all of it for the dead man she still loved, a man with whom Kit could never compete.

He did not look at her again. Just said the words that made her his wife in the eyes of the church and the law and heard her voice soft and husky make the same vows.

They signed their names in the parish book. No one commented that he signed Northcote and not North, just as they said nothing over the name spoken during the ceremony.

They were man and wife in law. For now.

A marriage made easily enough and to be undone just as easily when the time came.

He kept his heart hard and cold. Because it was the only way he knew to survive.

Kate brushed her hand over her skirt, the same black silk in which she had been married not seven hours since, as if she would smooth away invisible creases. The afternoon sun glinted in through the window of the corridor in the Admiralty building, lighting the men that sat patiently waiting seated on the rows of hard wooden chairs still dressed in their best from the morning. All of *Raven's* crew had come to support their captain and gain their share of the bounty.

The worn old gold band on her finger glowed in the sunlight, light and bright against the darkness of the silk. Her hand stilled. She stared at the ring that Wendell had put there, the ring that she had sworn never to remove. Kit's larger ring was looped on to a thin leather lace tied beneath the fichu. The gold lay between her breasts, hidden well out of sight alongside her heart. No one had noticed the switch so far and she hoped no one would, but she slipped on her small lace day gloves, just in case.

The slow steady tick of the tall clock in the corner of the room resonated through her body. It seemed that Kit had been in that office for an age. What if there was a problem? What if the Lord Admiral did not believe he had delivered them La Voile? What if they were refusing to pay him the bounty, with all his men sitting here waiting expectantly for their share of the hard-earned coin?

The air was too warm, the palms of her hands beneath the gloves already growing clammy. She smoothed a hand over her skirt again and was about to ask Gunner how long these things normally took when the office door opened and the young naval officer who had shown Kit in appeared once more.

'Reverend Dr Gunner, the first Lord of the Admiralty will see you now, sir.'

Gunner smiled his meek smile at the smartly uniformed younger man and, with a nod, rose and followed him into the office.

Eventually Gunner returned and then each of *Raven's* crew in turn were called within that office. The process took so long that Kate could feel her body tense all the more with growing worry. There was none of the usual convivial chatter and teasing. No jokes, just a feeling of absolute tension and importance, as if they all stood lined up at a cliff edge with a sheer drop on to jagged rocks beneath.

What if Kit had got it wrong and they meant to imprison her, after all?

What if they imprisoned him for trying to help her? She was an enemy of the state now, after all; a foreign combatant in their midst and that was before they knew anything of Le Voile. A feeling of panic twisted in her stomach.

'What will I say to them when it is my turn?' Little Tom, sitting by her side, whispered the question and looked up at her with a pale face and worry in his eyes.

She wanted to take his little hand in her own or put an arm around him, but she knew that would only embarrass the boy before the men of the crew. So she just smiled at him as if there was not a jitter in her body and told the lie calmly. 'There is nothing to fear. Just answer their questions with the truth.'

He relaxed and returned the smile with a nod of his head.

When Tom disappeared into the office and the crew all sat there in silence, she heard Briggs across the waiting room murmur, 'It's like the bleedin' Spanish inquisition in there.' And despite all she had told Tom she could feel the fear tighten in her lungs and tremble in her nostrils. Her hands clung tight together. She closed her eyes to try to control her nerves.

'Stout heart,' she heard Gunner whisper by her ear.

He was a kind man. A gentle man. A priest. And he did not know how much she was hiding, or how much Kit was risking, and all that was in danger of being discovered.

And then Tom came back with a relieved grin and the young naval officer was saying, 'Mrs North.'

In the expectant silence all faces turned to her and only then did she realise.

'Mrs North,' the officer said again and she realised that she was Mrs North and no longer Medhurst; no longer Wendell's name, but Kit's. Another pang of guilt twisted deep within.

Taking a deep breath, she followed the young officer into the first Lord of the Admiralty's office, to play her part in this masquerade.

*Just answer their questions with the truth.* In order to save herself and the man who was now her husband, Kate had to do anything but.

'So Captain North rescued you from *Coyote* and the pirate La Voile,' Mr Charles Philip Yorke, the

First Lord of the Admiralty and president of the Board of Admiralty, said once Kate was seated.

'Indeed, sir. He rescued me from Le Voile.'

And the significance of what she had just said was not lost on Kit. *Le* Voile.

Everything about her was easy, relaxed, confident. That same air that sat about her always, Le Voile, the veil, in truth, except in those few rare moments when the two of them were alone and she had let the veil drop away to reveal the vulnerability of the woman beneath.

She was feigning it. He watched her and felt that same respect he had always felt for her. She had more courage than most men he knew.

There was a silence while Yorke steepled his fingers and held her gaze.

Kate returned his gaze, calm and steady.

'And how did you come to be aboard *Coyote*?' Yorke asked.

Kit waited for her answer. There had been no time for rehearsals or to agree a story between them. He just had to trust that she would tell it in the same way he had.

'How does a respectable woman normally come to be aboard a pirate ship?' she said quietly and kept her gaze on Yorke's, almost daring him to be so insensitive and brash as to ask her the details of what everyone imagined the pirate had done to the woman he had abducted.

Kit reached his hand to hers and gave it a little squeeze. 'To discuss the details of the matter distresses my wife,' he said coolly and knew that he was not lying. He felt a wave of protectiveness for her. *My wife.*

Yorke cleared his throat. 'Of course.' He had already heard from his crew that La Voile had been seen treating her roughly on *Coyote's* deck.

'And once you were aboard *Raven* with Captain North...' Kit could see the way the man's mind was working. He thought that Kit had compromised her, taken advantage of her and been left with having to do the honourable thing by wedding her.

'I found a man of integrity and honour.' She glanced across at Kit, her eyes meeting his. 'A man whom I admire and respect.'

More lies or the truth?

Silence.

'And you were married only this morning. The day the nation learns that America has declared war on England.'

'We were,' she answered, unruffled by the unspoken implication in his words. But every man of his crew had told the First Lord of the Admiralty the same story—that their captain and Mrs Medhurst had declared their betrothal on their first day ashore.

Yorke gave a nod. 'Thank you, that will be all, Mrs North.' He got to his feet alongside Kit as she left, treating her like the lady she was. Only once she was gone and the door closed behind her did he resume his seat and speak again.

'I will have the remainder of the payment released to you and your men before you leave. There is, of course, no question of your wife being interned. You are deemed guarantor for her.'

Kit nodded. 'Thank you.'

There was a silence as Yorke's eyes raked his. 'I did not realise you were William Northcote's son.' He could hear the slight rebuke in the older man's voice and see the shift in attitude from respect to something very different. The first portent of what was to come.

'I did not expect that you did.' Kit bowed and returned to his men and his wife.

Within the rented house in Grosvenor Street Kate stood by the window, looking out over the quiet road. London, with its sprawl and its streets with rows of town houses with their stonework and Palladian style, was quite literally a world away from Tallaholm with its wide dusty single street and her wooden homestead out on the edge of town.

The bounty had been divided and *Raven's* crew paid their share. The cart with its great wooden butt and gruesome contents had gone. She did not want to think of what they would do to Tobias's body. No matter what she had thought of him, he was still a fellow American.

The day's difficulty had not been helped by having to feign a true marriage, before all those at the Admiralty and in the hours after. But she had done it both for fear that word might get back to the Admiralty and because she did not want to destroy the happiness that the crew and Gunner and young Tom had over the union. Gunner had taken Tom with him for the night, leaving the newlywed couple alone for their wedding night.

Now, as they stood in the drawing room of the house Kit had rented, she felt as nervous as the green girl in the rough-hewn bedroom of the farmhouse that Wendell had taken her back to after their wedding seven long years ago.

She turned to face Kit. 'So what happens now?'

He stood by the great marble fireplace, the toe of one boot resting on the fender guard, the wrist of one arm resting on the pale carved marble that made the mantelshelf. He looked not at her, but into the empty grate.

'Now we keep up the pretence of living as a happily married couple until the Admiralty's surveillance wanes and Gunner's business is concluded.'

'You think they really will keep their eyes on us.'

'I know they will. You are American. And I am—' He stopped abruptly, biting back whatever it was he would have said. 'My family might be genteel, but I am something of an untrusted entity.'

Because he had once been a pirate, she supposed. But they had trusted him enough to let him turn hunter.

'How long will it take?' Only once the words were out did she realise how they sounded—that she was desperate to be gone from him and on her way home to Louisiana. The latter was true, the former was not.

He turned then, and looked at her. 'A little over a fortnight.' His voice was cool.

She gave a nod, glanced away and, twiddling her wedding band, swallowed. She saw his eyes flick to her left hand and the gold ring upon her finger that was not the one that he had put there, before coming back up to her face. He made not one comment upon the exchange but his expression was as closed and as unreadable as the first day she had seen him standing on *Raven's* deck.

'Console yourself with the fact that we must play our parts as husband and wife only when we are being observed. Rest assured I will not inflict my presence on you a moment longer than necessary.'

'Kit…' Her fingers twisted harder at the gold band.

His eyes held hers, waiting, giving her the chance to explain. He could not know how much she wanted to, or at least try to. But even just to say the words would have been to betray Wendell and she could not do it. And in the stretching silence any chance was lost, swallowed up into something else.

He gave a bitter smile as if he understood, when in truth he understood nothing at all.

'Matthews, the butler, will give you a tour of the house and attend to your every need. If you will excuse me…?'

She should have stopped him. She should have told him.

He bowed and walked away, leaving her standing there. She heard the thud of the front door closing, its echo ringing in the emptiness of the house around her.

Everything was as she had wanted—she had been saved from internment, her passage back to Louisiana was guaranteed, Kit would annul the marriage once it had served its purpose, and he was leaving her alone, with her loyalty to Wendell. But she had never felt more empty and solitary.

She sat down in one of the drawing room's little

armchairs and looked at Wendell's wedding ring upon her finger. And she did not understand why when she was trying so hard to do this right, it felt so wrong.

After his business with the bank he walked to Whitechapel and stood there in the dusky light outside the place in Half Moon Alley where he had sold his soul to the devil and destroyed his world and that of his family. It was a shabby, filthy-looking hovel with boarded-up windows and the scent of piss and stale ale and pipe smoke hanging around the doorway. It always had been, but Kit Northcote had been too blind to see the reality. He had seen only excitement in a life of privileged boredom and the chance to make himself look big in the eyes of others.

The same two toughs loitered, leaning on either side of the doorway that led into the small smelly darkness within, like matching black-toothed sentinels. Their faces were scarred and unfriendly. Their eyes held nothing of recognition. They did not remember him, but he remembered them and everyone else who had been there that night. They sized him up, not sure what to make of his shabby sea attire, or Bob sitting on his shoulder, and, most of all, of the cutlass that hung by his side.

He had thought it would be difficult to stand here

and face it again, but it was not. He had thought he would feel that old terror that had haunted him for so long, but he did not. He felt almost disappointed in its ordinariness. Three years ago, it had been anything but. Extraordinary. Exciting. Dangerous. Just like the rest of Whitechapel that surrounded it. But the places that Kit had spent the intervening years made Whitechapel look safe and salubrious.

'Is Stratham within?' he asked, gesturing with his head towards the dark passage. The air seemed to hum as he waited for their reply.

'Who wants to know?'

'An old friend,' he said, and never took his eyes from the biggest man's gaze. He saw the man's eyes flicker down to where his hand, through force of habit, rested upon the handle of his cutlass.

When the eyes returned to his face once more, the man shook his head. 'You ain't been around these parts for a while, mister. Stratham's long gone.'

He should have been relieved, but what he felt was a curious sense of disappointment.

'You going inside, fella?'

'I will pass on the invitation, this time,' he said.

One of them gave a nod of acknowledgement. The other just watched him with sullen eyes. In the memory that had played a thousand times in his mind, they had been taller, bigger, tougher, and

Old Moll's Place a dark enticing den of iniquity. The men were not so very different from the man he had become, and Old Moll's just a hovel where Whitechapel men went to ease their hard lives. And the man, Stratham, whose face Kit could recall in detail, from his dark blond hair to his bright-blue taunting eyes and cold sneering smile, was gone.

He should not have been surprised. Someone had probably slipped a blade between the bastard's ribs in a darkened alleyway late one night; just as they should have done to Kit Northcote.

Whatever it was he had expected, it was not this. Stratham was gone. And Old Moll's was nothing. But he had done what he came to do.

He made his way back on foot, walking from the narrow dirty streets of Whitechapel with its poverty and danger all the way across town to the wealthy haunts of the *ton*. He walked the same streets he had walked three years ago, walking past places in which he had gamed and womanised and drank, past the homes of those who had been his peers and his friends.

The watch was calling midnight by the time he approached the house he had rented in Grosvenor Street.

No light burned behind the curtained windows of Kate's bedchamber. All of the house was in darkness save for the lantern left burning to guide his return.

He dismissed the footman who was curled up in the hallway chair waiting for him and climbed the grand staircase.

It was his wedding night, but he did not hesitate by the doorway that led in to where his wife slept. Instead, he walked straight past and on into the master bedchamber. But he did not go to bed. He stood by the window looking down on to the empty street. Tomorrow it would begin. All that he had returned to London to do.

He slipped the neatly folded piece of paper from his pocket and glanced at it. The money was earned. By hard honest labour.

Tomorrow it would begin and he would face it alone.

He thought of Kate Medhurst asleep in the room through the wall, not Northcote, but Medhurst.

And for all that he thought he had grown as a man, for all that he thought he had learned of himself in Johor, he realised that he had not learned that much at all. He had not learned that he would be jealous of a dead man.

## Chapter Twelve

Kate watched Kit across the breakfast table the next morning. They were married, living in the same house yet it seemed that there had never been a bigger distance between them.

He was polite enough, considerate of her welfare, but there was a part of him that was closed off to her, a part that she could not reach. As if they were two strangers rather than two people who had sailed across half the world together, who had shared their bodies and their secrets; who had risked their lives for one another.

Gone were the shabby leather coat, the cutlass and black shirt, the worn buckskin breeches and those kicked-in boots that looked as though they had walked a thousand miles. North the Pirate Hunter was gone and in his place sat Mr Kit North-cote, a gentleman she barely recognised. He was clean shaven, his dark hair cut short and tidy, his dark eyes guarded.

'You look like a different man.' He seemed like a different man. It seemed as if everything between them was different. 'You are a gentleman in truth.'

'Appearances can be deceptive,' he answered. 'I am no gentleman, Kate.'

'And yet your family is gently bred and one of the oldest in all England,' she said softly.

'It is, but neither of those facts makes me a gentleman.'

Her eyes moved over the dark tailcoat that was tight across his shoulders, the white shirt and cravat, the white waistcoat and dark pantaloons that were snug around the hard muscle of his thighs.

He seemed to read her thoughts. 'I arranged for a wardrobe to be readied along with the house when we landed at Plymouth.'

'This house was not always your home?'

'No.'

She thought of what Gunner had said about meeting Kit in Portsmouth. 'But you *are* from London?'

'I am from Johor.'

'And before Johor?'

'There was no North before Johor.'

'And Kit Northcote?'

'Kit Northcote ceased to exist a long time ago.'

'Then to whom am I married?' Her eyes held his, wanting to understand him.

He glanced pointedly at the worn gold wedding band upon her finger. 'Wendell Medhurst, I believe,' he said softly and, rising to his feet, threw a heavy purse of money on to the table between them. 'Speak to Matthews to recommend a respectable dressmaker. Buy yourself whatever you need. London society is a deal different from *Raven*.'

She stared at the purse, Wendell's name still ringing in her head.

'There is somewhere I have to go this morning. If you will excuse me, ma'am?' He bowed and made to walk away.

'I do not excuse you,' she said, stopping him in his tracks.

She rose from her chair and faced him with her heart beating so hard that he surely must be able to see it through the black-silk dress she was still wearing. She knew she had to stop him; she just was not sure how to do it. Everything was wrong between them and she needed to make it right.

'What of the Admiralty's spies? Or did you lie about them watching us?'

'I did not lie. I have not lied for the past three years.'

'Then what when they see you going out alone? Again.'

'They will follow me for my visitation and they will understand.'

A sense of foreboding whispered down her spine. 'Where are you going, Kit?'

'Home,' he said. Without her.

She held her head high, too proud to let him see how much that hurt.

He crossed the room until he stood right before her, so close that the toes of his slippers brushed the hem of her skirt, black merging with black to become one, as husband and wife were supposed to be.

'I have to do this alone, Kate.'

She nodded as if she understood, but she did not; not really. 'To warn them that you are married to an American pirate,' she said, trying to make light of it.

'I would give the world that it were so simple,' he said quietly. His eyes studied hers and in their dark depths she caught a glimpse of something so painful that it made her want to weep.

He leaned in and brushed a kiss against her lips. 'I would be proud were you truly my wife, Kate. Never think otherwise.'

And with that he walked away.

She looked down at the ring on her finger and at the skirts of her black dress, the symbols of her love for Wendell and, screwing her eyes shut, tried to conjure the memory of his face. But it was hazy and indistinct. The face that haunted her, the face she saw when she closed her eyes, and when she opened them too, was not Wendell's, but Kit North's. She pressed her hand to her heart to stop what was there from bursting out and making a mockery of the vow she had sworn: to stay true to her first husband.

As his carriage came to a halt in Berkeley Street Kit sat there for that tiny moment before the footman opened the door. This was it—the thing that had driven him through the years and made him choose survival over the easy darkness of death; the chance to right the wrongs he had done, at least in part. It had been over three years since he had last been in this street, outside this house. Three years and in one respect it felt like three times a lifetime, and in another, only three beats of his heart since he had turned his back on them and walked away.

Now the time had come. Kit had returned home.

The carriage door opened. Taking a deep breath, Kit stepped down from the carriage and went to face them, but even as he walked towards the bottom of the stone stairs that led up to the black-painted door he could see that his journey had been in vain. For where the gleaming brass door knocker should have been there was nothing. The striker had been removed, indicating that the family were not in residence.

He climbed the steps just the same, knowing that a caretaker member of staff would have been left in place. But the thump of the edge of his fist upon the door brought no answer. Only when he was this close did he see the street dust that clouded the black of the paintwork and the glass of the windows. From where he stood on the doorstep he could see into the drawing room. There was no furniture. Where paintings had once hung were only empty hooks. But most telling of all was that the red-patterned wallpaper he remembered so well had been replaced with something else. Of his family's possessions not one sign remained.

He made his way to the front door of the neighbouring house in the smart terraced row. This time the brass knocker was intact. He gave it a loud thud.

Old Carter, the Fredericksons' butler, answered.

'I am looking for the Northcote family. They lived next door.'

Carter looked at him suspiciously as if he had not a clue as to the identity of the man who stood upon his master's doorstep. 'I am afraid they are no longer in residence, sir.'

'Where have they gone?'

Carter's lips pressed firmer together. 'Away.'

'That much is evident. Might you shed any further light on their removal?'

'I cannot, sir.' Then Carter peered at him closer, screwing up his nose in the effort to see. 'Is that *you*, Master Kit?'

'It is, Mr Carter.' Kit held the old man's gaze.

'You look different, sir. I barely recognised you.'

Kit said nothing.

'So you came back, after all,' the old man murmured almost to himself.

'I came back.'

The old man just looked at him as if he had seen a ghost.

'My family's removal…?' Kit prompted, hoping that now the old butler had recognised him he would get on with answering the question.

For the tiniest of moments something flickered in the old servant's eyes, before he lowered his gaze to the toes of Kit's boots. 'As I said, sir, I would not know anything of that.'

'Is Mr Frederickson at home?'

'I am afraid he is not presently at home, sir.'

'And were he at home, would he be able to answer my question?'

The old butler still would not meet his gaze. 'I could not say, Mr Northcote. If you will excuse me, sir…'

'Of course,' said Kit coolly. He expected nothing less once people knew who he was. Contempt. Condemnation. Turning away, he made his way down the stone steps to where his carriage waited. His footman opened the door ready for him, but before Kit climbed inside he glanced back at where old Carter still stood watching. Carter was finally looking at him but, contrary to what Kit had thought, the look in the old butler's eyes was not contempt or condemnation, but pity.

The Fredericksons' front door closed with a quiet click.

And a cold finger stroked against Kit's heart.

'How did it go? With your family.' Kate saw the distant distracted look in Kit's eyes as he stood by the window looking out over the streets in the drawing room and recognised it as worry he would never admit.

'It did not. The house was empty. They have moved to reside elsewhere.'

Whatever resolution he had hoped to effect, whatever reunion he had planned, had evaded him. 'How will you go about finding them?'

The question seemed to pull him back from the dark place in which he brooded. His eyes met hers. 'Ever practically minded.'

She gave a shrug. 'It is my nature.'

He gave a little smile at that, brief and small, but real.

'My mother has a cousin in London, a Mrs Tadcaster. She will know where they have removed to.'

She nodded. 'Kit…what happened to make you lose touch with them?'

'Life happened. Change happened. Kit Northcote died.'

'And Kit North was born?'

He smiled again, but this time it was hard and bitter. 'Indeed. If you will excuse me, I will pay a call upon Mrs Tadcaster.'

Wasting no time. He might pretend a relaxed indifference, but she was not fooled. He needed to find his family. She could feel the tension that emanated from him at just the mention of them.

'Take me with you,' she said on impulse.

His gaze moved to the untouched purse of gold upon the dining-room table, before meeting her own.

'Unless you are ashamed of me,' she challenged softly, her gaze holding his, never backing down for a minute.

They looked at one another across that sunlit drawing room, all sorts of subtle tensions playing between them, until he said, 'If you would care to accompany me, I would be honoured to introduce you to my mother's cousin.'

'I will fetch my shawl,' she said, 'and bring Tom along for the ride. A boy needs fresh air, especially a boy used to sailing the ocean. '

He gave a nod.

She felt his eyes on her as she walked from the room.

Kit drew a similar response from Mrs Tadcaster's manservant as he had from the Fredericksons' butler. Making his way back to the carriage, he saw young Tom's face watching him and Kate's, so calm and strong.

'She left two days ago to take the waters at Bath and is not due to return for a couple of weeks.' He took his seat opposite Kate and Tom, seeing the boy's pride in the fact that Bob had settled upon his narrow shoulder.

'Will you wait that long?' she asked, the look in her eyes telling him she already knew the answer to her question. She thought like him. She was not a woman to sit back and wait for life to happen to her, but one who went out and did what was required.

'No,' he said. 'There are men one can hire to find people.'

She just gave a nod of understanding and did not ask for any details in front of the boy.

Tom stared around him with obvious curiosity and excitement, making Kit realise that Kate was right—a boy did need fresh air. Kit's problems were his own to solve. Neither Tom nor Kate should suffer because of them.

'What say you to a trip to the park?' he asked them both.

'Yes, please!' Tom grinned.

Kate's eyes met his in shared pleasure. She smiled. 'A trip to the park would be a fine way to spend the afternoon.'

'Hyde Park is just round the corner.'

The carriage rumbled round the park's paths, the breeze catching at the dark ribbons of Kate's bonnet and the tassels of her parasol. Her eyes were soft silver in the sunlight and there was something in them when she looked at him, which was often. The sunlight brought colour to the freckles that had faded across the bridge of Tom's nose.

The boy held up his face to the sun and took a great big deep breath of air. 'It smells different here, not a hint of ocean or waves.'

'What do you smell?' Kit asked.

'Grass and horses, dung and rot, chimneys and...' He sniffed again. 'Sunshine,' he finished.

They all laughed.

Kit stopped the carriage, and they climbed out and walked along the path. Bob flew off to some nearby trees and Tom ran off chasing him, detouring around every bush and park bench he could find.

Kit and Kate walked side by side, close but not touching.

Kit offered her his arm. 'Admiralty will be watching and we need to look the part.'

She accepted his offer, resting her fingers on the crook of his arm, holding on to him, as if they really were a couple who had just married for love.

'You were right,' he said. 'A boy needs fresh air.'

'It is good of you to have him here to live with you as a young gentleman.'

'If you could have seen him in that Johor gaol…' He swallowed down that awful memory, hardened his voice. 'This is just another part of his training. He has learned how to handle life at the lower end. Now he must be equipped with the means to deal with those from money and breeding, those who consider themselves his superior in every way.' He said it with cool dispassion, but Kate's eyes were soft when they met his and she smiled in a way that made his heart swell.

There were few people about at this hour—those exercising their horses, servants hurrying on errands, nurses with children in their charge—and none of them recognised him. It was a strange feeling. Nice. With Kate on his arm and Tom laughing and running about them he could almost let himself believe in this illusion they were presenting to the world. He could relax into it for those few moments and enjoy them for what they were. Reality would intrude soon enough. He could not defer it. The music must be faced.

He felt her fingers caress against his arm and his hand moved to cover them. And he thought how much he would give to have this masquerade be the truth.

At five o'clock, they were back in the carriage, but they did not head home.

The ease of what had been between them for those couple of hours seemed to vanish. She sensed the return of the tension within him.

He faced her, his eyes, so dark and filled with their secrets, on hers, and she knew something important was coming.

'We have to make our appearance in society sometime and the sooner the better.'

*Because the Admiralty's spies would be watching.*

She glanced at Tom, who was stroking Bob's feathers and feeding him some titbits, and listening intently for all it looked otherwise. Tom did not know their marriage was a sham and she could not burden the child with a truth that would destroy his happiness. With the boy's terrible background she was determined to protect and care for him in the little time they would be together, to let him experience something of what it was like to be loved and cherished, as every child should be, as her own little Ben, of whom he reminded her so much, was.

'And show them all how happily married we are,' she said with a smile, and held Kit's eyes, knowing that the irony of the words would escape the boy. 'What are you proposing?'

'Five o'clock is the fashionable hour for the *ton* to be seen here in Hyde Park. It will be quite the parade at Rotten Row.'

'I always did like a parade.'

'Kate, there is something that I should warn...' He glanced at Tom, then back at her, as if whatever it was that he wanted to say could not be spoken in front of the boy.

Tom glanced up directly at Kit at that moment, waiting to hear the words, silent, a slight tension about him.

Kit shifted his gaze to meet the boy's. He smiled at Tom. 'I should warn you both,' he said, 'that some of those we shall see are rather high in the instep.' Then paused, leaning closer. 'Very high in the instep, if truth be told,' he said, lowering his voice as if spilling a confidence to them both, and gave a grin that made him so devilishly handsome that it made Kate's heart skip a beat.

'Do you think you will be able to suffer a few curious stares?' he asked.

'Oh, yes, sir.' Tom smiled. 'It's a shame you are not wearing your cutlass and me my knife. I reckon we would draw even better stares then.'

'I reckon we would,' said Kit with that same grin that did strange things to her heart. He was still smiling when his eyes shifted to meet hers.

In their dark depths she saw that whatever lay ahead was not as easy as he was pretending. And she wondered as to the true words of warning he would have spoken had Tom not been with them.

Kate had not long to wait to fathom something of an answer.

It was, as he had said, a swarm of fashionable people. Most in open-top carriages with matching teams of bays like those that Kit had hired. Some were small groups of gentlemen on horseback. Some were women in a cacophony of coloured silks and bonnets, all expensive and elegant, perfect sophistication. The gentlemen's attire was very like that of Kit's—dark tailcoats, white shirts and waistcoats beneath, with matching neckcloths, and black beaver hats, black pantaloons and shoes for those who rode in carriages and buff breeches and shiny high-top black boots for those who rode. But their clothes had a look of expense and luxury, as if they had been stitched on to their bodies by some top-end tailor.

She thought of the pouch of gold that lay on the dining-room table at the house in Grosvenor Street and knew Kit's choice of tailoring was not due to lack of funds, but more what he deemed it important to spend his money on. She liked the fact he was not strutting and preening like the men all around them. Just the way he sat there, everything about him… He was more of a man than any of them.

How those fashionable people stared. And with Bob perched upon Tom's shoulder she supposed she could not blame them. A tame raven was a novel sight, after all. But then, as those long-nosed women and puffy-faced men stared, she saw something change in their expressions.

She saw that they recognised Kit.

There were no nods of acknowledgement. No waves, or friendly smiles. Just wide-eyed stares and disapproving tight lips and gossipy whispers behind fans and gloved hands. A ripple of shock spread out through the park, with the carriage that contained Kit and Tom and herself at its epicentre.

She held her head high and kept a slight smile on her lips as if it was all nothing more than amusing, and was both relieved and proud when Tom did the same.

Kit met the eyes of all those they passed. He did not look away. He did not smile. But he nodded an acknowledgement. Some returned it. Others turned their faces away in obvious slight. Neither response seemed to make a difference.

He showed nothing, but she knew that this was what he had expected, that what was happening was no shock to him. And his eyes when they met hers and Tom's were strengthening, as though it was the three of them together against the rest of the world.

When they got home, Tom dined with them as he did most evenings. It had been her suggestion upon their arrival at the house, both for the child's sake and as a means of alleviating the awkwardness of her and Kit dining alone. But the boy's presence was double edged, preventing both matters she did not want to discuss and those she did. She was forced to bide her time, to wait for a chance to speak to him alone. Dinner seemed to stretch on for ever.

At last it ended and the hour was late enough to send Tom to bed.

The footmen stood sightless and deaf against the wall.

The butler hovered discreetly by Kit's elbow. 'Shall I fetch the port, sir?' The man's eyes shifted to where Kate sat at the opposite end of the long, polished mahogany table.

Kit did not take his eyes from her, even though his words were for the manservant.

'No, thank you. My wife and I are going out to the theatre.' Then, to her, 'If you are feeling quite up to it, darling?' Playing the masquerade before the servants, for in truth what better place to set a spy than in the house that was supposed to be their home? Not him and her against the world, after all, only him. Behind closed doors she felt the distance he put between them.

'Perfectly,' she replied. 'If you will excuse me, while I change…'

From her Antiguan wardrobe she selected the deep-purple silk with tiny glass beads scattered over a low-cut bodice. For the first time, she did not don the black fichu to cover her décolletage, aware of how much skin she was exposing. But if all of London was going to stare and point and gossip over her as an American, then she would hold her head high and give them something worth staring at.

She tucked the necklace containing Kit's ring into her pocket and had the maid pin her hair up high at the back, then pulled a few strands free, winding them round her fingers and arranging the resultant tendrils against her neck and décolletage. Her neck was bare, the darkness of the dress exaggerating the pale nakedness of her shoulders and breasts. Nothing relieved the starkness of the dress or the skin it revealed…only the thin worn gold band upon her finger. Wendell would be shocked at her, she thought. She was shocked at herself. But the woman who looked back at her from the peering glass did not look shocked; she looked… powerful and proud and unafraid, and ready to face down the sneers of London's *ton*. Kate smiled, then went downstairs to where the man to whom she was married waited.

Kit stared at the woman who walked down that staircase of the house in Grosvenor Street and the sight of her stole the words from his tongue and the breath from his lungs. He had always thought her an attractive woman, but… He stared at her, as though he was some greenhorn and she, a goddess.

'Cat got your tongue, Captain North?' she said softly as she came to stand before him, but she must have known the sight she presented; that she was sensual and powerful and spectacular.

'You look beautiful,' he said, and could not take his eyes from hers. He leaned in and brushed a kiss against her lips and then whispered softly and slowly in her ear, 'The footmen are watching.' But that was not why he kissed her, or why he could not take his eyes off her.

She smiled that smile of hers, not fooled for a minute.

'Thank you, darlin',' she said, accentuating her American accent. 'You are kinda irresistible yourself.' She stepped in closer just as he had done and brushed the back of her hand against the fall of his breeches as she whispered in his ear, 'For the footmen's sake, you understand.'

With a smile that said she knew her power, she walked with a saucy wiggle out to the waiting carriage, leaving him standing there with an enormous and obvious erection.

His gaze shifted to the footmen and butler, who were all watching goggle-eyed, but who shifted their gazes immediately to pretend that they had noticed nothing.

He smiled to himself. Suddenly the prospect of the night ahead did not seem bad. Not with Kate by his side.

He walked out into the night to join her.

The Theatre Royal in Covent Garden was relatively quiet, which was not surprising given that it was only a matter of weeks until Parliament and the Lords closed for recess, and most of the fashionable and powerful families took themselves off from London to spend the hot summer months on their country estates. But the attention of the *ton* that were there that night was not focused on the theatre's stage with the players upon it, but on the box on the first level in which he sat beside Kate.

'Oh, my,' she said, 'we do seem to be rather a spectacle of interest.'

'We do,' he said. He had been prepared to face their scrutiny and condemnation, to suffer it as was his due, but this did not feel like suffering. It felt… He felt…buoyed by Kate, proud of her, sitting there like some beautiful Boadicea who could have felled them all with one sensual glance from those ocean-grey eyes, soft and gentle and yet wielding such power. All the men in the place were craning their necks to stare at her and he knew that every single one of them would be wanting her; every single one of them aching to be in his shoes, for all that they knew of him. It was not what he had expected to feel, coming back to swallow down his shame and humiliation.

The matrons of the *ton* were peering blatantly through their opera glasses, making not the slightest effort to hide either their disapproval of him or their jealousy of the woman by his side.

'I feel sorry for those players down there on the stage, acting their hearts out…' she began.

'When no one is looking at them,' he finished.

She smiled.

'All those shawls and fichus, all those…coverings you wore on *Coyote* and *Raven*, I think I understand them now,' he said.

'To protect me from the hot beat of the sun on one ocean and the cold bite of the wind on another,' she said.

'That is not why you wore them.'

'No?' She arched an eyebrow.

'No'. His eyes held hers. 'No man could resist if he saw you.'

She shook her head, but she laughed.

The lead actor's voice was resonating through the auditorium, but beneath it was the murmur of scandalised voices from the stalls below and the boxes all around them. A matron across on the opposite side of the theatre was pointing at him as she gossiped behind her fan, as if he were blind and could not see her. Above them, young Frew was hanging out of his box so far that he was in danger of falling. He saw Kate's eyes glance up at Frew before returning to meet his.

'Do you think he is reporting back to the Admiralty?' she asked.

'Frew fancies himself as a romantic and a poet in the fashion of Byron. But who knows who Admiralty are recruiting these days? Do not let him spoil the play for you.'

'But this is not about the play, is it? Being here. Tonight.'

'No,' he admitted.

She leaned closer to him, her eyes searching his. 'Maybe we should give them something more to gossip about.'

'What have you got in mind?' he asked softly.

She kissed him on the lips, a deep, gentle, passionate kiss that made him want to wrap his arms around her and lay her down right there and make love to her. To make her his wife in truth. To hold on to her and keep her by his side for ever.

He kissed her with the truth that was in his heart, with all that he felt for her. He kissed her as if he really were worthy of winning her love from a dead man.

The actor on the stage stumbled over his words, but that was not what drew the gasps of shock and disgust from the audience.

She broke the kiss and, looking into eyes, she smiled.

And, despite everything, he smiled, too.

She had faced them down. She had held her head high and been proud of being an American in their midst even though their countries were at war.

But now that they were alone, facing each other across the carriage as it rumbled over the roads that led from Covent Garden back to the house in Grosvenor Street, she could feel the change in the atmosphere. The darkness of the night was interrupted by regular-spaced gas lamps with their warm yellow glow. Every few seconds it flashed across the hard handsome planes of his face like that of a warning beacon over rocks. Her body thrummed with the knowledge of him, of the temptation he presented. The bodice of her dress seemed too tight and restrictive, her breasts too sensitive.

She could remember the feel of his mouth upon them, the stroke of his fingers over the skin of her hip, the thrust of him between her thighs. Turning her face away from the lure of those dark dangerous waters, she looked out at the passing sandstone houses, all uniform with their Palladian-styled fronts and black-painted window frames and glossy front doors. Beneath the long black evening gloves, she could feel the press of the old wedding band and moved her fingers to touch it, to turn it, to remind herself of vows once sworn that, at this moment, seemed so long ago that she could barely remember.

'I am sorry for exposing you to this, Kate. You should not have to suffer such scrutiny or be subjected to such harsh appraisal.' His voice was quiet in the darkness.

'I am not sorry. I am proud to be American.'

She heard the slight catch in his breath, as if he had given an ironic smile. 'They do not look at us because you are American.' She heard him smile again. 'They look at you because you are beautiful. But their attitude—the disapproval, the censure—it is because of me, Kate.'

She moved her gaze to meet his across the carriage once more. 'Why?'

In the silence that followed she did not think he would answer. And in that moment everything seemed to click into place and she knew that this was at the heart of everything that drove him, everything that he was. She did not ask the question again, just waited.

'Because of what I did before I left London.'

The words seemed to echo in the space between them.

'What did you do, Kit?'

The next flash of gas lamps showed him smile that bitter ironic smile, the one that hid the other things beneath. 'Do not ask me that question, Kate. Not tonight.'

Her heart was beating hard with awareness, with anticipation. She swallowed. 'Why not, Kit?' she asked softly.

'Because I cannot bear to tell you the answer. Because I want you with me for the little time we have together.'

'I am with you.'

'But you would not be were I to tell you. Trust me, Kate.' He smiled again, but the quiet darkness was in his eyes so that she believed him.

She nodded, knowing this was not the right time to push, but feeling a spasm of fear over what would cause North the Pirate Hunter, who had endured torture and thought it nothing, who could expel another man's life without so much as a blink of the eye, to speak in such a way. What he had done must be truly terrible on a scale beyond imagining. A chill crept across her skin.

'In two weeks Gunner will be back in London. In two weeks you will be on your way home to Louisiana and your children.' The distance was there again in his voice. Whatever ease and teasing sensuality was between them in public was lost in private, when temptations and truth and darkness returned to stand as unscalable barriers, reminding them that they were each in a place the other could not reach.

Wendell's name whispered in her ear. She turned her gaze to the passing houses.

They did not speak again.

# *Chapter Thirteen*

A man was leaving Kit's study when Kate came downstairs the next day. She leaned against the doorway, looking at him. She was wearing the black day dress and fichu, her armour back in place, shielding herself from him as much as every other man.

'Your family,' she said, not a question, but a statement. She was quick, intuitive. She understood too much. And gossip would reach her eventually. It was only a matter of time. The *ton's* censure he could bear, but hers? He turned his mind away from that thought.

'I will know their whereabouts by the end of the week. Collins is a Bow Street Runner and good at his job,' he said.

She nodded.

'There is a charity musical being held in Almack's Rooms this afternoon. Much of the *ton* will be there. Gossip will have spread following last night and our appearance in Hyde Park. It will not be easy, Kate. You do not have to accompany me.' He wanted to give her a way out. This was not her punishment to take.

'I want to,' she said.

Their eyes held and too many things stirred between them across that small distance, before she turned and walked away.

He listened to the sound of her footsteps on the hard polished floors.

One week and Collins would have traced his family.

Two weeks and she would be gone.

This was the way it was supposed to be, he thought, and focused his attention on the ledger that lay open on the desk before him.

Kate wore a dark chocolate-brown dress to the musicale, and forwent the fichu again. Ironically, in facing this London society that was Kit's enemy and hers, and opposite to everything that she had needed to be Le Voile, her strength lay in her sensuality and confidence as a woman.

Kit had been right in his warning. She slid her arm into his, presenting a united front to those vultures that circled them and felt the warmth of his fingers as they covered hers.

Rows of chairs had been set out within the ball-room of Almack's. Kate and Kit did not sneak like thieves into the back rows, but took seats right at the front.

She did not fully understand what this home-coming was about for Kit, but knew that, whatever was going on, part of it was a need to face them, to stand before them all and look them in the eyes. And given all he had done for her, it was the least she could do to stand by his side and help him. She did not want to think of the other reasons she was doing this, the complications in her heart.

There was a string quartet that played with a vibrancy and immediacy of emotion and an opera singer who sang with the voice of an angel of love, all of it of love.

Without thinking she toyed with the thin gold band upon her finger, feeling the tug of guilt and longing and the turmoil that struggled within her. Her thoughts moved from the woman who was singing to the man who sat by her side, the man with whom she had stood before a priest and spoken the same words that made a mockery of those she had spoken to another man a lifetime ago.

She glanced up to find Kit's eyes on her hands, where she touched Wendell's ring. His gaze, dark and too perceptive, moved to meet her own. He smiled, his cool ironic smile, and, returning his gaze to the musicale, did not look at her again.

Kit accepted a glass of champagne from the salver the footman offered and passed it to Kate. He did not take one for himself.

'Mr Northcote, is that really you?' The voice sounded behind where they stood.

'Prepare yourself,' he whispered in Kate's ear as he turned. 'One of the *ton's* biggest gossipmongers.' And saw her smile.

Mrs Quigley, a tabby of renown, had not changed in the years he had been away.

'It is, indeed, Mrs Quigley,' he said smoothly.

'How…surprising.' She smiled a sickly sweet smile. 'And yet here you are, with your lovely companion.' She looked at Kate, still smiling, the question burning in her eyes.

'Here we are,' said Kate with a naughty twinkle in her eye. He could have sworn she was making her accent deliberately more American.

Mrs Quigley's eyes widened, the fervour of excitement of this latest discovery practically choking her.

'May I introduce my wife?'

Mrs Quigley pressed a plump white hand to her breast. 'Your wife?' she breathed.

Kate leaned forward, as if to confide a secret to

the tabby. 'It was a love match,' she said in a voice loud enough for all around to hear.

The room was quiet enough to hear a pin drop. The women were practically straining closer and tucking their hair behind their ears all the better to see and hear what was unfolding in their midst.

'How—' Mrs Quigley scrabbled for an acceptable comment and found one '—romantic.'

'I thought so,' said Kate, and stroked a hand against his arm.

It was all he could do not to laugh at the way the woman's eyes riveted to the small gesture with a fascinated horror. It was with obvious effort that she managed to draw them away long enough to ask Kate the question, 'And do my ears deceive me, or are you not of these shores?'

'You noticed.' Kate smiled. 'I'm American.'

Mrs Quigley practically choked on that revelation.

'How...nice,' she managed to say.

'Isn't it just?' Kate smiled again.

'I heard tell you had a boy with you, a boy from the west country.'

'You heard correctly,' Kit said.

'Not America?'

'Not America,' said Kate.

The speculation in Mrs Quigley's eyes was obvious. If the boy was not his wife's... But even she was not crass enough to ask the question outright. Instead, she changed the subject.

'We did not expect to see you again.'

'Evidently not,' he said.

'Where have you been hiding all these years?'

'Here and there.'

'Such a shame over what happened.'

Kit said nothing. This is what he had come back to face and face it he would.

'Your family losing the house and moving to a… less fashionable…neighbourhood.'

'Quite,' he said as if he already knew and indeed, in a way, he did.

'And your mother's death—my heartfelt condolences on that.'

The world seemed to stop. His blood ran cold. A knife cut through the wall of his chest, exposing the scars of his heart for all to see. He schooled his face to show nothing.

'Such kindness, Mrs Quigley.' He knew he should move away. He knew he had to mingle, to face them all down. But he could not move. He just stood there. Frozen. Exposed.

*His mother was dead.* The words did not seem real. None of this scene seemed real. Except he knew it was. He deserved this, all of it. But his mother…she had deserved none of it.

'Kit,' Kate's voice sounded. He felt her hand

thread through his arm, catching hold of him, pulling him up from the dark waters closing over him. Her eyes met his as she threw him the life line. 'I am feeling a little...hot. Would you be so kind as to escort me home?' And in them was strength and understanding.

'As you wish.' He turned to the tabby who was watching every nuance of their interaction with avaricious eyes. 'Excuse us, Mrs Quigley.'

He led her across the room, out into the fresh air and space of the street. Their carriage drew up, the footman jumping down and opening the door.

They climbed inside.

He was in control again, closing it all over, knowing this was just a part of it, telling himself he should have been prepared for such an eventuality.

The door slammed shut and they were on their way to Grosvenor Street.

He stared out at the passing streets, streets he knew so well, streets that were a part of his life, a part of his childhood.

'Thank you,' he said without taking his gaze from the houses and shops and carriages, from the horses and the men and women.

'I am so sorry about your mother, Kit.' Her words were as gentle as her hand that took his.

'So am I.' His voice was hard.

He withdrew his hand from hers because he

feared what he would do if he did not. He feared what he would tell her. He feared what he would reveal. He feared he would break every damn vow he had ever made.

He thought of those vows he had sworn. This was just a part of what must be faced, all of it by him alone. Kit Northcote was dead. It was Kit North who had come back. And Kit North who would do what must be done.

Now that they were alone again he was shutting her out as ever he did. Kate knew that. But this time it was different. This time he was hurting, really hurting. For all his cool hard veneer she had seen the truth in that unguarded moment in Almack's Rooms when he had learned so cruelly of his mother's death. He was hurting, but the hurt seemed only to harden his resolve, to make him harsher and more determined to do whatever it was he had come here for, facing down London's society, running the gauntlet of their censure.

The rest of the journey was conducted in silence but when the carriage stopped outside the house on Grosvenor Street he took her hand in his and helped her down from the carriage, his fingers entwining with hers as if he would never let them go. She held to him, and he to her, proclaiming their union to the world.

She glanced up into his eyes and he did not look away, just held her gaze and, stopping still, touched his mouth to hers. He kissed her with an excruciating sweetness that belied all of his coolness. And she slid her arms around him and kissed him, too, her lips offering the comfort her words could not. She kissed him in the middle of that respectable street, oblivious to all else except the need to reach him. She kissed him. And when the kiss ended, their eyes just held, clinging to that moment they both knew would end when they stepped out of the public eye into the privacy of their home.

He raised their still-entwined fingers to his mouth, brushed a kiss to her knuckles and led her inside.

Tom came running down the staircase, abandoning whatever tasks Kit had set him to, as soon as the front door closed.

'Captain North, Mrs Medhurst.' He smiled, oblivious of the mistaken name.

Kit said nothing, but she saw the tiny tightening of his jaw before he spoke to the boy. 'As part of your duties it is necessary that you learn to ride. It is a most useful skill in life. How about we start the lessons this afternoon, in Hyde Park?'

'Yes please, Captain, sir!' Tom looked delighted as he stared up at his hero with admiration, belatedly remembering her. 'If that's all right with you, ma'am?' The boy glanced over at her.

'It's all right with me,' she said, but she wondered if Kit was not doing this in part to avoid her.

'If you will excuse me,' Kit said to her with a stiff bow.

She said nothing, just watched him walk away pretending that he had not just learned that his mother was dead and that his family had been forced to move due to reduced circumstances; pretending that everything was all right.

It was the same when they returned later that afternoon. Tom was there then and at dinner so that she could say nothing of it. Kit behaved as if nothing at all different had happened today, but he made his excuses and left before it was time for the boy to retire for the night.

She heard the front door close and knew he had gone out. From the window she watched his dark figure descend the stone steps. There was no waiting carriage or horse. He walked off along the street to merge with the darkness.

Kit was not going anywhere. He walked, just walked, because he needed to be alone. And he did not know what else to do. He walked every damn street in London, trying to straighten the thoughts in his head. He walked until his steps had returned him to the house in Grosvenor Street and the woman who waited inside.

There was no light behind the curtains of her bedchamber. She slept. At least one of them would.

He had spent three years getting back here. Three years for a chance to make it right. Except he was too late. It would never be right for his mother. She was dead and gone, never knowing how sorry he was, never learning how much he regretted it all.

He made his way quietly up the stairs and into his bedchamber. A bottle of brandy and a single crystal tumbler still sat on his bedside cabinet. He kept it there, the same set as in his study, to tempt him, to know the strength of his resistance. Now standing there in that moonlit room, for the first time he lifted the bottle, held it in his hand and stared at the neatly printed label, seriously contemplating breaking the wax seal and prising the cork from the slender glass neck.

He missed the rich sweet taste of brandy. He missed the burn on his tongue and in his throat and stomach. He missed the oblivion it could bring, the numbing of the senses, the escape that he had lost himself in so many times after he had realised the magnitude of what he had done on that terrible night three years ago. The pain bit all the deeper for knowing there was now a part of it that he could never undo. His mother had deserved better, so much better.

He sat the bottle back down in its rightful place and walked to stand by the window, staring down on to those streets he knew so well. He deserved the pain. Every damn bit of it. And God help him, he would take it like a man and keep his mouth shut from whining.

Kate sat in the chair in the darkness of her bedchamber.

She knew Kit was in there alone. She knew he was shutting her out. And she knew why, at least in part.

Beneath the push and pull of her thumb and forefinger Wendell's wedding band slid this way and that around her finger, the habit so engrained in her across the years. Normally it soothed her. Tonight it did not. There was a tightness in her throat, an ache in her chest.

The scene from Almack's Rooms was there in her mind, just as it had been there all night. Every time she shut her eyes she saw that moment again, when Kit had stood there and heard that his mother was dead from the lips of a gossip; stood there with his face a mask of cool dispassion hiding the truth beneath. She felt his pain as sorely as if it were her own. And she knew he needed her for all he refused to admit it. But if she went to him this night…if she offered him comfort, she knew what would happen between them. And if they made love, there could be no annulment. And if she went to him knowing that, what did it say about how she felt about Wendell?

*Betrayal.* The word taunted her and it was true because she could feel his presence fading. And she had loved him, with all her heart. She still did. He was Ben and Bea's father. And she missed him. And she missed her children. She missed them so much that there was a hollow of aching deep inside her. But Kit was on the other side of that door.

He was such a strong man. She had never seen him weaken, not in all that he had endured. He pretended he did not feel, but she knew that he did.

In a fortnight Gunner would be here to take her home, leaving Kit here alone.

The barrier between them seemed higher than ever. But there was a way she might reach him. And after everything they had been through, he deserved to know.

She toyed with Wendell's wedding band upon her finger and rose from her chair.

A light knock sounded from the connecting door from Kate's bedchamber.

She did not wait for an answer, just opened it and came to stand there.

He knew from the fact she was wearing not her night robe, but the black dress that mourned the passing of her real husband, that she had been waiting for him to return.

'You should go to bed,' he said, his voice unnecessarily cool. He did not want her to see him like this.

'So you can shut me out?' she said.

'What is it that you want, Kate?'

'To talk.'

'About what? My dead mother? The things I have done? Your journey home to Louisiana?' He shook his head. 'If so, you are wasting your time.' He made to turn away from her.

'None of those things,' she said, stilling him. 'I came to talk about Wendell.'

He stood where he was and watched her walk right up to him. 'I think I already know all I need to about Wendell.'

'No, Kit, you do not,' she said, and looked up into his face.

He knew he should turn away from her. He knew he should insist she go back to her room. But he did neither of those things. He just stood there and waited for what it was she had come to say.

'I loved him. I still do.'

'As I said—nothing I do not already know.'

'When he died, I swore a vow that I would stay true to him and him alone, that there would never be another man for me. It is the main reason I became Le Voile. Because I had sworn that I would never marry again. I needed to support myself and my children financially.'

He swallowed, only now fully realising the position he had put her in by bringing her here, by marrying her, even if it had been with the best of intentions.

'I have never told anyone of my vow,' she said.

In the same way he had never spoken of his. Vows were private things. They were sworn in blood and kept in secret. No one understood that more than Kit.

'I know some folks would not deem such a vow binding. They would say it was made in a moment of grief and offer all sorts of excuses to get me out of it. But a vow is a vow.' She stopped, and met his eyes, facing him squarely while she told him this most private of truths. 'If I break it...'

'If you break it, you would not be the person you are. It would turn you into someone else altogether,' he said. 'Someone you do not want to be.'

'Yes.' She nodded, her eyes caressing his face.

'I understand. I have sworn a vow or two myself.'

The silence hissed with his chance to tell her, but

he could not. Because he could not bear to see the look on her face if he did.

'Thank you for telling me,' he said.

'There is more, Kit.'

He waited, not hurrying her, giving her the space she needed, even if he was not sure he wanted to hear the rest of it.

'Before you there was only ever Wendell. And now, there is not. I feel things for you. Things that make me feel like I am betraying him.'

So he said the words she needed to hear. 'Our making love, our sleeping together, it was just to satisfy our bodies' physical needs. Lust, not love. Wendell would understand. Your heart is intact, Kate. You have not betrayed him.'

'Lust, not love?' she whispered.

'Yes.' But he looked away to tell the lie.

She reached her hand to cup his cheek, turning his face back to hers. Tears leaked from her eyes, glistening like crystal as they rolled down her cheeks in the moonlight.

'But, you see, the problem is that my heart is not intact, Kit. I still love Wendell, but I love you, too. No matter how hard I have tried not to. I have to tell you. I have to make you understand.' Her voice was thick with emotion. 'I cannot break my vow to Wendell, but I love you, Kit.'

He pulled her into his arms and held her, cradling her against him, pressing his face into her hair. 'I love you, too, Kate.' But he did not deserve her love. And once she discovered the man he had been, once she learned what Kit Northcote had done, she would not love him any more.

He wanted to carry her to his bed. He wanted their bodies to merge. He wanted to show her the truth of his feelings with his body, but he could not be so selfish. 'But you know we cannot make love. There could be no annulment if we did.' He spoke the words into her hair. 'And we both have our vows.'

'I know,' she whispered and he felt the sob she stifled in her chest. 'But I don't want to be alone, Kit. And I don't care what you say, I know that you cannot be alone tonight. I want to be with you.'

'I want to be with you, too, Kate.'

She looked up into his eyes and he held her face in his hands and carefully captured each of those precious tears.

'We cannot make love, but we can hold one another,' he said.

'We can hold one another,' she echoed softly.

He took her hands in his and led her to his bed. They climbed beneath those covers and he held her. And she held him. All through those long dark hours of the night. And when she finally fell asleep in his arms he was not sure she had not been right. He was not sure that he could have made it through this night alone.

The next morning when Kate awoke, Kit was gone.

When she finally caught up with him at the breakfast table it was as if none of it had happened, not last night, not their admissions of love, not the death of his mother. All of his barriers were once more intact, built so high she wondered if she had ever really succeeded in finding a way through them, if he had ever really lowered them at all.

He smiled at her, but it was his smile that showed he was hard and tough, and strong and emotionless. The first three were true, the fourth, she knew for a fact, a lie. She knew it in the kind way he spoke to Tom, even now.

He took her and Tom around London in his carriage all that day, buying them ices and chocolate from Gunter's Tea Shop. The relationship between him and Tom was changing; the little boy seemed to have found a way to pierce through Kit's armour, for all that Kit would deny it. And even though the way it was between her and Kit was a masquerade, a pretence, the way his hand was warm around hers, the way his lips brushed her cheek, the way his eyes caressed her body and that secret smile that spoke volumes to all those around that stared so, it felt real. Or maybe it was just her own wishful thinking.

Regardless, she did not think, she just embraced the illusion and enjoyed their time together, acting out all that was the truth of what she felt for him. Laughing with Tom, hugging the boy, linking her arm through Kit's, wiggling her hips when he was watching, looking at him with eyes that said she wanted to loosen his neckcloth and lead him to her bed and do all sorts of wanton things. Everywhere they went people stared—and the black sheep returned, his American wife and the boy they were whispering was his adopted son of questionable origin, gave them something worth staring at and they had the time of their lives in doing so.

They took dinner at a chophouse, then bought iced cakes that they ate in the carriage on the way home. According to the baker the cakes were replicas of the very same sponge iced doves served at the Prince Regent's latest banquet but they all agreed that the doves looked more like white versions of Bob.

'No more cake,' she said to Tom as if he were her own little Ben, 'or you will make yourself sick. You have icing all round your mouth. Come, let me wipe it clean.' She pulled her handkerchief at the ready.

But Tom beat her to it, wiping the sleeve of his new tailcoat, that was identical to Kit's, across his mouth, to leave a nice white trail of icing over the black superfine. 'All done.'

'Tom!' She pulled a face.

Tom grinned like a Cheshire cat.

She looked at Kit and the two of them shared a laugh.

'This is like having a mother and father,' Tom said. 'We're like a real family, aren't we?'

But they were saved from a reply by the carriage coming to a halt outside the house in Grosvenor Street and the footman opening the carriage door.

Tom jumped down and raced up the stone steps to the front door of their home. Kit stepped down, then offered her his hand to assist her.

*This is like having a mother and father. We're like a real family, aren't we?*

Their eyes met and held, and there was a tightness in her chest and a lump the size of a boulder in her throat, and the prickle of tears in her eyes.

'What is that you are saying, Mrs North? You cannot wait to get me inside and upstairs?' he said, naughty play-acting for the Admiralty spies and the rest of London, distracting her from Tom's words and all they meant so that she would not betray them both by weeping. He threaded his fingers through hers. 'Very well. I acquiesce.'

She smiled and stoppered the tears. But when he turned away and tugged at her hand to take her with him, she resisted, pulling him back to her, knowing what would happen once they were inside and free from the eyes of servants and watchers, and needing this closeness with him, feigned or not, to last that little bit longer.

He came to her, stood close, indecently so, looking down into her face. 'We are attending a dance at the Argyle Rooms this evening,' he said quietly.

She nodded.

The teasing sensuality had vanished from them both. Their gazes held and all of the world around her seemed to vanish. She looked into those so serious, so strong, so deep dark eyes and her heart was aching so much.

He leaned in and kissed her. Not a teasing playful kiss. Not a kiss that was all hot hard desire. A kiss that was nothing of masquerade or pretence, but serious and honest. A kiss that told her that he understood and felt the same.

A discreet clearing of the throat sounded from the butler who stood nearby.

The kiss ended and the moment was over. She could no longer defer the inevitable. He released her hand and she followed him up the stone stairs into the rented house, holding on to the thought that they would not be inside for long. There was still this evening's outing to come. She knew he would dance with her. She knew he would hold her close. And probably even kiss her again.

And that at least was something.

In the Argyle Rooms that night Kate was wearing a deep midnight-blue silk that revealed just enough of her figure to torture all of the men in that dance room, and him, with all that would never be theirs. It was not play-acting when his eyes were hard and hot upon her, or when he stood that little bit too close or let his fingers brush against hers.

It was not play-acting when he led her out on to the dance floor and waltzed with her before them all, their bodies moving together, as natural and rhythmic as they had been in bed.

She was a natural seductress, lowering those long dark lashes, then meeting his gaze with boldness and strength. This woman who had defied a pirate's world of masculinity and hostility and rivalry to reach the top. This woman who could weave the ultimate illusion and hold true to a vow. He wondered if she would be able to sustain the pretence once she learned the truth about him. It was something of which he did not want to think, not right now, when the scent of her was in his nose and the satin of her skin beneath his fingers. He was all too aware that the grains of sand were slipping too fast through the hourglass, but he held to these small precious moments, committing them and everything of her to memory.

And then he raised his eyes from her face to glance across the floor and saw Devlin.

## Chapter Fourteen

Kate felt the sudden change that rippled through Kit's body, the tightening and tensing of muscles, the honing of attention that came when one sighted the enemy. Following his gaze, she saw the four tall dark-haired men who stood tight-lipped and cold-eyed at the corner of the room watching them, waiting like the four horsemen of the apocalypse. The last notes of the music sounded.

She curtsied.

He bowed.

The dance was over. She had the sense that something else was over, too—the waiting. Whatever battle he had come back to fight involved those men.

'Friends of yours?' she asked.

'With whom I must reacquaint myself.'

Alone. Four against one was hardly fair odds. 'Introduce me,' she said.

He looked into her eyes, as if weighing her words. 'Very well,' he agreed at last.

Tucking her hand into the crook of his elbow, together they went to face the men.

'Devlin,' he said to the tallest, most arrogant looking of the men and gave a small nod of acknowledgement.

*Devlin.* The tortured words of a nightmare whispered again in her mind and she felt an instant dislike and wariness towards the handsome-faced man.

'Monteith, Bullford, Fallingham.' He named them all in turn.

'Northcote,' the man he had called Devlin replied. 'Or is it North? There seems to be some dubiety over which name you are going by these days.'

Kit smiled his cold hard smile and said nothing.

She could feel the bristle of animosity in the silence that followed, feel the coldness that existed between them and wondered why Kit was even here talking to them.

'So you have come back.' Devlin's tone was arrogant and dismissive.

'As you see.' Kit's eyes were cold and hard, but that same hint of a smile played around his lips.

'And creating quite the scandal.' Devlin's eyes flicked to her.

She returned his gaze with frosty dislike.

'I succeeded in that before ever I left,' Kit answered. 'May I introduce my wife?' he said to them. Then to her, 'His Grace the Duke of Monteith, and Viscounts Devlin, Fallingham and Bullford,' he introduced each of them to her. 'My oldest friends, darling.'

Blue-blooded aristocracy and nothing of friends if the way they were looking at him was anything to go by.

They all bowed, the perfect noblemen, but it was not North they called her. 'Mrs Northcote.'

The atmosphere was thick enough to cut with a knife.

'Perhaps your lady should avail herself of the withdrawing room.' Devlin's eyes were fixed on Kit.

'Thank you kindly for having such a concern over my welfare, Lord Devlin, but I have no need to visit the ladies' withdrawing room.' She stepped a little closer to Kit and eyed the viscount coldly. 'You can say whatever it is that you want to in front of me.'

Devlin looked at Kit.

She saw the tiny muscle flicker in Kit's jaw and knew that he was not as cool as he was pretending. His eyes slid to hers, holding them for a tiny second so that all of the world seemed to roar between them in that moment, before he returned his gaze to Devlin and gave a nod.

'You should not have come back,' said Devlin.

'I disagree,' Kit said smoothly.

'Why are you here?'

'I have my reasons.'

'Whatever they are, you are no longer welcome in London, Kit Northcote.'

Kit smiled. 'No doubt.'

'Go back to wherever it is you have been hiding these three years past.'

'Not yet.'

'How dare you speak to him like that? You have no idea—'

'Kate.' Kit's warning stopped her.

'You have not told her. She does not know.' Devlin laughed and it was a cruel sound that sent a shiver all the way to the tip of her soul. 'I suppose I should have expected nothing other from you, Northcote.'

With a nod of his head, Devlin and the three other noblemen turned their backs in a way that was clear to all who watched was an insult.

But Kit did not leave. He stayed with her in those Argyle Rooms, dancing with her, remaining in that spotlight of disapproval and gossip, smiling his cool hard smile, his hand warm and possessive against the small of her back, but there was something in his eyes when he looked at her that frightened her, something that told her that they were both standing on the brink of something terrible.

This time when eventually they left and travelled home, there was no teasing sensuality, no loitering by the carriage, no kissing. Only that tight-wound sense of foreboding and the haunting echo of the mocking words that Viscount Devlin had spoken.

*You have not told her. She does not know.*

Neither of them spoke, not until they were in the drawing room of the house in Grosvenor Street with the door firmly closed and the curtains drawn and the staff dismissed for the evening.

A branch of candles burned upon the mantelpiece.

He stood by the fireplace, staring into the dark hearth with its carefully built pile of coal and kindling unlit upon it.

She came to stand there on the Turkey rug behind him.

'So, Kit,' she said softly.

He glanced up into the looking glass above the mantel, meeting her gaze in it. 'So,' he said.

Their eyes held.

'I deserve their contempt,' he said. 'I am not the man you think me, Kate.'

'Whoever you believe yourself, whatever heinous crime you have committed in the past, have you not punished yourself enough?'

'No.'

'I know you, and you are good and strong and a man of integrity.'

He laughed, a bitter cynical sound, and shook his head. 'No, Kate, I only wish that I were, but Kit Northcote is none of those things.'

'So what is he?' she demanded.

He turned to face her, holding her gaze. 'He is a liar, a cheat and a coward.'

She shook her head in denial.

'Yes,' he said.

'What did you do, Kit?'

'I was an arrogant weak wastrel who did nothing save drink, womanise and game. Three years ago I went to a gaming hell in Whitechapel with Devlin and the rest of my friends and gambled away my father's fortune. And when it was done, I ran away like a coward and left my family penniless, ruined and shamed.'

She stared at him. 'You were young and reckless, you made a mistake—'

'No,' he cut her off. 'You do not understand. I sold my soul to the devil, Kate.'

She felt a shiver run through her.

'I cheated,' he said. 'In that gaming hell, I cheated and I was discovered. I should have paid with my life—it is what they do to men who cheat at cards in Whitechapel. I deserved it. But the tough I played against struck a bargain—everything on one turn of the cards. I lost everything—my father's money, my honour, my soul. Devlin and the others swore an oath that they would never reveal the truth of that night—that I had cheated. And they never did.'

A small silence hissed.

'So now you know the truth of me,' he said quietly, and there was a terrible grimness in his expression.

'Now I know the truth,' she said.

She saw the regret in his eyes, the guilt...the self-loathing...and at last she understood. All that lay at the heart of him, the terrible burden he had carried through the years. And what it was he had come back to London to do. And it made her chest feel tight and crushed beneath the weight of sorrow. The tears spilled from her eyes. 'Kit...' There was so much she wanted to say.

The drawing-room door opened and Tom stood there in his nightshirt, his eyes moving from her to Kit and back again, the smile on his face fading to be replaced with concern. 'Is everything all right?'

'Everything is just as it should be,' said Kit as he walked from the room, tousling the boy's hair as he passed him in the doorway.

'Ma'am?' Tom stood there staring at her, shadows of fear in his eyes.

'Captain North is right,' she said, wiping away her tears. 'I was just telling him how much I missed my children at home in America.'

'You have children?'

'A little girl who is four years old and a boy who is not so much younger than you.'

'What are their names?'

'Why don't we go down to the kitchen and I will warm us some milk and tell you all about them.' She put an arm around Tom's thin shoulders and guided him towards the stairs.

There would be time to speak to Kit later.

Kit stood by the window of his bedchamber, staring down on to the moonlit street. The hands of the clock on the mantelpiece showed a quarter to one.

He heard the soft knock on the connecting door between his bedchamber and Kate's, but he made no move.

'Kit,' she said quietly through the wood.

But he could not bear to see the disgust and pity in her eyes. It turned out he was still Kit Northcote, after all, still that same coward. He might face down all of London. But he could not face down Kate Medhurst.

He heard the rattle of the handle, but he knew

for certain that the door was locked and the key removed from her side.

She did not persist.

The silence that followed was loud.

He stared out over the London streets, wondering where his father and sister were, wondering how the hell they had managed all those years with ever-diminishing funds. In his pocket the bank cheque was neatly folded. Soon Collins would trace them; soon he would make the little reparation he could.

Kit might have told her his deepest darkest secrets. He might have laid his soul bare before her. But it had changed nothing. In the morning they sat at the long mahogany silver-set table in the dining room with Tom between them as if it had not happened. She realised that everything was rolling on like an unstoppable carriage running down a hill, heading towards a destination she could not change.

He discussed the day's schedule, the planned visit with Tom to an art exhibition at the Royal Academy with a smooth ease.

She did not know how he bore it. How he kept going, as if their whole world were not imploding. As if he felt nothing. But she knew he felt. And she knew that this was more of a torture to him than to her, facing what he had fled from, trying to right the wrongs. She also knew if she was going to reach him it was never going to be by a direct approach.

Within the main exhibition gallery at the Royal Academy of Art Kit and Kate stood before a massive, framed oil painting of naval ships in fast pursuit of a schooner. Tom was a little distance away, a frown on his face as he examined a painting of a ship of pirates being apprehended by a British naval frigate.

'Perhaps we should be looking at some still-life oils of flowers and fruit,' Kit said by her ear, knowing this was safe because they were in public.

'Or pastoral scenes of the English countryside,' she replied. 'Scared the Admiralty will hear of our racy preferences in art?'

'Terrified,' he said.

She smiled.

And so did he.

'That schooner has a look of *Coyote* about her,' she said.

'She does,' he agreed, and felt the brush of her fingers against his.

She did not look at him, only at the tall-masted ships, the billowing canvas sails and spray of ocean waves. 'Are you keeping any more dark secrets from me?' she asked.

'Were not the ones last night enough for you?'

'Nowhere near enough,' she said, and turned her face to look into his. 'I have not changed my mind over you.' Threading her fingers through his, she leaned in closer until he felt her breath, warm and sensual against his ear. 'Even if you do lock your bedchamber door against me.'

His eyes met hers and it was not pity he saw there or disgust. It was acceptance. It was strength. It was love. He raised their joined hands to his mouth and pressed a kiss to her fingers.

'Just in case the Admiralty are watching?' she asked.

'No,' he answered. 'I do not give a damn if they are watching or not.'

They stared into each other's eyes.

She knew the worst of him. She knew who he was, what he was. And she did not judge him.

'Are those King's navy men going to hang the pirates?' Tom asked in a loud voice.

'It looks like they are going to, doesn't it?' Kate replied as she pulled Kit to examine the picture Tom was worrying over. She lowered her voice, 'But I happen to know that they escape.'

'Are the pirates villains?' the boy asked.

'Some pirates are, but not those ones.'

'Not like the ones that captured you.'

'Not like the ones that captured me,' she agreed.

'You must be very glad that Captain North rescued you and captured their captain.'

'Very glad, indeed,' she said, and her eyes met Kit's again.

She knew and still she looked at him like that.

'No more veils,' she said.

'No more veils,' he echoed.

No masquerade. No pretence. Everything between them was real. Now, and for the days they had left together.

'Thank you, Kate,' he said quietly

'For what?' she asked, and held his eyes with that old defiance and strength so that he smiled to see it. 'Now, sir, we should take this boy to see some more peaceful paintings of the world.'

'How about Venice?' He smiled. 'There is a Canaletto exhibition in one of the smaller rooms.'

'Perfect.' She smiled.

The small room that led off from the main exhibition hall was covered with intricately painted canal scenes of Venice, all blue skies and translucent green water that reminded her of the ocean back home in Louisiana. There were magnificent pale sandstone buildings and red-tiled spired churches, and grey-domed cathedrals, but what drew her attention the most were the dark boats that crowded the canal water. Mostly small rowing boats and ferries and hooded dark gondolas, but larger sailing barges, too.

The room was quiet compared to the main exhibition hall. Only a single woman stood there, dark-haired, respectable, dressed in a pale-blue walking dress and cream spencer, her attention all on the painting before her, seemingly caught up in its scene.

Kit glanced at the lone figure and kept on walking. But then Kate felt the check in his step as he looked again at the woman.

Beneath her hand she felt his arm tense, felt everything about him still.

The woman only then seemed to sense that she was not alone. Glancing round, her eyes widened and fixed on Kit. She stared as if he were a ghost.

'Kit?' the woman whispered.

'It is good to see you, Emma,' he said quietly.

*Emma.*

'Oh, Kit!' The woman flew to him, wrapping him in her embrace, staring up into his face. 'Kit!' She wept and pressed her face against his chest, while he held her.

Tom stared in confusion. 'Who is that lady?' His hand crept into Kate's. He looked at Kit fiercely as if he were betraying them both.

'That lady is Captain North's sister.'

'Oh,' he said, and visibly relaxed. 'I suppose it's all right then if she hugs him.'

'I suppose it is,' said Kate with a smile.

'I never had a sister,' Tom said wistfully.

'Maybe you will one day,' said Kate, for she did not doubt that Tom truly had become something of a son to Kit. When she had gone home to Louisiana and Kit was with another woman. Just the thought made her want to weep.

'I would like that.' Tom smiled.

She nodded, not trusting herself to speak.

A tall, muscular, fair-haired man walked into the little Canaletto room. Kate knew by his fine-tailored, expensive clothes that he was a gentleman, but the scarred eyebrow above his sky-blue eyes and the air of danger about him suggested otherwise.

'Emma?' the man said.

'Oh, Ned, it is Kit! He has come home at last!'

But when Kit's eyes rose to see the man standing there everything changed.

'Ned Stratham?' he said in a soft dangerous voice.

Emma released her hold of him and moved to take the man's arm.

Kit's eyes were arctic as they went between his sister and the man.

'It is not what you think, Kit,' Emma said quickly.

'Ned is my husband. We have been married these six months past.'

'Your husband…?' Kit did not look at his sister, only at the man who stood by her side. The promise of violence was suddenly thick in that little room, along with danger and tension. Kate knew something was about to explode.

'Kit,' she called his name, trying to prevent it, but knowing enough of warring men to realise it was fruitless. She reacted instinctively, her outstretched arm shielding Tom, backing him against the wall, away from where the little group stood. 'Kit!'

'You bastard, Stratham!' he whispered.

Ned Stratham knew what was about to happen, too, for in one swift move he had placed his wife behind him. 'Get out, Emma,' he said in a harsh London accent unlike any of the others Kate had heard in the *ton*.

But Emma was shaking her head. 'No, Kit!'

'Me, Stratham, yes, but not my sister,' Kit growled. 'She was innocent of any wrong, damn you!' And he launched himself at Ned Stratham.

'No!' screamed Emma and tried to grab her husband back. 'Do not hurt him, Ned!'

Kate ran to Kit, putting herself between the two men, moulding herself to him as a barrier so that he could not reach Stratham. 'Look at me, Kit.' She took hold of his face, steering it to hers. 'Look at me,' she commanded, knowing she had to break the death lock in his eyes before he would hear her.

She could feel the raggedness of his breath as his chest rose and fell hard against her breasts, but she did not let an inch of space open up between them.

'Think what you are doing, Kit. Think of your sister's reputation. Think of Tom who is watching.' She lowered her voice to a whisper. 'Think of your vow…'

He took a breath and she knew she had got through to him. His eyes finally met hers.

'There are better ways to do this, Kit,' she said quietly.

His nostrils were still flared with the scent of violence, his eyes dark as the devil's. She could feel the tension that strained through every muscle of his body. But he nodded and swallowed. His gaze shifted to the crowd that was staring in fascinated horror from the doorway before moving to Stratham again.

'My wife is right,' he said stiffly.

Emma's face was powder white, her eyes dark and huge in her face. She looked shaken. Stratham stood slightly in front of her, everything of his stance protective towards her.

'You, too, are married?' his sister asked.

Kit gave a nod.

*In name only.* The words seemed to taunt Kate. She slid her hand into his and held on tight.

'Your wife *is* right,' Emma said. 'Please, both of you—' her eyes shifted to take in Tom '—and the boy. Come home with us to Cavendish Square so that all of this might be explained.'

Kate looked at Kit.

He gave a nod.

Kate took Tom's hand in hers. The other she placed in the crook of Kit's elbow and let him lead them out through the silent crowd.

They did not speak another word until they were in their town coach, following after that of Stratham and his sister's toward Cavendish Square.

'Who is he?' she asked.

Kit looked into her eyes. 'He is the man I played against that night in the gaming hell.'

Her blood ran cold and her heart went out to his.

'Oh, Kit,' she whispered and understood his reaction in the art exhibition. 'Maybe it is not as it seems.'

'Maybe,' he said, but he did not look convinced.

In a drawing room at the back of a massive mansion house in Cavendish Square the two couples sat facing each other on dark-red-and-gold-striped sofas. Tom was outside in the garden, playing in the sunshine with a puppy and a footman that both belonged to Ned Stratham and Kit's sister.

Four tea cups filled with tea sat untouched on the occasional table between them.

The servants had vanished out of sight.

'It is not what you think, Kit,' Emma said again. He saw where her hand rested upon Stratham's. 'I know who Ned is. I know what he did. And I know what you did, too.'

He closed his eyes at that and felt Kate's hand tighten around his.

'And I still love him, Kit. Just as I still love you.'

'Even knowing the truth of what I am?' he asked.

'What are you other than my brother?'

'A fool, a cheat, a coward,' he supplied.

'We've all been a little of those in our lives,' said Stratham.

He looked at Stratham.

'I own my share of the blame,' Stratham said. 'If I could go back and undo that night in Old Moll's, I would.'

'The blame was mine, Stratham, all of it. I went to look for you in Whitechapel earlier this week to tell you. I know they would have lynched me were it not for your intervention. But Emma is a different matter.'

'I know you will never believe it, Northcote, but I do love her. And if you were not her brother

I'd break your damn neck for what you've put her through.'

'Ned,' Emma chastised softly.

'If you ever hurt her, I will be the one breaking necks.'

Stratham smiled. 'You've grown some balls, Northcote.'

The two men looked at one another with a grudging mutual respect.

Kate rubbed her fingers against Kit's, her gaze touching to his before saying to Ned Stratham, 'It looks like you have a delightful view of a wonderful garden. May I...?' She got to her feet, gesturing towards the further of the two windows in the room.

Stratham was already on his feet, understanding what it was she was doing.

Kit needed time and privacy to talk to his sister and discover what had happened in his absence. He needed to learn the details of his mother's death and his father's welfare and whereabouts.

'I would be delighted to show you the view, ma'am,' said Stratham. Kate smiled at Kit and Emma, too, before she walked with him to the window at the far away end of the drawing room.

'A beautiful house and garden,' she said.

'Thank you.' said Stratham. 'A fine boy.' His eyes were on Tom running the length of the lawn with a glee that matched that of the small, brown, scruffy dog by his side.

'Yes.'

They could hear the soft murmur of voices and knew that Emma Stratham had moved to sit by her brother's side.

'Kit rescued him,' she said. 'As he rescued me.'

Stratham said nothing.

'Do not judge my husband so harshly. He has suffered in ways you could not begin to imagine.'

'And you think that Emma did not? You have no idea what he left them to. So do not seek my sympathy, for him I have none,' said Stratham and switched those cold too-blue eyes to hers.

'It is not sympathy I seek. Sympathy would kill him.'

'I am glad to hear it.'

She held his cold gaze fearlessly. 'You are the one who has no idea. My husband did something foolish, but he has paid a thousand times over. He is a good man. If you knew—' She stopped, aware she had probably said too much already.

'He has a loyal wife.'

*A loyal wife.* Stratham's words cut right through everything in that moment. It was not Kit North to whom she was loyal. Or the little boy who played so happily on the lawn outside that window. In a matter of days she was going to walk away from them both and sail to the other side of the world. Nor was she even really his wife. It was all feigned, all an illusion, a marriage in name only. She swallowed hard and forced the thoughts away.

'As Emma has a loyal husband.'

Stratham said nothing, but she saw the flicker of his eyes to where his wife sat weeping by Kit on the sofa, and the way they softened for the woman and hardened with threat at her brother. Kate's gaze moved to Kit, taking in the hard line of his jaw and the way those dark eyes stared straight ahead and her heart contracted hard as if it had been punched, and a band of iron seemed to tighten around her chest, for she knew that Emma was telling him of their mother and she knew, despite all that it appeared otherwise, inside he hurt much more than his sister. He blamed himself as the cause of it all.

Kit did not tell her what his sister had revealed of the family's life following his departure. And Kate could not ask, not while Tom was present.

But that evening he went to visit his father and she read stories to Tom and played cards with the child until his bedtime. Afterwards the hours stretched on without Kit's return and her concern grew all the more.

A single candle burned on her bedside cabinet. She waited by the rain-flecked window of her bedchamber and watched for his return, worrying until at last, when she had all but given up hope, she saw the familiar dark figure upon horseback come trotting down the rain-soaked road that shimmered in the light of the gas lamps.

She heard the outside door shutting, heard the quiet tread of his booted steps on the staircase. Tensing in anticipation, she stared round at that door, willing him to open it, but he did not so much as hesitate outside her bedchamber, only walked straight on past to reach his own. Her heart wilted. She turned aside, leaning on the window sill, staring down on to that same wet, dismal, dark street, telling herself not to be such a fool, that it was better this way for them both.

A single rasp of knuckles tapped against the door connecting their chambers and her pulse leapt at the sound of it.

The door opened softly and then closed again behind him.

She turned to face him.

His face was pale, his eyes black in the candle-light. The rain had soaked his hair, making it cling dark and sleek to his head. Raindrops sat wet on his face and across the black superfine of his coat, like a scattering of crystal beads. He just stood there and said nothing, but she could sense his devastation.

She came to stand before him. He had brought with him the scent of rain and dark night and their chill. She could feel it emanating from his damp clothes without even touching him.

'You waited up for me,' he said quietly.

She nodded.

From the pocket of his coat he took a piece of white paper folded in half. It was soft with dampness. Opening it out, he looked at it.

'He would take not one farthing of it, just as Emma refused it, too.'

She stepped closer and glanced down at the paper; it was a banker's cheque made out for thirty thousand pounds.

'All that you have earned since Johor,' she said softly.

'I thought if I could give them back the money I had lost, with interest, too, that it would go some way to repairing the damage...' He shook his head as if he had been a fool.

'My father said he did not want the money, but he no longer lives the life of a gentleman. He has a house in Whitechapel. He owns and runs a dockyard, employs men and spends his days in an office there.'

'That is a worthwhile pursuit. To provide employment. To have purpose.'

'So he says.'

He looked at her. 'How they suffered, Kate. My mother was a lady, used to a life of ease and comfort. She died of consumption in Spitalfields, penniless, seeking employment as a pieceworker!'

His pain was a living, breathing, tangible thing. It caught in her chest, sharp and painful as a blade sliding between her ribs.

'My father, a gentleman from one of the oldest genteel families in England, worked as a labourer in a dockyard. My sister, who should have been dancing at Almack's and laughing with her friends, was a serving wench in a chophouse and is married to a tough from Whitechapel. Because of me. And nothing I can do will ever change that.' The wetness on his cheeks was not just raindrops. 'I broke their world apart and I cannot fix it, Kate.'

She closed the distance between them and slid her arms around his waist, looking into his face.

'You cannot,' she said, 'because they already fixed it for themselves, Kit.'

His eyes clung to hers.

'Your sister is married to a man whom she loves and who would lay down his life to protect her. Did you not see the way they look at one another? Everything about her radiates happiness. And he seemed to me to be a very wealthy man. Your father is pursuing a life of meaning and purpose. Was he sullen, resentful, resigned to a frugal life in Whitechapel?'

No.' Kit's gaze shifted to the distance, reliving the details of the night. 'He seemed…content.'

'They do not take the money, Kit, because they do not want it.'

His eyes moved back to hers.

'And as for your mother. Trust me when I tell you she would never have stopped loving you. I am a mother, Kit, I know. And I know, too, that she would have forgiven you. As your father and sister do. As you must forgive yourself.'

'I did not come back for forgiveness.'

'I know. You came back to face them all, to face what you did, to acknowledge your mistakes and make recourse. And you have done that.'

'And it changes nothing, Kate. There is no closure. I swore I would never be Kit Northcote again. But I am. I changed my name, but I cannot escape him. I never will.'

She took him in her arms and he wept, this strong implacable man who had endured the worst of tortures, who had risked his life time and again to save hers and others. This man who was the most integral, honest man she had ever known. She held him and kissed the tears from his face and looked into his eyes.

'Kit Northcote and Kit North are the same man, Kit. They always have been. They always will be.'

She peeled off his wet clothes and her own, until they stood there naked and exposed.

'And I love him, perfectly imperfect, just as he is,' she said, and led him to her bed.

'Kate...' But she touched her fingers to his lips to silence him. Even now, when he was bleeding and hurt, all his hopes shattered, all his defences ripped aside to expose him, naked and vulnerable, he was putting her needs before his own.

'Don't,' she said. 'Just a physical need,' she whispered the excuse for both of them.

'Just a physical need,' he echoed, complicit in the lie.

Gently she pushed him back against her pillow and straddled his body, covering him with her warmth. She kissed his eyelids and his nose. She kissed his lips and his throat, and every single one of the scars that marked his body. And then she took his long hard length into her, merging their bodies as one.

Looking into his eyes, she rode him, soft and slow at first, building harder and faster, taking him in deeper. Because she needed him and he needed her. And this act of passion and love was the only thing that could drive away the ghosts and the guilt and make them forget the ache in their hearts...for this night at least.

## Chapter Fifteen

Kit watched as Kate smiled her easy confident smile, and chatted and joked with Tom at the breakfast table the next morning as if nothing were wrong. But it was a play-act. She could barely meet his eyes across the table for all she was pretending otherwise. Echoes and shadows of their intense lovemaking throughout the night hung heavy and long between them. The very air vibrated with the knowledge of what they had done and its far-reaching consequences. But she was pretending for the boy's sake, feigning a happiness and normality she did not feel. Her tension was as tangible as his own, at least to him. He was no longer fooled by that smile.

When Tom finally left for his riding lesson Kit half-expected Kate to make her excuses and rush out after him, not wanting to be alone with the man who was now her husband in truth. But she just sat there, her focus all on the white tablecloth, her face pale from lack of sleep, the smile and all other pretences fallen away now that the boy was no longer with them. Kit waved the servants away, telling them to close the door behind them. Even then she could not look at him.

The small clock on the mantelpiece ticked its fast steady rhythm. Outside the heavy wheels of a delivery cart rumbled past, with the clatter of horses' hooves. The sky was a cloudless summer blue. Clear white shafts of sunlight spilled through the window, highlighting the golden streaks within the soft brown of her hair.

'Last night...' she said. Her voice was quiet, sober, gutted. Her eyes shifted from the tablecloth to her unused cutlery. 'It was just a physical coupling...just a physical need...for us both.' Reiterating the lie she was telling herself. She ran a nervous finger along the blade of the knife, rocking it so that it flashed silver and glinted like the blade of the knife she had worn strapped to her thighs, like his cutlass, like the glitter of the ocean before the bow of a ship. 'It changes nothing.' She closed her eyes, momentarily, as if she were gathering strength. And when she opened them she swallowed and said the words again, stronger this time as if that would convince herself. 'It changes nothing.'

Her eyes finally rose to meet his so that he could see all of her guilt and confusion and split allegiance. 'You understand what I am saying, don't you?' Her brow was creased with worry, her eyes shadowed with the conflict that raged within.

'I understand, Kate,' he said softly. 'A vow is a vow.'

'Yes.' She swallowed. He could see her every breath, see the dip of her eyelashes, the way her teeth bit at her lip so hard as to make it turn white. She dropped her gaze to the table once more.

Somewhere in the distance a door slammed shut.

'You loved Wendell. And Wendell loved you.'

She nodded, but did not look at him again.

'He loved and protected you. And he wanted you and your children to be happy and healthy and safe.'

'Yes.' The word was a broken whisper.

He could walk across that room and pull her up into his arms and kiss her. He could scoop her up into his arms and take her to his bed and love all the pain away from her. He could raid her heart and claim it as his own. But that would be to use force and desire against her and it would not solve her conflict. For the resolution her soul required, she needed time. Time to make the choice herself. Time to say her farewell. Except that time was running out.

'Gunner has written to say that his business has concluded early. He will be here the day after to-morrow.' He lifted the opened letter that lay on the table before him and, rising from his chair, walked the length of the long dining table and sat the letter down before her.

She glanced up into his eyes, the look in her own shaken and haunted.

'We have accepted an invitation to Arlesfords' ball this evening, but I can send our apologies.'

'No.' She swallowed, and turned her face away. 'We must arouse no suspicions in the Admiralty's watchers, not so close to my departure.'

'As you wish.' His face felt grim, his jaw tight. His gaze lingered on her face for a moment of silence, but she would not look at him.

Three days to go, if he included this one. Was it long enough? And if not, was he really just going to let her sail out of his life as surely as she had sailed into his heart?

A curt bow of his head, then he turned and walked away.

The ballroom in the Duke of Arlesford's town house was packed to the gunnels. The French windows at the rear of the room were open, allowing the sweet dark night air to seep in and the edges of the crowd to spill out on to the stone terrace and beyond, and for the more illicit, down the stone steps into the hidden secret recesses of the garden. But the open windows and stir of the gauze curtains did little to relieve the heat and press of London's *ton* at the fashionable event.

Kate felt a bead of sweat trickle down between her breasts. She fanned herself with the black-feathered fan and was glad there was so little material in the black evening dress. The bright glow of a thousand candles set in the huge crystal-tiered chandelier above their heads brought a glitter to the beads encrusted on her low-cut bodice and a shimmer to the swell of pale décolletage exposed above its tight support.

She held her head high, met all the nosy disapproving stares with confidence and pride and amusement that belied the conflict that churned within. Standing united with her man. Her and Kit against them all, knowing the truth of what was between them, knowing that in two days she was going to have to walk away from him, just like everyone else here was doing. And the knowledge was killing her inside. She wondered how long she could keep the smile on her face.

They were feigning the truth. Neither of them able to say the words, just standing there together.

The music started for the very last dance of the evening—a waltz. She felt his fingers brush against hers and her whole body tingled and sparked from that one tiny touch and in her heart she ached all the more for him.

'We should dance.' His voice was low, his breath warm and caressing against her bare shoulder.

She did not trust herself to speak, just nodded and let him lead her out on to the dance floor. He pulled her indecently close and, unmindful of the crowd and the eyes that watched with such censure, they looked deep into one another's eyes and let their bodies move together to the music, savouring this last closeness, this last public play-act of all that was real. And she clung to it, as she clung to him, wanting these last moments to last for ever. But too soon they ended.

They stood there on that floor, their eyes locked together, even when the music had finished. Until the scandalised murmur of voices grew louder and one of the musicians cleared his throat with meaning. And they could no longer defer the end of the dance, the end of the evening, the end of Captain and Mrs North.

He led her from the dance floor, would have led them from the room, but Devlin stepped out of the crowd to block their way.

The viscount's eyes glittered from having imbibed too freely in drink. His cheeks were faintly flushed. The other three tall, dark-haired gentlemen who had been Kit's friends, looking even more foxed, flanked him.

'Leaving so soon, Captain North, or should I say young Northcote?' Devlin loomed over Kit.

'You are drunk, Devlin. And, yes, we are leaving. So step aside and let us pass.'

'You really have no shame, do you? Coming back here, with your Yankee wife and your west-country bastard. Would the tavern wench who spawned him or your darling wife have opened their legs so readily if they knew the truth of—?'

Kit reacted in an instant. Before Kate realised what was happening he grabbed Devlin by the lapels of his coat and rammed him against the wall. Kit's face was hard and focused and an inch away from the viscount's.

'You can slight me and insult me, and call me every name in the book, Devlin. You all can, for God knows I deserve it. But my wife is another matter. You will apologise to her, right here, right now, or I will—'

'Leave it, Kit!' Kate pulled at his arm. 'It does not matter. Let us just go home.'

But he never shifted that steely gaze from Devlin's. 'Oh, it matters,' he said softly. 'And Devlin will beg your forgiveness.'

'Never,' said Devlin. 'What are you going to do about it, Northcote? Run away?'

A silence was spreading over the ballroom as people began to realise what was happening and turned their eyes to the spectacle.

Kate watched the cold dispassionate focus sharpen in Kit's face and felt a tremor of fear ripple through her.

He released his grip on Devlin, smoothing down the creases he had made in the front of Devlin's tailcoat. Stepping back, he half turned, smoothing a hand through his hair, composing himself.

Devlin was still sneering as Kit's fist hit him hard, first on one cheek and then the other.

'Were I wearing gloves I would have peeled them off and slapped you across the face, but you get the idea...' said Kit, never breaking his focus from Devlin's. 'I call you out, Devlin. Name your weapon.'

Devlin wiped the blood away that trickled from the corner of his mouth. He smiled, but it was a cold smile and his eyes were narrow and filled with a chill that matched Kit's. 'Let us finish what you started, *boy*. I choose fists.'

There were gasps and whispers. She heard someone say in a stage whisper, 'Devlin is a champion pugilist. Northcote does not stand a chance.'

Devlin heard it, too, and he smiled as he glanced at the man by his side, 'Bullford will act as my second.'

'Of course I will, old man,' Bullford mumbled.

'But is there any who will act as yours, North-cote?'

The silence was resounding.

Kate made to step forward, but a dark-haired, pale-skinned man beat her to it. He was smartly dressed in the same austere dark tailcoat as the rest of the men there, the same white shirt and waist-coat, the same neatly tied white cravat. But on his finger was a ring in the shape of a silver wolf's head, and from it glinted a pair of emerald eyes as green as his own.

'I will be Northcote's second.'

Kit's eyes slid to the man's. 'Hunter.' He gave a small nod of acknowledgement to the man.

Kit glanced at Devlin one more time, before offering Kate his arm.

She placed her hand upon its crook.

A path opened up through the crowd before them.

Together they walked that gauntlet, out and along the road lined with stationary carriages until they found their own.

Only once they were safe inside, the door closed and the wheels rumbling along the roads that would take them back to the house in Grosvenor Street did she speak.

'Do not do this, Kit, please,' she pleaded, reaching her hands to his.

'You think I will just let him insult you?'

'It means nothing.'

'Your honour means everything.' He would fight all of London to defend it. To the death. He hoped she understood why.

She raised his knuckles to her lips and kissed them. 'We could go away...' She looked into his eyes.

'Run away together?' he said softly and, raising her left hand to his lips, pressed a kiss to the centre of her palm. 'Only for you am I tempted. And only for you do I refuse.'

She looked at him and the tears leaked from her eyes. But she made no more pleas. She understood, at last.

He moved across the carriage to sit by her side and wrapped an arm around her.

There was only silence and their entwined hands for the rest of the journey.

There was no time to talk to Kit. No time to tell him that she loved him and knew what he was doing for her, for them both. No time to share the comfort of their bodies one last time. They had only just arrived back in the house in Grosvenor Street when Hunter's carriage drew up outside.

The butler showed him into the drawing room where she stood by Kit's side.

'Tomorrow at dawn by the burnt oak on Hounslow Heath,' Hunter said.

Kit gave a nod. 'Thank you, Hunter,' and from the way the two men looked at one another she knew that Hunter had been there that night in Whitechapel.

Hunter inclined his head in acknowledgement and then slid a narrow green gaze at her.

'You may speak freely in front of my wife. We have no secrets.'

There was a small silence before Hunter gave a nod. 'You know that Devlin is an ardent supporter of John Jackson's Academy of Pugilism in Bond Street. He is barely out of the place these days.'

'So I hear,' said Kit with a smile.

'He is angry with you, but he also blames himself for what happened that night. We all do, but Devlin more so.'

'The blame was all mine,' said Kit.

'Largely, but not all.'

'All,' said Kit firmly.

Hunter smiled.

'Will you take a drink?'

'Thank you.'

She saw Hunter raise an eyebrow when Kit poured his guest a brandy but himself a lemonade, but he said nothing.

'Kate?' Kit looked at her and she felt her heart

warm that he did not just dismiss her but would have included her in this.

She shook her head with a smile, knowing that the two men had the past to talk over and understand and resolve, and that it would be done a deal easier without her presence. 'I will leave you two gentlemen to your discussions.'

She stood by the window of that bedchamber, as she had done so many times before, looking out into a darkness that mirrored all that was closing around her.

Kit's words of earlier that day seemed to whisper in her ear. *Wendell loved you...he wanted you and your children to be happy and healthy and safe.*

Wendell. She looked down at his ring on her finger, as worn and faded as his image in her memory. A vow was a vow. To stay true to him always. There was so much love in her heart for him and for Kit. How could so much love hurt so badly? She knew that she was breaking Kit's heart as surely as she was breaking her own.

'Oh, Wendell.' She whispered his name in the darkness and closed her eyes as the tears spilled to roll down her cheeks. 'What am I to do?'

In the chill of the night darkness she felt a warmth envelop her and a feeling of peace and reassurance descend upon her. And in that darkness she thought she caught the fleeting scent of Wendell, so strong and real that she opened her eyes without a single doubt that he would be standing before her.

But the room was empty and the scent was gone.

'Wendell?' she whispered his name and, closing her eyes, tried to sense his presence as she had done so often in the early days of losing him. But there was nothing left any more. He was gone. And she was alone.

She looked up at the star-scattered sky, like diamond angels in the deep dark blue of the heavens, and as she watched one of the stars shot across the sky to disappear elsewhere.

And she understood in that moment. She knew she had her answer.

*Wendell loved you...he wanted you and your children to be happy and healthy and safe.*

She had stayed true to him. She always would. By being happy, by living, by loving.

Kit was right, it was what Wendell would have wanted, for her and their children.

Wendell had stayed by her side long enough to weather the grief and deliver her the right man. The vow had stopped her being forced into marriage. It had made her test Kit and herself, in every way that was possible. And it had proved that their love was real and true.

She eased the worn gold band from her finger

and placed a tender kiss upon it before stowing it safely in her sea chest. Then she took Kit's ring from her pocket and slipped it on to her finger.

She stripped off her black dress of mourning and donned the white nightdress.

The connecting door between their bedchambers was not locked. She closed it quietly behind her and climbed beneath the covers of her husband's bed to wait for him in the darkness.

There were things she had to tell him before he left to face Devlin. Important things, before Gunner came the day after tomorrow.

Kate opened her eyes and realised that she had must have fallen asleep for a few minutes. But the blackness of the night was beginning to fade. Across the room the window showed that the inky hue of the sky had lightened to a deep blue. In the far corner of the heavens the first hint of day bleached it lighter still. A chill ran over her scalp. Her heart gave a stutter.

She glanced at the other side of the bed where Kit should be and saw the smooth undisturbed sheets. Her heart raced off at a hard frenzied gallop. The bedcovers were thrown aside and she was off running down the stairs, barefoot, her hair and white nightdress flowing long behind her.

'Kit!' she shouted his name. 'Kit!' so loud that it echoed all the way down the stairs and around the hallway. But the drawing room was empty just as she had known it would be. Two empty glasses sat there, one still containing some lemonade, the other drained of brandy.

Her heart was hammering so hard she felt sick.

She glanced up to find Matthews, the butler, standing there. 'Where is he?' she demanded.

'Captain North and Mr Hunter left some fifteen minutes ago on horseback.'

'Have the carriage made ready immediately.'

'Yes, madam.'

Even if she left right now, just as she was, she would not catch him. By the time she got there he would already be bare-knuckle fighting with Devlin. For her and her honour. Fighting for a woman who had refused him as her husband, who he believed was going to sail away and leave him.

She had seen the look in Devlin's eyes when he looked at Kit. And she knew that he was a man trained in using his fists. Her blood ran cold with fear for her husband, for all that she had not told him, for all that he still believed.

She stared at the two glasses, so like another two glasses aboard a ship on a night that now seemed a lifetime ago. And then she smiled and went upstairs to ready herself for the journey to Hounslow Heath.

* * *

Dawn was only just creeping across the sky above the burnt oak on Hounslow Heath, but Devlin was already waiting there, along with half the crowd from Arlesford's ballroom.

Kit smiled grimly to himself at the sight of all those expectant faces. They were about to see a whole lot more than they had bargained for.

No matter who Devlin was, no matter what Kit had done, no matter humiliation and shame, and dishonour that could never be undone, there was one thing he knew with absolute certainty—he was not getting out of that ring, he was not going to stop fighting, he was never going to walk away until Devlin had withdrawn his insult to Kate. He had no honour left to fight for. But for her honour he would give his life.

With Hunter by his side he walked right up to Devlin and Bullford until he stood close enough that none of the crowd could hear the words exchanged.

'You are not alone, Hunter? My, my, I thought young Northcote here would have been halfway across England by now,' sneered Devlin.

'Enough,' snapped Hunter. 'You insulted his wife, damn it!'

'And he insulted every damn one of us!'

'This is not about that.'

'Is it not?' said Devlin softly, then spoke to Kit. 'You have had this coming to you for over three years, Northcote.'

'I have,' Kit said. 'But you will apologise to Kate or I will punch the life out of you until you do.'

Devlin laughed. 'You think because you have built yourself a few muscles you are a match for me?'

'No. I am a match for you because Kate is my wife and I am not going to walk away until you apologise to her.'

Devlin did not laugh at that. His old friend just looked at him as if he did not believe the words. But he would believe them soon enough.

'Ready yourself, gentlemen.' Gentleman Jackson, the man who had built his wealth and position out of bare-knuckle fighting and was the acclaimed authority on it, came to stand between them.

Devlin walked to one corner of the makeshift ring, Kit to the opposite.

Devlin removed his hat and gloves and passed them to Fallingham, before Bullford helped him to remove his coat and the subsequent layers beneath.

Kit, like Devlin and most of the others present, was still wearing last night's clothes. He began to strip off his guise as a gentleman—the black tail-coat, the white waistcoat, the white neckcloth, passing each item to Hunter. Without pausing he pulled his shirt off over his head.

The gasps sounded all around. Fingers pointed. A woman screamed. Another fainted. Voices whispered.

Kit ignored it all and walked into the ring to face Devlin.

Devlin's gaze dropped lower, wandering over the scars that marred Kit's body. Dawn was here in truth, leaving nothing of the night to obscure them.

'Apologise,' said Kit grimly.

Devlin just looked at him. 'Make me.'

Kit put his fists up and went for him.

Kate squeezed her way through the crowd that seemed out of place here in the remote spot on a wind-blown heath at the break of day. They did not step aside for her; they barely noticed her. All their attention was riveted ahead with a macabre fascination and excitement that disgusted her. She could hear the sickening punches—the thuds and crunches and grunts that made her stomach drop and quiver with dread. Part of her knew that the backs of too many tall, dark-coated gentlemen and black-caped ladies that blocked her view were a mercy, but she had to get to the front.

'Excuse me.' She pushed her way through until

she caught sight of the men in a fighting ring. And the sight stopped her dead.

They were both stripped to the waist and knocking hell out of each other. Despite the chill in the air their bodies glistened with sweat and with smears of blood, neither fluid obscuring Kit's tattoo of scars with the fresh one on his shoulder, a warrior pattern more magical and meaningful than any ink could ever be, exposing him for what he was—strong, fearless, honourable. His expression was all cold, relaxed, relentless focus, just as it had been that first day on *Raven*. North and Northcote, one and the same. Tragedy and suffering had burnished away the weakness and the boy to leave only the strength and the man.

The blows were relentless and delivered with a violence that shocked even her, who had been a pirate captain. Grinding a man down with fists was so much closer and more personal than a bullet or a blade. It took something extra to use yourself as the weapon to deliver the punishment.

Devlin was taller with a longer reach and he had the finesse of training, but finesse and training and height counted for nothing against full-hearted, rock-solid determination. Kit did not even attempt to avoid Devlin's fists. It looked as though he stepped right up to them, into them, almost as if Devlin was not punching him, as if he were not a man but a training sandbag that felt nothing, was nothing, but an automaton coming in close to deliver deadly punch after punch to Devlin's body.

Devlin's right fist landed again hard against Kit's mouth, the splatter of blood from it spraying those who were ahead of her in the crowd, making some of the women shriek with a terror and delight that repulsed Kate. Devlin followed fast with a left hook that drove her husband down on to his knees before walking to his own corner of the ring as if he had won.

But Kit got back on his feet and wiped the blood from his eyes. 'Apologise,' he said to Devlin.

Devlin glanced behind him and saw Kit standing there.

A strange expression crossed the viscount's face. He looked at Kit for a moment longer, holding his gaze as if really seeing him for the first time. Then he gave a nod of acknowledgement and came again at him with his fists.

Devlin held nothing back. But Kit was relentless, soaking up punch after punch as if they were nothing, and driving his own fists hard against Devlin's body and face as if his arms would never tire.

Devlin knocked him down again.

Kit got back up. Came back at Devlin, swinging his left hook up into the viscount's nose. Punching and being punched.

The blood was everywhere.

Bone-crunching thuds—each one Devlin landed on Kit's body was as if it had struck Kate's heart. It was intolerable, unbearable. But still it went on.

She pushed her way through the remaining bodies to get to the front. Wanting to be there for him. Needing to support him. But Kit's focus was complete, honed, sharp upon Devlin.

'Apologise,' he demanded, his breaths ragged as Devlin's.

And the fight continued.


Devlin leaned against him as much as Kit leaned on Devlin. The two of them supporting one another in that fist-against-ribs hold, like two dogs with jaws locked together.

Their gazes fused, neither backing down.

But something was different in the way that Devlin was looking at him.

'North, after all,' said Devlin with grudging respect.

Kit smiled. 'Northcote,' he said.

Gentleman Jackson pulled them apart, warning them to keep the punches clear.

Devlin got his fists up.

Kit went in again until this time it was Devlin down on his knees.

Kit walked up to the man who had been his friend and, reaching down to him, helped him up.

The two men looked at one another in silence, before Devlin gave a nod and Kit hit him again, the effort almost costing him his balance.

Devlin staggered.

The two of them were still on their feet, just, but bent over, panting with exhaustion, leaning their hands on their knees, their eyes still fixed on the other.

'I was wrong about you,' said Devlin.

Kit said nothing. Just waited for Devlin to recover enough to hit him again.

Devlin stood upright.

Kit stepped forward, fists at the ready.

But Devlin raised a hand to stop him, his eyes holding Kit's as he spoke the words loud and clear between his ragged breaths. 'I take back my words of last night and apologise for any insult dealt.'

'It is not me you have to apologise to, Devlin,' he said and let himself look at Kate for the first time since her arrival on the heath.

She was standing at the edge of the ring. There was blood in his eyes but nothing would have obscured her. For she stood there in that crowd of dark coats and capes in a dress of bright yellow silk, a ray of Caribbean sunshine in the gloom of a London day. The dress he had bought for her from the

Antiguan dressmaker. The dress that was nothing of mourning and all of celebration.

Devlin staggered over to stand before her. He bowed. 'Mrs North.'

'Mrs Northcote,' she corrected him, saying Kit's name with pride.

Devlin gave a nod. 'Mrs Northcote,' he said. 'I most humbly beg your forgiveness, madam.'

'I accept your apology, Lord Devlin.'

Devlin bowed again and came back to Kit, offering a handshake.

Kit accepted.

Devlin gave him a gruff clasp. 'Welcome back, Kit, in truth.'

Kit gave a nod.

Bullford hurried in and, putting a shoulder beneath Devlin's armpit, helped him away.

'A moment, please,' said Kit quietly to Hunter who stood ready by his side to offer the same service.

And then he walked to stand before his wife.

Their eyes held and hers were wet with love and pride and tenderness.

He let his gaze move down over the bright yellow dress, where the wind moulded it to her body, before coming back up to her eyes once more.

She reached out her left hand and he accepted it, taking her slender fingers in his swollen-knuckled, bloodstained ones, touching the wedding band there as she had done so many times. His eyes caressed the thick, heavy, new band and how it gleamed upon her skin. And he smiled as he raised his eyes to hers again.

She was smiling, too. 'You should get dressed, Mr Northcote,' she said. 'At least until we get home.'

He laughed and, relinquishing her hand with some reluctance, turned away to where Hunter was waiting, to do as his wife bid.


In the privacy of Kit's bedchamber, Kate stripped off her husband's clothes and washed away the blood and bathed the cuts and the discoloured bruises that were already beginning to show.

'Kit Northcote...' she whispered as she gently held a cold damp cloth against the swelling of a cut on his eyebrow, her eyes holding his.

'Kate Northcote.' He took the cloth from her and set it aside, pulling her gently into his arms.

Neither of them offered another word of explanation. They did not need to.

He just kissed her and undressed her so that they stood naked and exposed in the full glare of the daylight, not a single barrier remaining between them.

She reached out and, taking hold of his bruised

hand within hers, placed it over her naked breast. 'My heart is all yours…if you want it.'

He smiled and slid his hand up in a gentle caress to capture her to him.

'I want it,' he murmured and kissed her again. 'You have no idea how I want it.' And then he lifted her up and laid her down gently on top of his bed, and there, in the bright sunlight of the London morning, he loved her, filling her body with his, taking them both to a place of sweet union, looking into each other's eyes as she softly cried out his name, as he spilled his seed within her, as their souls became joined in truth.

Afterwards, as they lay in each other's arms, skin to skin, he took her hand in his, looking at his ring upon it again in wonder and happiness.

'It was time to let him go,' she said softly.

He nodded, his eyes holding hers.

'I think he would have liked you, Kit Northcote—pirate hunter, Englishman and all.'

'I think I would have liked him, pirate, American and all.'

She smiled. 'My heart was hurting with loss, now it is full of love for you.'

He kissed her with such love and tenderness. 'You do know that I am never going to let you go.'

The tears prickled in her eyes. 'Gunner is coming tomorrow and we both know I cannot stay here. My children…my home…the war between our countries…' She stared into his eyes. 'What are we going to do, Kit?'

He smiled and kissed her fingers. 'There is nothing here in London for me anymore, Kate. I have done what I came back to do. I am stripped bare of armour and pretence. I am Kit Northcote and everything I am, flawed and damaged as it is, I offer to you. To be your husband and father to your children and Tom, and any others that come along. To be yours wholly and in all ways, for ever, and live out our lives in Louisiana…if you will have me.'

The tears were spilling from her eyes in earnest now, for this man whom she loved so much. 'But an Englishman in Louisiana at this time of war… it would not be easy for you.'

'Nothing worthwhile ever is,' he said with a smile. 'So, will you have me, Kate Northcote?' he asked softly.

'I will have you a thousand times over.' She kissed him with all the love that was in her heart.

'I had better tell Gunner he is not needed, after all, unless he wants a one-way trip with us on *Raven*.'

She smiled and so did he.

And then they made love all over again, merging their bodies and their hearts, merging their souls and their futures. Knowing the preciousness of life and love, and that whatever challenges lay ahead they would face them together. Pirate and pirate hunter, American and English, a union forged in steel and blood and a love that surpassed all.

\* \* \* \* \*

# MILLS & BOON®

## Why shop at millsandboon.co.uk?

Each year, thousands of romance readers find their perfect read at millsandboon.co.uk. That's because we're passionate about bringing you the very best romantic fiction. Here are some of the advantages of shopping at www.millsandboon.co.uk:

* **Get new books first**—you'll be able to buy your favourite books one month before they hit the shops

* **Get exclusive discounts**—you'll also be able to buy our specially created monthly collections, with up to 50% off the RRP

* **Find your favourite authors**—latest news, interviews  and new releases for all your favourite authors and series on our website, plus ideas for what to try next

* **Join in**—once you've bought your favourite books, don't forget to register with us to rate, review and join in the discussions

### Visit **www.millsandboon.co.uk**
### for all this and more today!